WRONG BED BABY

A SMALL TOWN FRIENDS TO LOVERS ROMANCE

CRESCENT COVE
BOOK 10

TARYN QUINN

Wrong Bed Baby
© 2021 Taryn Quinn
Rainbow Rage Publishing

Cover by LateNite Designs
Photograph by Lindee Robinson Photography
Models: Mairi Van Dyke & Brian Boynton

First print edition: September 2022
ISBN Print edition: 978-1-940346-75-5

I can't go back to yesterday because I was a different person then.

ALICE IN WONDERLAND

ONE

MOVING SUCKED.

Moving because your bachelor pad for half a decade was being torn down by Gavin Forrester, the hotshot big time developer in town who wanted to build more condos, *really* sucked.

But getting a hefty payment to help compensate for the inconvenience of moving helped ease the pain. Slightly.

"You gonna get a move on or just keep staring into the back of this SUV like it holds the answers to good sex?"

I didn't even glance at my best friend Lucky. I knew he'd be looming over the back of my vehicle to show off his biceps to maximum advantage, just in case any ladies happened to wander by.

"I know the answer to that," I muttered. "And it involves me and a glass of merlot."

"That's how you warm yourself up? You sound like a chick, but hey, do what works for you, man."

I had to laugh. "Shut the hell up, Roberts, and grab the other end of this hutch."

He elbowed me out of the way. "You might prefer group activities, but I can handle this one on my own, son." He hefted up the handcrafted oak piece built by my older brother August with a grunt.

1

The sound made me grin as I stepped back and waved him toward the propped open door to my apartment building. "By all means. I'll just stand here and cool off with a refreshing beverage." I popped open the cooler and grabbed a can of lemonade before flipping open the top. "Ahh. Tastes good," I said as I took an exaggerated swallow.

In a truly spectacular feat, Lucky managed to flip me off before hauling the hutch toward the open door.

Music suddenly spilled out, loud and unrepentant. It wasn't something you'd hear on the local station either. This was a sinuous, exotic beat, the kind that brought to mind warm breezes, a gorgeous sunset, and an even more gorgeous woman belly-dancing with a colorful snake wrapped around her upper torso.

I took another drink. Or maybe that was just me.

Lucky didn't seem to pay it any mind as he barreled through the doorway and headed up the stairs with his latest bulky item of furniture.

I turned toward the back of the SUV to take stock of what was left. In short, it was a lot.

This wasn't the first trip I'd made over here, but we were in early innings. My new apartment was still mostly a barren wasteland. I'd skipped hiring a moving company, considering I hadn't had far to go and could call on a number of fit dudes like myself to help out.

Oddly enough, most of them had become suddenly unreachable despite knowing for weeks the days I'd planned to move. August would be over later after work, but I couldn't count on any of the rest of the slugs I knew. As if wives and children and gainful employment could keep them *that* busy.

Whatever.

Lucky, however, used any attempt to show off and looked at carrying heavy furniture as the best opportunity going. So far, his plan had not borne much fruit, although a couple of the gooey-eyed young baristas at Macy's coffee shop had come out a few times to offer us refreshments. Lucky hadn't been too keen on any of them, since most of those girls were barely legal.

He had some standards. Not a lot, mind you, but some.

He jogged up beside me as I was dragging out the small bookcase that doubled as a nightstand in my bedroom. "Dude, there's some kind of chick party in there, and I think they're stripping."

I snorted and set my bookcase on the pavement. "I think heat stroke has finally warped your brain." I swiped my forearm over my sweaty forehead and grabbed for my already sweating can of lemonade. "It has to be ninety out here."

"Ninety-five," he informed me, flashing me his smart watch. "Not that you've been doing much to get sweaty, you lazy fuck."

I shrugged. "Conserving energy for when the help is gone is a valid strategy. We both know you'll only stick around as long as there's a chance you'll get laid."

He waggled his brows at me. "I didn't know that was on the table."

"Not in your fondest dreams, pal. I don't care if you unload every piece of furniture by yourself and decorate too."

"I don't fucking decorate. That's what sisters and girlfriends are for. You've got one."

"A sister? Definitely. Not that she has enough time for that shit. She's not even around right now, remember?"

My baby sister Ivy was in LA with her husband and their baby daughter Rhiannon for a week, which had been a tactical error on Ivy's part since we were smack dab in the middle of a heat wave. Her ice cream truck Rolling Cones would've made a killing if she'd been open for longer than the banker's hours she kept the truck operating on while she was away. She had a good crew to help her, but she preferred shorter shifts when she wasn't around to manage things. If she'd been able to stay open until 10 pm on these sweltering nights as she usually did, she probably could've funded Rhi's college education.

Not that her fancy rich husband needed any help with that.

I wasn't bitter, toiling away on a teacher's salary. Mostly because I loved my kids. I enjoyed their curiosity and enthusiasm and sometimes even their mischief-making. Aug claimed my affinity for children came from the fact that I hadn't matured past twelve myself, but I would've said at least thirteen. Maybe fourteen on a good week.

In any case, I was happy with my lot. I wouldn't have minded a bit more green to grease the wheels, but then again, who would?

Lucky tied back his long hair, swatting away the sweaty pieces sticking to his neck. "Yeah, Ivy's getting used to that high-rolling life. Next thing you know, she'll move out there. Probably get a pad on the beach. That'd be something to have a place to crash at on the west coast, huh?"

I didn't say anything. My family was close. Sure, we had our occasional spats like any other. Now and then, we didn't speak for days at a time. Life got busy.

But I didn't want to lose my sister across the damn country. I definitely didn't want to only see my niece on FaceTime and for occasional vacations. I was her favorite uncle. The fun one who'd hired a clown for her last birthday—Lucky, of course—and helped her whip up and down the sidewalk on her tricycle. She'd had a small accident and busted open her lip on account of the raised lip on the sidewalk, but she'd healed fine, right? And she had a hell of a story for the kids at playgroup. You know, for when she could talk coherently.

She was a sentient toddler now, so I was enjoying my little RhiRhi more with each passing month. But infants were another story. My other niece, Vivian, was a bit younger, so we were still working on communication beyond *goo-goo gaa-gaa*.

I wasn't one for babies. Nope, never. Not my bag. I preferred kids once they got past the drooling and excessive pooping stages.

Lucky straightened and grabbed a soda for himself, popping the top. "Well, if Ivy can't help, then you gotta get your mom involved. They live for that stuff."

"Are you kidding me? She's on like fourteen town committees. She barely has time to sleep, when you factor in her work at the gallery. Besides, who says I need a damn decorator? I didn't at my old place."

He laughed and took a long drink. "Yeah, and it looked great. *Not.* Most of the rooms didn't even look lived in. You can't do that in a swank place like this, man. Forrester's taken all these apartments up a notch." He let out a belch. "When you invite over that sexy chick who strips for tuition, you don't want to make her sit on the floor. Then again, if you do, I have a better chance." He nudged my shoulder. "I still owe you one for the Sanders' sisters."

He'd imparted so much in that barrage of information, I didn't even know what to unpack first. "Uh, the Sanders' sisters were almost a year ago."

"Hell no. They were this spring." He frowned and drank more. "Weren't they?"

"Try last fall. And I didn't hook up with both, just Judy. You just didn't like that they both weren't immediately bowled over by your baby greens."

"Says you. What happened with you guys?"

I shrugged. "We went out a few times. We're still friends. Just no spark."

"But she's smokin'. Doesn't that count for something?"

I shrugged again and finished off my lemonade, feeling like a class A chump. How could I tell him I was developing an aversion to casual dating? Not because I wanted something serious. Hell no.

Lucky and I were Crescent Cove's original bachelors. When all the single men around us tumbled like timber for the whole marriage and babies scene, we stood strong. We didn't want any of that. Pleasures of the flesh were enough for us, thank you.

No commitment. No stress.

No way, not in baby central anymore. How could you possibly enjoy a no-strings hookup in a place like the Cove? We'd become known across the northeast for ease in procreation. The damn town bird might as well have been the stork.

I gestured to the remaining items left in the back of my SUV. We'd packed that sucker like a Tetris game, taking advantage of every millimeter of space. "You going to help me with this stuff or what?"

"*Help?* I've been carrying most of it while you stand around out here sipping lemonade like a southern belle." To show off—as usual— he picked up my bookcase under one arm and grabbed another small shelving unit with his other hand. Then he winked at me before heading inside.

Since I knew quite well his posturing probably had to do with the woman he'd mentioned probably innocently dancing in her own apartment, I grabbed a couple of small end tables and followed him toward the sexy music.

After we went upstairs, I stepped around him to open the door to the hallway before we continued on toward my apartment. The music only grew louder as we walked.

Apartments branched off in two directions. There were only a few on each floor, and for now, there were three levels. There was still room for more on the very top floor, but Forrester was taking his time there, gauging interest, before he decided to make it one big place or split it up like the other ones. On the roof, there was a communal gathering space for all the tenants' use.

This property right across from the lake was in a prime location, what with Macy's Brewed Awakening on the bottom floor and the Cove's real estate market booming. I'm sure Forrester liked being the hottest ticket in town.

"Holy shit," I mumbled as I walked into the back of Lucky, who had stopped dead outside my door.

And who could blame him, because the door across the hall was cracked open, just enough to reveal a scantily clad blond winding around a pole that had been drilled into her floor. Or attached there somehow, well enough to support the gyrations she was doing around it.

To it.

"Told you," Lucky said smugly, panting slightly from what he held. He appeared to be glued in place and had not set it down yet.

"Does she realize the door is open?"

I was fervently glad that it was, even if I felt a bit like a pervert watching her. Her eyes were closed as she moved to the music, so she didn't know we were out here, but she *was* dressed—albeit in a minuscule way.

When Lucky didn't reply, I tried again. "Since the door is open, maybe she wants us to see?" It was a mostly hopeful question.

My conscience was screaming now. I had a sister and a niece and of course a mom. I taught kids. Spying on her wasn't kosher.

Unless she had some exhibitionistic tendencies and didn't mind if we peeped on her. At least she wasn't naked.

I would just keep telling myself that.

"I cracked the door open a little, wanting to see where the music was coming from," Lucky admitted, voice low. "She hadn't latched it though. I'm not *that* bad."

"Asshole." I jabbed the pointed corner of one of my end tables into his back.

He grunted and dropped the bookcase on his toe. His unholy bellow of pain made the gorgeous blond stop dancing, just as I set down my furniture and moved toward her door to firmly pull it shut.

Well, that had been my intention anyway. I didn't make it all the way to closing the door, because her face fucking slayed me.

I could admit I hadn't noticed it before, as occupied as I'd been with her fluid movements. She was seriously coordinated. Flexible. Hot as fuck. But then she just had to have a stunning face to match, with fiery eyes—color undetermined from this distance—and full lips and enough cleavage to kill a man who'd been abstinent for, oh, close to eight months now.

The last woman I'd asked out had ended up engaged to the chief of police within weeks. So, that kind of gave a reading on the state of my love life.

"What in the goddess are you doing?" she demanded, lowering the music and marching to the door at a rate of speed sufficient to make all the dangling threads from her top flutter over her abs.

She had a twinkling jewel in her navel. I was reasonably sure the beam of light from it had rendered me cross-eyed. Possibly altered some of my bodily functions as well.

That was as good an excuse as any for my current...pants predicament.

"Eyes up here, pal." She tapped her forehead. "Were you breaking in?"

"Hardly. The door was open. I was shutting it for you. Never know who's around."

"Wind did it," Lucky muttered from behind me.

I glanced back to see him leaning against the wall, gripping his foot. His boot was lying sideways on the floor.

I probably should've felt guilty, but he knew better than to pull stunts like that. Nudging a door open wasn't cool. She didn't know us. The last thing we wanted to do was scare her or make her feel uncomfortable. And I was her new neighbor, for fuck's sake. If he made things weird between us, *I'd* be the one dealing with the fallout.

"Look, we apologize." I cleared my throat. "The music lured Lucky to your apartment, and the door wasn't latched, so he made an ill-advised decision to open it. *We* apologize," I repeated, glancing back at my best friend, who nodded with a sigh.

"Sorry, ma'am."

"Ma'am?" She frowned and crossed her arms. "Just how old do you think I am?"

"Barely legal?"

She arched a brow at my quip. "Since I suspect that's your attempt at flattery, I will say you're both wrong. I'm not old enough to be called ma'am, though who is? And I'm also not young enough to remember having a fake ID to get drinks. Although I rarely imbibe to excess." She flushed. "Well, unless bestie service calls."

"How do I call you through that bestie service?" Lucky pulled on his boot and flashed her a winsome smile. "Truly, you won't meet a friendlier guy in all of the Cove."

"She's new in town. Don't scare her off already. At least I assume." I gave her a smile of my own. One far less toothy than Lucky's.

"I'm fairly new to actually living in town, but I've worked here since last year." She squinted at me. "Are you sure we haven't met before?"

"Unless I was drugged unconscious, there is literally no way I could forget meeting you." It was probably the most sincere thing I'd ever said, but Lucky snorted out a laugh just the same.

She just kept squinting. "I've seen you before. Are you—" She snapped her fingers. "August."

I scowled. "I'm definitely not August. If you think I am, I'm leaving." Not that I could go far.

Across the hallway. Yeah, that would soothe my wounded ego.

"His reputation as the hotter brother is on the line," Lucky informed her. "Mind you, the only one who ever said he was hotter was Caleb himself, when he was preening in the mirror."

"Caleb." She rolled the name around in her mouth as if she was tasting a fine wine. "I definitely can tell the difference between you."

Was that a subtle dig? Or maybe not so subtle? I threw back my shoulders and puffed out my chest. I didn't think I was the equivalent of a body-building male model like my best friend, but I cleaned up quite well.

I'd definitely never gotten any complaints.

"August has a picture of you guys on his desk," she continued. "You two and your sister."

"How do you know August?" I wasn't over being compared to him, even if it had happened my entire life.

I wouldn't have said I suffered from middle sibling syndrome, but I had to admit I got testy sometimes. August was one of those guys who did everything well. He was a supremely talented craftsman, a good friend to practically the whole town, and now he had a perfect little happy family with Kinleigh and their baby.

But that was neither here nor there.

"I work for him. Well, technically, I worked for Kinleigh, before their stores and everything else merged." She spun a damp curl around her finger. "They're so happy. It's lovely to see."

I grunted. As did Lucky when he picked up the furniture he'd dropped, along with my end tables, and somehow managed to heft them all into my apartment in one trip. Then he banged the door shut.

"What's his problem?" she asked.

I turned back to her and sent up a silent apology to Lucky. Technically, he'd spotted her first, even if that spotting had been through shady means. Bro code and all that.

But I was the one who was moving into this building. She was my new neighbor. I was honor bound to chat with her and get to know her while she looked so attractively sweaty.

Okay, so side benefit.

I lifted a shoulder. "His paper plane has been unexpectedly grounded."

"Don't think its made of paper. Unless he's one of those who stuffs toilet paper rolls in his jeans. Do guys really do that?"

I had to grin as I leaned against the jamb. "Guys really do a lot of things, though I think socks are more common." I shrugged. "Sorry, can't say definitively."

"Oh, right, because of course you've never needed to do anything like that."

I didn't bother to hide my smirk. Hey, she'd continued this particular line of conversation, not me.

"If I was the ogling sort, I'd just look to see myself. But I prefer a little mystery."

"What's your name, Mystery?"

"Luna."

"Nice to meet you." I held out a hand and she clasped it after a moment. I waited for sparks. Expected them, for some weird reason. When there was nothing, I frowned. "Do you have a last name?"

"Nah." She released my hand with a satisfied smile. "I'm like Madonna. Who needs more than the first?"

"Us ordinary people who teach school, for one. I don't want my students calling me Cal."

"But that's what the hip teachers do, isn't it?" She smiled again, this time in a much less practiced way. "What do you teach?"

"Second grade at the Catholic school."

Her expression warmed exponentially. "It's Hastings."

"What?" Why was she so damn beautiful? It shouldn't be legal.

"My last name is Hastings."

"Mine is Beck." I rubbed the back of my neck as Lucky turned on the music in my apartment and started singing along loudly.

Since when did he like Sinatra? Or like butchering Sinatra, because wow.

Her lips twitched. "I know that. You know, August and all. But thank you for the confirmation."

When I lingered in the doorway, not wanting to leave just yet, she arched a pale brow. "Since you're just moving in, you can't need a cup of sugar."

"Oh, you'd be surprised what I might need. You don't happen to have any children you'll be enrolling at school?"

"No."

"Any husband to help you make those nonexistent children?"

She glanced over her shoulder at her fully furnished apartment. I couldn't see much with her blocking my view, but the place felt relaxed and serene. Much like the woman herself. "Appears not."

"How about a boyfriend?"

"Are you auditioning?"

"I'd like to know what the audition consists of before I sign up. If it involves that shiny pole over there..." I gestured into her spacious apartment, which seemingly had the same layout as mine. "Regrettably, I'll have to pass."

"Let me think about it and get back to you."

I knew a brush-off when I heard one. I needed to seal the deal. "Why don't we discuss it over lunch tomorrow? I'll cook," I offered, before remembering that my apartment was half empty and the rest was a disaster zone.

"A second grade teacher who cooks," she mused, tapping her irresistibly glossy lips. "In the package of an outrageous flirt. Very interesting."

"I wouldn't say I'm outrageous. Exactly. More like persistent." I flashed her a grin. "So, what do you say?"

TWO

 Luna

WHAT DID I SAY? THAT HE WAS TROUBLE.

I managed not to say it aloud. Yet.

Caleb's eyes crinkled adorably. He was in that ambiguous age group of twenty-something, but he had a nice level of scruffy beard that made my palms itch to touch. I was always a sucker for a guy who didn't scrape his face raw every morning. But there was nothing soft about him.

He was angular at the jaw and with that slash of smiling mouth. Ultra-white teeth told me he took care of himself, but the holey T-shirt in faded green didn't give me any details about his personality. In fact, he screamed bro-dude.

I leaned on the door and let him see a little bit more of me. Not that I needed to since he'd already sneakily looked in on me, although I was pretty sure that was his friend's doing more than his. He'd seemed almost panicked about the fact that his tall, brawny pal had opened my door.

As he should've. That wasn't cool.

There wasn't anything other than an inherently good vibe coming off of Caleb. Even if he had an underlying frat guy air. The big, hair metal guy also seemed on the up and up. I saw him in the café a lot, and I was pretty sure he was more an exuberant puppy than problematic. Not that I wouldn't bust his chops later for being a creeper.

Guys needed to be taught that a woman's space was sacred, as were our bodies.

"Think you can keep your friend on a better leash?"

He grimaced. "Yeah, that was fuck—er, freaking stupid of Lucky."

Lucky. Why did that name suit him? It fit the overeager puppy thing he had going.

I couldn't stop a laugh. "Censoring yourself because you're a good Catholic boy or..."

"Because you're a lady."

"Well, thanks. But I gotta go."

My endorphins were on hyperdrive from a long dance session with my pole, and it had been a damn long time since anyone had made me want to say yes. I wasn't being conceited when I said I got hit on constantly.

I worked in retail. Men and women approached me with wild abandon most days. I enjoyed it, even played into it for a sale. But something had made me throw up my shields the moment Caleb stuck his hand out.

Trouble.

His charming smile said harmless, and that he was a teacher should have done the same. But I'd learned to listen to the little voice who told me to close the damn door.

She was usually right.

But part of me always wanted to rebel. Especially when his aura had such a cheerful sunny hue with a lovely little buzz of creative red along the edges.

"Wait, you didn't answer me."

I gave him a half smile and closed the door in his face. I'd make the decision another day.

"You know you're intrigued," he said through the door.

He didn't sound annoyed. That was always something a woman

had to worry about when tossing back an overture. Especially since this dude was going to be living across from me.

I pressed my palm to the door over the oil sigils I'd painted on them. For protection, for peace, and most of all, for contentment. My home needed to be a safe space, especially for all the healing work I had to do. The door was warm from his energy.

"Guess we'll find out," I said just loud enough for him to hear.

Spinning on the balls of my feet, I put the delicious Caleb Beck out of my mind. I'd worked up a light sweat and needed a quick shower before I met up with the girls on the rooftop.

I rushed into the bathroom, stripping as I went. I didn't have time to deal with my crazy hair, so I shoved it under a shower cap before I slipped under the water.

I was looking forward to hanging out with the ladies in my building. It was a new space that had just been finished at the end of spring. It was going to be blazes hot up there, but I was pretty sure the ever eclectic Bess Wainwright was going to make sure there were cool drinks and food. She was the ultimate entertainer.

Gavin Forrester, the owner, had some sort of renovations going in this apartment building all the freaking time. But it was too damn hot to do much right now since we were in the thick of a late July heat wave.

Not the smartest time for my new neighbor, Cal the hottie, to move in. Probably why there wasn't an army of his fellow frat buddies —or even his brother—helping him.

Then again, August was the sort of man who picked up the slack at the end.

He was forever doing that for Kin at the store. The guy had a million balls in the air between custom work and his new furniture venture with his wife. But he was always there to help out when she got a wild hair about moving stuff around the store. One of the reasons why I loved working there so much. It was never the same for very long and kept me from getting bored.

I'd moved into this apartment building after I'd started working at

Kinleigh's Attic—now Kinleigh and August's Attic, the combined storefront for both August's furniture and Kinleigh's eclectic store.

Since having their baby, they'd ended up going all in on the baby furniture deal. Kids' furniture, vintage toys, and clothing had taken over half the store. I'd really gotten into helping Kinleigh embrace her new calling. With the baby boom taking over the town, things for children were in high demand. And Kinleigh was nothing if not an astute businesswoman.

I finished rinsing off and tucked my huge cotton bath wrap around me. While I drip-dried, I quickly did my usual skin care deal with crystal-infused oils and toner, plus some lotion from my favorite shop in Luna Falls. I never thought I'd find witchy products I didn't have to go online to buy, but there were a surprising number of shops a few towns over.

I padded into my bedroom and hung up my towel, then I slipped into a light robe as I tried to figure out what to wear. I hated running the air conditioning in my apartment, but it was too blessed hot to deal without it. In fact, I wondered if we should reroute our little meet-up to Bess's place.

Her apartment was big enough to cover all of us.

I picked up my phone to text her when one came in from her with a photo of her handiwork on the roof. Yep—scratch that.

Quickly, I replied to her that it looked amazing and pulled out a pair of cutoffs and a cute rainbow tie-dye tank top with a duo of daisies over my nipples. It amused me enough to pair it with some daisy earrings, necklace, and some citrine crystals. I tied a few more around my wrist and opposite ankle. Then I found my daisy sandals at the back of my closet and embraced a little more summer child energy with some sparkly makeup.

I checked in with Kylie and Tabitha, the other women in my building who were part of our girls' night. We all agreed to meet with tarot decks, water, and notebooks in hand.

Damn if they weren't adorable.

I wandered out of my bedroom to my small living room. I'd embraced the boho chic style in the open floorplan of my perfectly-sized apartment. Plants and herbs I used in my practice dotted the shelves I'd put up. Macramé hanging planters held easy to care for greenery and added to the serenity of my space.

I gathered a few supplies from my bookcase and filched a few crystals from my altar to help with the nerves that would be sure to pop up. I said a quick prayer of thanks to the goddess Brigid for her knowledge and for borrowing from her altar.

Moving to the plethora of divinatory items I had displayed in my corner alcove, I choose a few straightforward tarot decks for the evening. Then I closed my eyes and let my intuition tell me which oracles to bring with me.

I laughed when I opened my eyes to find a daisy bag under my fingers. "Freya, are you giving me a sign for the evening?" She wasn't a goddess I prayed to. She was the goddess of love and fertility and most often associated with daisies and their purity.

I wondered if there was an offering in the lake to her because damn if this town wasn't exploding with fertility. I laughed and shook my head as I stuffed all my things in a retro canvas bag with a pair of vintage roller skates embroidered on it.

I grabbed my cell phone, my water jug to combat the alcohol that would surely be in my future, and my keys. When I opened the door, I found the hulking piece of man-bun in the hallway.

His charm glowed as surely as his ultra-tanned skin. "Hope there was no hard feelings for my bonehead move."

I grinned up at him. "Nah. Sorry my music was so loud."

"Oh, believe me, it was no problem."

I twirled my keys on my finger. "Glad you enjoyed my workout."

Lucky hooked his thumb on the edge of his workout shorts. Mostly to show off his sin lines, I was sure. I enjoyed them, even if he didn't give me the little buzz that his friend had. "Workout? So that's not your..." His other hand tugged at his beard.

My eyebrow arched. "My... Oh." I laughed. He thought I worked the pole. "Dude, I've talked to you a few times at the café. I work at Kinleigh's."

"Oh, sure. I knew that."

I laughed again. I couldn't help it. "You do know that it's a large workout craze." I stepped closer to him. "I could snap your neck with my thighs."

He swallowed. "I'm down with trying that."

"You would be." I tipped my head. "Is that supposed to be a pick-up line? 'Hey, are you a stripper?'"

"No. I mean, it wouldn't bother me if you were." He cleared his throat. "Equal opportunity and all that shit."

"I'm so glad. Catch ya around, Slick." I passed him and headed for the staircase.

"Hey, I didn't mean anything by it," he called after me.

I just waved him off.

And that was why I was a single. Men were utterly ridiculous. The fact that he went with 'yo, I'm cool with you being a stripper' as his opener made me want to weep for humanity.

My cell phone buzzed in my hand. I looked down at the screen and shook off my mood. Tabitha was asking if I was still coming. I could practically feel her uncertainty through the text. I shot off a quick reply that I was on my way up the stairs.

Music greeted me as I opened the door to the roof. It was early evening, but since we were still in the clutches of July, sunset wouldn't be for hours yet.

As I'd feared, Bess had gone all out. Huge umbrellas kept the worst of the sun off of the table she'd set up with fruit and a charcuterie board in the shape of a star. White candles were lit all around the food in the center as well as in groupings of various heights on the smaller tables she'd set up with crystals.

I laughed as I walked to the little group waiting for me. "Did you buy out the whole shop?"

Bess flushed, then patted her hair. "The ladies at Moonstone and Obsidian were very helpful."

"I bet." I was certain Georgia, the proprietress, saw Bess and led her right into temptation. She was a savvy businesswoman, and Bess was probably like a gift from the goddess. Luckily, Georgia was also proud of her shop. The crystals were all of good quality.

"Well, this is a good way to charge all your new babies."

"Oh?" Bess moved to stand beside me. She was wearing a gorgeous siren red and black caftan that flowed around her surprisingly bomb-ass body. A few crystals glinted from her neck and ears, along with some decidedly more expensive diamonds.

"Yes. Charge your cards in the moonlight and your crystals in the sun. Some also like to do the crystals by the moon, but in my opinion, they get most of their energy from the sun."

She touched the jagged tip of a tower of amethyst. "I'm not sure why they bring me so much happiness, but they do. And I agree, the sun makes them sparkle. Anything that happy should go together, right?"

"Exactly."

Tabitha Monaghan came up behind me and peered over my shoulder. "Do we need to buy that many," she whispered.

I pulled her forward, laughing at the notebook clutched in her arms. She owned Sugar Rush, the cake and confections shop in town. She'd moved into the building just before me. We'd bonded over wrestling her Christmas tree down the stairs. Chicks had to stick together.

While Forrester seemed like a pretty good landlord, his maintenance guy wasn't on the property. And little things like helping a damsel in distress weren't high on the coverage on our apartment app. If it wasn't leaking, on fire, or broken, we were on our own.

It was pretty much how Tabitha, Kylie, and I had banded together.

"Taking notes?"

Tabitha pushed her glasses up her nose. "I have many questions."

"I might have answers. Probably better ones with some of that sangria I saw on the table."

Tabitha brightened. "Oh, it's very good. I found the recipe on Pinterest. Mrs. Wainwright made margaritas too."

"Bess, dear." The older woman waved her off. "I'm already old enough to be your grandmother. Don't make me feel any older."

"Right." Tabitha flushed. "It was really nice of you to put this together for our class."

"I like to do it up in style." Bess swayed lightly. "I also got a few of these for the next few days. I purposely did not move to Florida because I dislike this sort of heat." She picked up her margarita and went back to the main table. "Now let's eat then we can have our little class."

Kylie Fisher burst through the door, looking decidedly disheveled. She tried to brush her hair out of her face. "Sorry, I'm late. I got...detained."

Tabitha sat down in a chair on the right side of the table, then stacked cheese, pepperoni, and some sort of pickled thing. "You mean Justin detained you."

I grinned. "Ah, young love."

Kylie nibbled on her lower lip. "He's very distracting."

"So's that hickey on your neck," Tabitha said with a sigh before munching on her mini sandwich.

Kylie slid into the chair next to her. "Well, we can get you a guy, right?" She glanced over at me. "Can we practice a love reading maybe?"

I folded myself into one of the big round chairs. "Well, that's half of my client calls." I pulled my romance reading deck out of my bag, then tucked the canvas bag behind me. "Let's start with what questions should we ask."

"Will I find love?" Kylie asked.

I pointed at her with my hand full of cards. "Don't be greedy. Ask the universe that and you'll make trouble."

Kylie's eyes went wide. "Oh, no. I got my man. No one else can have him."

I started shuffling. "When you're asking the cards a question like that..." I flipped a card. "You get something like Two of Pentacles. While not a bad card, it doesn't give you many details. This could mean you'll find someone who will balance you. Kinda a meh reading though. And from what I know about Justin, he balances you, girl, but that probably doesn't apply to Tabitha. So, you asked a vague question, and the cards gave you the wrong answer."

Kylie frowned. "Okay, so more like, will Tabitha find a man soon?"

"Better, but still, soon means different things to everyone. Soon could be tomorrow or this year."

"Can you get super specific?" Tabitha asked, her pen poised.

Something niggled deep inside of me. Teaching was heavier than I thought it would be. I could turn them away from the cards, or draw them in closer. I'd done my research when I'd first gotten into reading cards, but there was such a feel to being a tarot reader. You could learn the meanings of the cards, but if you didn't trust yourself to interpret them, you'd never go beyond spouting off definitions by rote.

"Tarot can sometimes help there. The suits can offer some insight for timing, but you could do something tomorrow that will change everything. That's why Tarot isn't the be all end all for divining. It was actually created to be a game for the bored rich."

"Isn't everything?" Bess asked from the head of the table. She was sitting back, relaxed, with a big goblet of an icy pink drink.

"Rather accurate, right? But when it comes to love, things can be ever in flux. One of my favorite Tarot teachers always says nothing is ever fixed in stone. The tarot cards tell a story, but you write the ending."

I didn't know why that in particular was hitting me hard tonight, as if the universe wanted me to keep that in mind going forward.

Not that I ever let myself forget it for long. But we all needed reminders now and then.

Even the one teaching others.

"That's true." Tabitha started scribbling in her notebook. "So, the more direct questions will get a direct answer."

I grinned. "As direct as tarot can get. The cards like to call you out sometimes, and other times, they are vague. Let's try something like, has Tabitha met the man she's going to get involved with?"

I shuffled and closed my eyes. I hadn't intended on doing a reading for anyone tonight. Normally, I had a few rituals I did to prepare, but this was just friends talking over drinks.

Speaking of that...

I opened one eye. "Tabitha, can you pour me some of that sangria?"

"Oh, sure." She got up and went to the big pitcher.

With her studious energy redirected, I centered myself and focused on the question. She was a sweet girl with a bit of loneliness in her eyes.

I pulled the Ace of Pentacles and The Moon. The deck I was using had a dreamy feminine vibe focused on empowerment. Both images mirrored one another. Our fair Tabitha was just starting her journey. And it didn't really include a man yet from what I could tell. She probably wouldn't like that answer.

But half of my job was giving people answers they didn't really want. It was up to her to work through it.

Tabitha set the goblet of golden sangria full of apples, pears, and raspberries. I smiled up at her and closed my fingers over her hand. "Love is sometimes blocked for a reason."

She swallowed and looked down. "Maybe."

I firmed my grip, watching her aura vibrate between a blue that told me she was feeling very sad and alone and a golden sweetness. I tapped the cards I'd set down on the table. "Maybe you're just at the beginning of the journey to find your guy. This Ace is always a sign of good things to come. But you have to trust yourself."

"I'm not really great at that."

I smiled up at her. "We'll teach you how to get started, okay?"

She nodded. "I'd like that."

Impulsively, I stood and hugged her. I didn't share my personal space with just anyone. She didn't seem to know what to do at first, then her arms looped around my back.

"Oh, I need to get in on that." Kylie jumped up and wrapped around Tabitha's back until we were all giggling like lunatics.

"Okay, that got heavy." I dabbed at my eyes. "The heat is probably getting to all of us."

A loud bang from the front of the building had all of us moving to the half wall. I peered down and found Lucky and Caleb wrestling with a marble-topped table.

We were too far away to hear what they were saying, but I went on my tiptoes when Caleb stepped back and lifted the bottom of his T-shirt to wipe his face.

"Why is that so hot?" Tabitha was craning her neck too.

"I wish I could tell you."

Bess came up beside me. "Because that boy has abs for days, that's why."

I laughed and looped my arm around Bess's. "That he does. And arms and shoulders."

"Teachers didn't look like that when I was a girl. Hell, most teachers were women unless they were professors."

"Well, women are the smarter gender anyway. But I'm sure he does well enough."

Bess patted my hand. "You're right there, my dear." She took one last look over the edge and shook her head. "They are pretty, but today is about us girls, not sweaty men."

Kylie brushed her finger over one of the wilted flowers dotting a planter along the half wall. "Sweaty men always have a place as far as I'm concerned."

"Wait until you're over sixty, Kylie," Bess said and floated back to the table.

Kylie glanced at me. "Pretty sure I'm always going to want a sweaty guy. Especially if he's over me."

I laughed. "C'mon, you don't like to be on top?"

Kylie's eyes sparkled. "Sometimes. But Justin sure looks good when he's pinning me down." She winked and followed Bess.

Tabitha's eyes were wide. "Did she say pinning?"

I laughed. "She sure did."

"Have you done that? I mean, been pinned?" She crossed her arms over her middle, fascination and surprise tingeing her voice.

I grinned. "I tend to do the pinning."

A delighted laugh bubbled out of Tabitha. "I'm so glad you helped me with my Christmas tree. I never would've had the guts to meet someone like you if we hadn't bumped into each other."

"Like me?" I gave one last look over the wall and enjoyed Caleb's flexing biceps before I steered Tabitha back to the table.

23

"So outgoing and sure of yourself. I could never be like that."

"Fake it til you make it, girl. And add in a little self care to believe you're worth it." It had taken me a damn long time to find myself, but I'd become a helper for a reason. Maybe being a teacher was more of a calling than I thought.

The Universe was a weird and wonderful thing.

I gave her an encouraging smile. "Let's learn about those cards. They can help a bit."

She nodded. "I'm ready."

Her spirit made me grin. "You sure are."

"Hey, what do your cards say about finding love?" Kylie asked before biting her lip. "I mean, for you. You're single, right? Or you don't want to go there right now."

I shuffled again to give my hands something to do. "I'm open to whatever happens."

Within reason, I added mentally.

And hey, if pinning was involved, maybe I'd just take that as a sign from a benevolent goddess.

THREE

 Luna

"Wakey, wakey."

I fumbled for my phone. Wait, that wasn't my phone. "Ugh, Ry?"

"Did you forget something?" Ryan Moon's voice came out of my speaker.

We both had our Alexa devices set up so we could drop in on one another. I'd thought it was a good idea when I made her set it up.

I rolled onto my back and quickly kicked my foot out to touch the floor of my bedroom to stop the spinning.

"Did we have a podcast?"

"We did, but we can reschedule." She paused. "Are you sick?"

I pulled the pillow over my face. "Maybe."

"I can't hear you."

I flipped it back. "Maybe."

"That sounds more like hungover."

"Maybe."

Ryan's husky laugh filled my bedroom. "What did you do last night? I thought you were just getting together to talk about tarot with some people."

"There was sangria and margaritas and finger food."

"So, more drinks than eating going on, huh?"

25

"Ugh. Yes." I rolled up to a seated position and the room only shifted a little. I may still have been drunk. "I think Tabitha dumped way more than just wine into that sangria."

"Well, if you make it right—or like half the Pinterest recipes—there's usually triple sec in there too."

"Ugh. She did say it was from Pinterest." Based on the taste at the back of my tongue, I'd bet it was more like brandy. It never, ever treated me well. "Would you hate me if we skipped it tonight?"

"No big. We can do it tomorrow. Want me to bring over the hangover cure?"

"Oh." I sighed as I rubbed my stomach. "You don't mind? I mean, technically I could walk across the way to the diner."

She laughed. "Nah. I'm bored anyway. I'll be there with a meatloaf special."

"You're the best."

"As long as you're aware of that fact, the bestie status is sound. See ya in a bit."

I dragged myself out of my bed and padded to the bathroom. I looked like death dipped in glitter. Somehow I'd lost my shorts and kept my bra—which was usually the first thing I took off—and had one sandal on.

"You're a mess."

There was no fixing that without a shower. I stripped off what was left of my outfit from the night before and scrubbed my face, hair, and person. It was still as hot as the surface of the sun according to my phone app so I dragged on a pair of boxer shorts I'd stolen from an old boyfriend and a tank top. I put my hair up into space buns to get it out of my face.

By the time I stumbled into the kitchen, I was slightly better. Post coffee and Tylenol, I was closer to human. I switched to lemon water to rehydrate for the wine I was sure that was in my future, then forced myself to settle on my yoga mat and stretch out the rest of the kinks from drunk sleep.

Which was definitely not the best kind of sleep.

I got a text from Ryan that she was around the corner, so I jumped up to set my small table and put on some music. Feeling a little more like myself, I danced around the room to my favorite boy band. They were infectious and had surprisingly well-written songs, and I didn't even care that I was staring at the wrong end of twenty as the British dudes of One Direction became my dinner playlist.

I heard a noise in the hall—what amounted to a yowling cat singing along to "Stockholm Syndrome", and fumbling at my doorknob.

"Man, I knew your voice was terrible, Ry—" I opened the door.

A very sunburned and slightly unsteady on his feet Caleb Beck was at my door. He was frowning and looking at his keys then back up at me. "Oh, sorry." He swayed a bit and smiled. "Hey, it's my favorite neighbor." He leaned in. "Gosh, you smell good."

I put my hand on his chest and pushed him back into the hall. "Wrong door, Romeo."

He frowned down at his keys again. "Well, that's why it didn't work." Then his gaze tripped over my very braless chest and down to my legs. "Have mercy."

I laughed and turned him around. "Okay, Uncle Jesse. Your place is that way."

He glanced over his shoulder with an exaggerated whisper. "Sorry. I really shouldn't have had that third beer on the fairway. Damn Lucky and his craft beer. I got a little lost."

"I hope you weren't driving."

"P'shaw. No. I'm a resp-respons—respectable teacher, and I would never do such a thing."

I took his keys from him. "Good to know."

He leaned against the wall beside his door, his flyaway overlong hair in his eyes. "You are really pretty."

"Thank you."

He reached out for my hair, flicking the little curls sticking out of my space buns. "Are you wearing pigtails?"

I unlocked his door and handed him his keys. "I am."

"That shouldn't be hot."

"And yet I'm a-freaking-dorable."

He laughed. "You are." His eyes were soft and sweet and a lot unfocused. Much as I'd been last night with my friends.

"And so are you. Didn't realize you knew all the words to One Direction."

He shrugged and tried to straighten up, but ended up leaning on the wall again. "Seven-year-olds will always love Harry Styles."

"So do twenty-something-year olds."

"Don't tell anyone," he was back to the exaggerated whisper, "but some of the songs are pretty good. Catchy. Especially this one." The end of the song floated into the hallway. "Hey, do you want to kidnap me?"

"Not really."

"Aww." He hiccupped. "I'd be a good captive. I clean up after myself." He shouldered open his door to show off his pristine apartment save for a few boxes in the corner. They must've done a lot of arranging last night. He even had a rug that was surprisingly not beige propped up against the wall. "I'm housebroken and everything."

I crossed my arms over my chest. No, my nipples were not reacting to a male who had his shit together. Or that even when he was a tad drunk, he made me want to lean in and take a good whiff. He just had to smell like bergamot—spicy and warm. One of my favorite essential oils, of freaking course. "Good to know." I took a big step back. "Think you can manage now that you're in the right apartment?"

He held on to the door to steady himself. "If I said I needed help out of my clothes, would that be too forward?"

"Yes." But I couldn't stop the bubble of laughter from escaping.

He sighed and hung his head. "Okay. I think I'm good."

Dammit, he really was adorable. A rumpled golf shirt was half untucked from his khakis and his face was almost glowing red. My witchy self couldn't leave him in that state. And I didn't want to think about undressing him too much, but I held up a finger. "Wait a second."

"Did you change your mind?"

"No."

Disappointment creased his brow. "You sure?"

"Well, I'm going to help you but not to get undressed."

I stepped back just in time for Ryan, my best friend in all the world, to appear in the hall with two bags and her eyebrows raised almost to her hairline.

"Hello." She glanced from me toward a swaying Caleb. "Did I interrupt something?"

I huffed out a strangled laugh. "Ryan, Caleb—Caleb, Ryan."

She gave him a small nod. "Hey."

I took one of the bags and crossed my apartment. "Caleb, wait one second." I dumped the bag on my small kitchen island and crossed to my mini apothecary. I'd had to make up a little something for my own sunburn the other day. I snatched the little jar off my shelf and ran back to the door.

He was waiting just outside my door, a polite smile on his face as Ryan blocked the threshold.

I rolled my eyes and elbowed her aside. "Take this."

His brows were knit once more. "What's that?"

"A mix of aloe and cucumber lotion."

He lifted it to his nose and sniffed. "Why would I want this?"

"For the sunburn that is going to hurt like a bitch when you're not so numb."

"Oh." He gave me a sweet smile. "Thanks."

"You're welcome."

He leaned to the side a bit. "Are you having Rusty Spoon food?"

"We are."

He sniffed the air. "Smells good." He rubbed his flat belly. "I could sure use some fries." He sighed. "And Mitch's meatloaf."

Ryan crossed her arms under her chest and gave me a long look. "Happens to be Luna's favorite too."

"Only for hangovers," I said and pushed Ryan back inside the door. "Okay, Caleb. We'll see you later."

"You don't want to share?" His expression was hopeful.

He was far too attractive for his own good. Or mine.

29

"Nope." I closed my door, then pressed my forehead against it. He was way too cute and I would not be charmed.

"He's pretty cute."

Of course Ryan had to agree with me. Then again, we agreed on a lot. Minus our preferences in men. Those usually diverged.

"He just moved in." I gave her a breezy smile and went for the bags. "Thanks for the hangover food. I am finally starving."

"So, we're not going to talk about the hottie next door?"

I unearthed one of the tins from the bag and peeled back the paper top. "Fries come to me." I reached for the paper bowl of gravy and took them both to the table.

"That's very interesting. Not even going to deny that he's hot?"

I shoved two more fries in my face. "I mean, you have eyes, and you know," I stopped to chew, "attraction is subjective."

"I didn't mention I was attracted, just that he was hot." Ry grabbed a plate and unloaded her food from the containers to eat like a human.

I stared at my fries and picked out an extra long one. "You're not attracted?"

Ryan set her plate down, took down glasses, then unearthed my electric wine opener from the drawer. She knew where everything was since she'd helped me move in, and she was at my apartment almost as much as she was at her own. "Jock dudes aren't exactly my style. They actually aren't usually yours, either."

I sighed. "No, they aren't. And he's not a jock—he's a teacher, actually."

Ryan filched a fry from my tin. "Is that right?"

I pressed my lips together, then blew out a long breath. "He's a second grade teacher at a freaking Catholic school."

She choked. "Excuse me?"

"I know. That seems crazy, right?"

I filled her in on the meet from the day before as she poured us wine then dug into her scrambled eggs and corned beef and hash with hashbrowns. I was pretty sure our food didn't really go with the bottle of cabernet she'd brought over, but neither of us minded.

Her plate and glass were half gone by the time I'd caught her up with everything. And I'd finally cracked open my meatloaf with mashed potatoes and gravy. Because one carb wasn't enough for the level of alcohol I'd had last night—and would be imbibing with her visit.

"Leave it to you to have two dudes interested in you precisely eleven seconds after they meet you."

"How did you get there?"

Ryan rolled her eyes as she cupped her large glass in her long fingers. "Lucky? The tall dude, right? With the hair metal hair?"

I snickered. "Yes, that's pretty much him."

"You said he was blaring music after you and hot for teacher were talking in the hall?"

"Yeah. Sinatra. Insane."

"Yeah, he was blaring the music as a dick move. He probably thought he called dibs."

"What? Where do you get that?"

"I mean, I can pull out the cards to be sure, but you know…psychic."

"Shut up." I stabbed at the buttered green beans buried under my meatloaf.

"And you were doing your stripper pole thing? I mean, c'mon." She gave me a look over the rim of her glass.

"It wasn't on purpose, and the tall one was the one who interrupted me. I wouldn't have even gone out into the hall—"

"Please. You so would have gone out there."

I tossed a fry at her. "Okay, I would have gone out to see if they were attractive. It's been drought city over here. But still, they started it."

Ryan's gaze narrowed. "How did they interrupt you?"

I huffed out a breath. "Caleb was trying to protect my honor—or something stupid like that. The door was open."

"Your door was open?" She sat back in her chair. "Since when?"

Uh oh. "I didn't lock it."

She set down her glass with exaggerated slowness. "He opened the damn door?"

"He's harmless."

"Except he might not have been." Ryan stood and paced.

"I get it." When she whirled to look at me, I held up a hand. "I lock my door now. Even if he's sweet."

"So, the teacher opened the door?"

"No, his friend. My music was blaring, and well, I was doing that complicated workout routine I saw on YouTube last weekend..."

Her brow arched "The one where the chick climbed to the ceiling?"

I gave a little shrug. "You should see the bruises on the insides of my thighs. But yeah, I did it."

"Huh. No shit. Congrats. Still doesn't mean he could open your goddamn door."

"No, and Caleb gave him hell about it. But they're both harmless. I know Lucky from town and the store."

"Yeah, but do you really know anyone? We listen to the same podcasts, dammit. Especially Asher Wainwright's local one." She shivered. "Small towns are only safe until some slasher moves in."

"I know, and I'm careful, I promise. The construction crew wasn't here all week, and I just got a little lax. It was nice not to have strangers all over the building or making noise."

She sat back down and picked up her fork. "All right."

I reached over and placed my hand over hers. "I'm fine. Really." I sent a few comforting vibes her way and watched her relax by degrees.

I loved how protective she was of me. We were both on our own most of the time, and we'd defaulted to watching each other's backs. But we both liked our space, so we'd never gone the roommate route.

We understood the need for boundaries—especially with our work. Being a healer of any sort was draining. For as many love readings we both did for our tarot clients, there were darker aspects to helping someone on their path of self-awareness. We weren't therapists per se, but sometimes we felt like we were. A sacred space was important, and for both of us, it meant one that included alone time.

Especially when I also dealt with the public on the retail end of things at Kinleigh's shop and to a lesser extent, the Ladybug Treasures line that was part of their storefront. I definitely needed time to decompress, and Ryan understood that, although she was a bit more freewheeling with her employment status than I was.

Last week, the reading I did for her on our tarot podcast had said she had some hot sexing action coming into her life—potentially. Then the day after that, her cards had indicated a surprise opportunity. I'd told her she should try hanging around my apartment while the workmen were here since most of those guys were fine, but she'd yet to take me up on my offer.

Hey, two birds, one toolbelt, why not?

"So, now that you know all my dirty details. What's been up with you?"

Ry shrugged. "Same old. April's been squirrelly lately."

"April?" Our mutual friend was as far from chaotic as you could get.

"Yeah. I'm not sure what's up with her. Maybe she's about to meet someone. The energy around her is all fizzy and frazzled."

"April Finley? *That* April?"

Ry kicked back in her chair with her wine resting on her middle. "I know. April usually has a schedule to take a crap—at least I'm pretty sure."

I snorted as I rose to clear the table. "And that's all?"

She focused on her glass. "Yeah. I think the restlessness is just catchy. And it's summer."

I knew summer wasn't exactly Ryan's favorite season. Her mom usually made a surprise visit and threw her life into chaos. As much as she gave April shit for her orderly existence, Ryan wasn't much better.

I refilled her glass. "How about we go up and watch a trash movie on the roof?"

"On the roof?"

"Yeah, they finished the communal space up there. Have some couches, a fake fire pit, and a projector you can hook up to whatever streaming service you have."

"So, what you're telling me is that I can watch FDR on a very large screen?"

I laughed. "So, I should make popcorn?"

Ryan rushed out of the kitchen to where I kept my iPad then came back. "Do we need to bring this?"

"I think I just have to log into their system up there."

"Man, score." She rubbed her hands. "I'm ready for boys to fight over Reese."

"You know those two boneheads aren't fighting over me, right?"

Ryan grinned and took out the second bottle of wine she'd stashed in my fridge. "Right, but it made me want to watch *This Means War*. Something delicious about two dudes fighting over you."

"Yeah, but it's the suck in real life." I pulled out my air popper and all the fixings for sweet and savory popcorn.

"Says you." She sat and crossed her mile-long legs. "What would it hurt if you did try them both out?"

"I'm not really looking to try either of them out, thanks." Though the idea of it made me hum just a bit.

But not when it came to the hair metal best friend. He was sort of a meddling puppy who would probably chew on your shoes and shit in your garden.

Caleb was a different story. I just wasn't sure if it was one I wanted to let play out.

FOUR

CLEARLY, I WAS A NATURAL AT THIS WHOLE MOVING IN THING.

I shelved a bunch of books in my bedroom nightstand and then rolled out the boho chic area rug I'd just picked up at my sister-in-law's place. She'd tried to explain what exactly boho chic meant and why I wanted it for my new digs, but in the end, I'd shoved my credit card at her and tuned out.

Who needed a decorator? Not me. I was a thoroughly enlightened male who was not day drinking ever again. Possibly not night drinking again either.

Alcohol was bad. Especially when you rarely drank so when you did, you made an ass of yourself in front of the gorgeous new neighbor you'd already looked like an ass in front of previously.

I blamed Lucky, as I did for many of the social failures I'd endured in recent years. He had the tolerance level of a herd of buffalo, and he knew I didn't so he enjoyed mightily encouraging me to "let my hair down." Since I had a reasonable length hairstyle, unlike my best friend —I'd let it grow out for the summer, so I looked woolier than usual, beard included—it meant something different for me.

It meant I had to be smart and keep my damn hair up, or whatever the equivalent was, whenever I had a chance of seeing Luna. The likelihood she'd allow me to make her my famous eggs Benedict was shrinking by the hour. It wasn't exactly an ideal lunch offering, but I wasn't counting on an opportunity to make her breakfast anytime soon.

At least not after spending the night. Yeah, right.

We'd met up in the laundry room earlier today, just as we had a few days ago after my tipsy proposition in her doorway after golfing with Lucky. At least I was pretty sure I'd propositioned her then, though the details were vague. I just remembered her smile, the one that indicated she believed I was a few crackers short of a sleeve.

God only knew what had come out of my mouth in her presence. Somehow she reduced me to a hormonal dude with no game whatsoever.

And that was when I *wasn't* drinking.

On our laundry room meetups, I'd managed not to act like too much of a jackass. We'd made casual, easy conversation, the kind that usually happened between neighbors. Talk of the weather—still hot as balls—and our work and our detergent preferences to get our whites brighter. All typical, low pressure topics.

I'd nearly asked what she used on the purple teddy mixed in with her underwear before sense had briefly reappeared.

Handily, she'd had on jeans and T-shirts that didn't overtly reveal her navel piercing or her super long tanned legs or any of her many assets below the neck. Of course her face was a damn knockout too. But she was also fun to talk to with a great sense of humor as we discussed some of our other neighbors, an eclectic bunch I was still getting to know.

Basically, we talked like people who had no remote interest in sexual congress with each other.

That was probably true on her part.

I opened another box and crammed more books on my shelves. These were easier to fit, since they were some of my college texts that had particularly resonated with me. Poetry volumes from Rainer Marie Rilke were mixed with a true crime tale I'd picked up a few months ago about a college teacher who stored bodies of several of the college co-eds he taught in a freezer on his property in the woods.

That had been suggested reading from Asher Hamilton's locally set true crime podcast, which I'd started listening to entirely on accident. So far, I'd read some creepy shit, usually when I couldn't sleep at night, which probably explained why I rarely got back to sleep afterward.

One way or another I had to get back in the game sexually. Back when I'd cured my occasional insomnia with non-self-administered orgasms, I'd gotten a lot more sleep.

Spotting my bottle of antibiotics on the nightstand, I popped one and chased it with water. Had I taken one yesterday? I didn't think so. I swallowed another with more water and wiggled my foot.

Yet another moving casualty. I'd stepped on a damn nail while carrying in more boxes and had to get a tetanus shot and a round of antibiotics since naturally, the wound had looked nasty and hurt like a bitch. My toe was wrapped up now and didn't ache much anymore since it had been a few days.

Assuming Lucky didn't drop another futon on it out of spite over the Luna door opening situation.

He was still holding a grudge, though I'd made it clear she thought I was about as appealing as the large ficus tree I'd helped her carry in last night. Turned out when a guy spent an unnatural amount of time at his window watching for a certain woman, he could be of some service.

Actually, I was fairly certain she had more warm and fuzzies toward the ficus that she'd named Sir Anthony.

I didn't ask. I didn't want to know.

My cell buzzed in my pocket and I dragged it out, spotting our neighbor Tabitha's name. She'd graciously loaned me a couple of pieces of bread for French toast when mine looked more like a science project than the delicious artisan bread I'd picked up at the grocery store. I was pretty sure the limping had also made her feel sorry for me.

Luna hadn't been home, so I'd gone knocking on other doors until someone had taken pity on my growling stomach. In return, I'd taken down some of Tabitha's recycling, for which she'd been very appreciative. Then she'd given me her number out of neighborly consideration.

Or else she liked men who occasionally listed to one side.

"Hey, what's up? Is it your turn to ask to borrow bread?"

"No, I bake my own."

"Oh, is that why yours tasted so delicious?"

When she giggled, I frowned. Did she think I was coming on to her? Did my vocal cords agree? "I mean, it was good, but bread's bread, you know."

Her laughter stopped. "Uh, yeah. I know. I'm pretty much a bread aficionado."

"Me too. But some days, I'd eat a stale cracker if it filled the hole."

"I know how that is."

I rubbed my forehead. I really needed to get laid if I was finding a conversation about bakery goods to be too suggestive between new neighbors.

Unless one of those neighbors was Luna. Then I'd be happy to discuss varieties of grain products until she wanted to sample my breadstick.

"So, um, how's your boyfriend?" Hopefully, Tabitha would have one, and I wouldn't have to wonder if she was scoping me out for a possible hookup.

Not that she wasn't beautiful. She absolutely was. She had long, wavy caramel-colored hair and a sweet smile. If I hadn't seen Luna first, I probably would've been up for trying her rolls and the rest of the contents of her bread basket too. But Luna was...holy fuck.

And since I'd turned over a new leaf about not dating in the Cove, I was highly selective. Casual or not, there was no way I'd tempt the diaper-pushing fates by getting to know two different women at one time. That was asking to be a guest star on an episode of *Maury Povich* right there. If that show was even still on.

Nope, not happening.

"My boyfriend?" Tabitha sounded puzzled.

"I mean, a pretty lady like you must have one, right?"

She laughed softly. "Oh, no, I don't. Not even close. It's so hard to meet someone nice, you know? I don't want to do online dating. So many creeps on there and I don't want any dick pics."

"Yeah, there was just a killer on one of those sites too. He used a machete to chop off—" At her gasp, I cleared my throat.

Apparently, with some women, talking about murder and mayhem was a deterrent too. Good to know.

"Okay, now I'm definitely not trying one of them, even if I'm alone until I'm one hundred and my girly bits wither and disintegrate." Then she gasped again. "Oh, God, did I just say that?"

I had to laugh. "Also the way I'm feeling right now. Sorry. My ineptitude knows no bounds lately. I blame the drugs." That was most certainly a joke, but she didn't know me well enough to understand the only drugs I was on were antibiotics and Advil.

Yeah, I'd just quit while I was ahead with this one.

"So, what's up?" I asked, bravely forging ahead despite the many signs not to.

"There's this thing. Tonight."

Uh oh. "Uh, sorry, I probably can't make any things."

"It's on the roof." She rushed ahead. "In that cool gathering place up there. Have you been? If not, you should come tonight. Luna is having a thing, kind of a small dinner party, but I was thinking that—"

"Yes. Definitely. I can go." She'd just said the magic word. Granted, it would've been better if Luna had invited me to her *thing* herself, but I wasn't easily deterred. "What time?"

"Oh, really?" Tabitha's voice rose. "You can go? It's at eight."

"Sure. Sounds good."

I immediately felt bad. I really hoped she was just being friendly. But if not, maybe I could get Lucky to help her out.

Not like *that.* I wouldn't sic my horndog best friend on a sweet, innocent woman. But he had friends who weren't quite so openly on the make. Maybe I'd see if he could invite a couple guys to come over too, to help make up for my lack of availability.

Assuming she wanted me, because c'mon. With my sterling track record, it was likely.

"Can I bring someone? I mean, a guy. Or a few?"

"Oh."

I hastily expanded on my question. "Not as a date. Or like a poly thing. I'm a one-woman man. At least now, since I have a new resolve." *And a healthy fear of procreation.* "So, anyway, can I bring a couple friends? Attractive ones. Ones you would be happy to have at your party. Or Luna's."

Not that I wanted Luna to be too happy with them, for obvious reasons.

Tabitha said something I couldn't quite make out, and I swallowed a groan. For fuck's sake, what was my deal lately? I used to be smooth with women. Just not since I'd been breathing the air in the Forrester Apartments.

"Um, sure. A couple friends should be fine. It's not really a party, just a small get-together."

A call from Lucky came in. Perfect timing.

"Got it. Just a couple people." More chances for me to get to know Luna better, though of course I'd talk to Tabitha too. She seemed like a fun person.

I quickly thanked Tabitha again for the invite and ended the call and switched to Lucky.

"Hey, free tonight?"

"Do you know how to say hello?"

"Hello. Free tonight?"

"Depends. If you need help matching your shams to your drapes, call a chick who cares."

"How do you know the word shams?" I only knew it because Kinleigh had used it today when I'd been in the shop.

And no, I hadn't bought any. There was a decorating point of no return, and I was certain that was it.

"I know things, okay?"

I smirked. "A woman told you, huh?"

"Possibly my last girl asked me not to rip her shams while we were…conversing. What do you have in mind for tonight?"

I explained the Tabitha situation, which made Lucky laugh hard enough to fracture something.

"You honestly think she's into you?"

"Why is that so hard to believe?"

"She could be being polite. If she wanted to put the moves on you, why didn't she ask if she could come up to eat your toast crap?"

"She's shy. And it's not 'toast crap', it's French toast."

He snorted. "Right. I think she's just being nice, but whatever, I can gather the boys."

"Not a crowd," I warned. "She said Luna wants it to be small."

"Luna, Luna, Luna. You are whipped, my friend. And taking Tabitha up on her invite only to try to get in tight with Luna is sketchy as hell."

"I know that," I said irritably. "Why I'm bringing you and a couple of your friends. That way she'll have other options. Decent dudes, Lucky. Got it? Besides, I am just getting to know everyone. Not trying to have sex."

He started laughing again, even harder than before. "Right. I'll see how many are available. Free booze?"

How many was not a phrase that seemed to indicate a couple friends. "Like two. Max three. And yeah, I assume there will be alcohol—"

He hung up.

I frowned and stared at my phone. Already I was getting a bad feeling about this. I should never have trusted Lucky to invite a few guys. We had many of the same friends, and I'd taken a shortcut to avoid texting people because I'd wanted to empty a few more boxes before I headed upstairs. I wasn't finished unpacking.

Eh, too late to worry about it now. He'd figure it out. Besides, it was short notice, so how many guys could he round up that fast?

Answer: a hell of a lot, as I found out a few hours later.

I managed to get through the contents of a bunch more boxes and then showered off the dust and sweat before pulling on some khaki shorts and a T-shirt. As my hair drip dried over my shoulders, I remembered I'd intended to make an appointment to get it cut, since school would be starting in a little over a month.

Before that, I'd have administration days and meetings and all that fun stuff and I'd have to tuck my Wildman Jack look away until next year. Winter break wasn't long enough to go full-on bearded or to let my hair go. The curls were out of control in this humidity, and hell if I used product in it. I was about ready to shave all the shit off.

I stopped in the kitchen to grab a bottle of...well, not wine, since apparently, I didn't have any. Why hadn't I gone grocery shopping yet? I didn't even have beer, a fact I'd not noticed until this very moment.

What I did have was a dubious looking bottle of coconut rum. I didn't know where it had come from. I certainly didn't drink that stuff. But it was rude not to bring an offering, and I was already running late.

Hmm, maybe Lucky could—

Nah, I'd asked him for enough already. Last thing I needed was for him to bring a keg to Luna's shindig.

To try to make the rum look like a better hostess gift, I slapped a bow on the side of the bottle that had fallen out of a box of Christmas crap and been trampled underfoot. I rubbed the footprint off and tried to perk it up then shrugged.

It was the thought that counted, right?

I tucked it under my arm and stepped out into the hallway, smiling as I heard the music coming from upstairs. It wasn't loud, just enough to indicate people were enjoying themselves.

Hopefully, I would too.

I grimaced as I headed down the hall then upstairs to the roof. My foot looked stupid with my bandaged toe sticking out of my sandal but it was too damn hot for real shoes. Not to mention I wasn't stuffing it into a toe box quite yet.

Just before I opened the door, the music switched to that Luna-style sexy stuff that had lured me the first time I saw her.

I grinned. Auspicious sign.

I opened the door and blinked at the softly lit space. There were colorful pillows and flickering candles and that low, erotic music offset by easy feminine laughter. A few women were roaming around or clustered near each other in the oversized round chairs that doubled for sun worshipping. The table held a serious spread of food, most of it light and summer-friendly. A lot of watermelon and delicate finger food.

My stomach growled. Where were the meat and potatoes?

Then Luna stepped forward in a loose romper-looking one-piece thing the exact color of the cantaloupe in the fruit platter, and I forgot all of my hunger needs except one in particular.

For her, backlit by candles and with the breeze fluttering in her long hair.

Surprise made her smile falter. "Caleb? What are you doing here?"

Tabitha popped up from a seat near the wall that surrounded the rooftop space. "I invited him. Hope that's okay. And...oh." She lifted her hand to her mouth on a self-conscious laugh. "Guess I was too late there, huh?"

I didn't know what she meant, but I made an effort to drag my gaze from Luna long enough to smile at Tabitha. "Hey. Thanks for inviting me. Sorry I'm late." I held out the bottle of rum toward Luna, who arched a brow.

"Is this your drink of choice?" She took the bottle from me, eyeing it with...not distaste exactly, but definitely not with excitement.

So, she wasn't a rum chick. Noted.

"No, it's a hostess gift. For your party," I explained when she continued to examine the bottle.

"For my party?" She glanced at Tabitha before looking at the bottle again. "How kind of you. Imagine if you'd delivered it before the best by date of," she bit her lip, "June 2015."

I cleared my throat. "You know how liquor is. I let that age."

"Hmm. Yeah, thanks." She set the bottle on the floor under the table.

Defiantly, I bent to pick it up and grabbed a colorful glass from the stack of them. "I'll have it then. This is the good stuff."

"By all means. Start us off." She waved her fingers at me, and I was nearly certain she was trying not to laugh. As was Tabitha.

I filled a glass and tossed it back shot-style, figuring it would hurt less if it went down fast. The sickly sweet alcohol burned when it hit my stomach, and I nearly gagged from the over-the-top, well, girlishness of it. I didn't know any dudes who would drink this.

Hell, I didn't know why *I* was drinking it.

But it didn't stop me from exaggeratedly smacking my lips as I tipped more into my glass. "Damn, tastes even better than I remembered. Bottoms up," I managed before I gulped down more rum.

"You are a game one." Her smile softened around the edges as she shifted to look at Tabitha. "Did you invite anyone else?"

Her cheeks reddened. "No, just Caleb. I didn't know I shouldn't."

Luna waved a hand. "It's perfectly fine. This is the spot for neighbors to get to know each other. It's not a huge building. We'll be in and out of each other's pockets whether we want to be or not."

Well, that didn't sound particularly promising, but I was a guy who preferred to look on the optimistic side. "Yes, and sometimes you just need a couple of pieces of bread."

At Luna's questioning look, Tabitha explained my visit.

Luna let out a light laugh. "If you need bakery goods, she's the door to knock on. She owns Sugar Rush. Best Half Moon cookies you'll ever taste. We take those cookies very seriously in the Cove."

"Aww, thanks, Luna. And if you want incredible tarot readings, great fashion tips or creepy true crime tidbits, she's your woman." Tabitha shook her head. "Guess you have that in common."

"Which one?" Luna asked curiously, her sexy blue eyes sparkling in the candlelight. "Let me guess. The fashion tips? Do you know of any hot new designers or have any tattoos in interesting places?" Her voice turned into a purr on that last part.

Not that I needed any encouragement from her direction to get harder than stone.

When I didn't immediately reply, she shifted to toe off her sandals, angling her body just enough for me to glimpse what appeared to be a daisy tattoo high on the back of her thigh.

My mouth went dry, leaving me no choice but to gulp more rum.

"I'm not big on fashion, but I'm a fan of tattoos and especially true crime. You'd be surprised how many ways you can brutally kill your neighbor with common household items."

As Tabitha covered her mouth, I drank more rum in the hopes of shutting myself up.

Luna, however, seemed amused. "Oh, you must be a fan of Asher's podcast then. You have to meet Bess. She's his—" She broke off and blinked down at my foot. "What happened to you?"

I swallowed repeatedly to try to get that hellfire taste out of my mouth. "Huh?"

Luna crouched in front of me to lift my leg. She eased my sandal off and propped my foot on a chair before touching it gently.

I swayed and it wasn't entirely from my lack of balance. Her touch felt like heaven. "Nail." I could barely speak.

"Oh, no. Your bandage is frayed. I can fix you up better than this." She stroked the side of my foot and I swayed again, because now my balance was affected by the urgent weight between my damn legs. If I didn't topple over, it would be a miracle.

What was it with this...goddess? That was the only appropriate word. Even her golden hair appeared to be glowing in the shimmering light.

"We can go—" She didn't get anything else out, because a sudden clattering of feet climbing the stairs disturbed the low-key environment.

My head was swimming from a mixture of rum and Luna, but I knew without a doubt that I'd made a serious error in judgment.

Not the first time when it came to my best friend. Probably not the last either.

I would never, ever fucking learn.

The door to the roof burst open and Lucky appeared, flanked by a whole heck of a lot more than a *couple* friends.

More than half a dozen. In fact, I was pretty sure the stairwell was clogged with quite a few of Crescent Cove's bravest. Maybe some of the finest too.

Didn't want to leave out any of the first responders, after all.

Luna's mouth dropped open as she rose and stared hard at me before swinging her gaze back to Lucky and his band of loud-as-hell merry men. "What is all this?"

Lucky held up a six-pack and motioned to the crowd behind him. "We came to party, womenfolk!"

FIVE

BELATEDLY, I REMEMBERED THAT CHAOS FOLLOWED LUCKY WHEREVER he went. Usually because he invited it and fed it slices of watermelon and shots of tequila.

In this case, he doled out a lot of both, acting as a master of ceremonies of sorts although he had not been invited by the woman holding the gathering. She hadn't invited me either, and from the looks she occasionally slid my way as she tried to salvage the night, she had not forgotten that tidbit.

"So, our fair Tabitha invited you, you said?"

Glumly, I poked at my watercress and cucumber mini sandwich with the plastic skewer I'd stolen off a drink. Not mine, since I was trying to slow down. I hadn't had all that much, all things considered, but after pounding that straight rum, I'd begun at a distinct disadvantage. Add in that whole lack of tolerance thing and I didn't feel too hot.

And so far, I'd spent most of my time talking to Bess Wainwright, a woman who was at least forty years older than me. She was lovely, no doubt about that, and she had a sharp wit and a great sense of humor, but she wasn't really in my target group.

"Yeah." I ate some of the watercress and decided it wasn't as awful as I'd assumed. Though I'd really prefer a steak. "She's nice."

Bess was eating far more enthusiastically than I was. She speared a cube of honeydew with her fork. "She is. Not for you, hmm?"

In lieu of answering, I lifted my head to glance where Tabitha was leaning against the wall, a smile on her face as she spoke to Brady, the newest member of our police force. She was popping green grapes in her mouth as she chatted animatedly. I wondered if she realized he was watching the path of the fruit from the tips of her fingers until she bit down. That little flash of tongue before she chewed and swallowed.

It would've been an almost unintentionally erotic display, if my dick hadn't been in the midst of a depressive episode. My toe was too. Ever since Luna had stroked my foot and then abandoned me to the vagaries of my raggedy bandage, it had felt cold and sore. And since the temperature had to be in the mid-eighties even now that it was after nine pm, that said plenty.

Bess turned her head to follow my gaze and she nodded sympathetically. "Scooped by a man in uniform." She made a noise that reminded me of what my cousin's cat did at the window when she was trying to lure birds into her den. "Such a handsome one too. Look at how that shirt fits him."

"They buy them all a size too small so their muscles bulge." There was no keeping the irritation out of my voice.

Bess laughed and poured from a pitcher of some fruity drink with a decidedly alcoholic scent into her glass. "Our honorable firemen too? They also fill out their attire quite well. Not that you have anything to feel bad about in that department, Cal."

"Caleb," I corrected. "Only my mother calls me Cal, and she's not allowed to either."

"Noted." She didn't laugh openly, but I heard it in her voice.

I didn't blame her. I'd laugh at me too right now if it didn't make my head swim.

"Why do I have a feeling you aren't over here drowning your

48

sorrows in cucumbers because of Tabitha's appreciation for the men in blue?"

"No. I brought her that man," I mumbled.

Bess's dark brown brow arched. "You run a male delivery service? Can I place an order? I just want one for an hour." She tapped her chin with fingers winking with sparkly rings. "Or two. Then he can run along home. Much easier that way."

I had to chuckle. "Actually, Lucky brought all these dudes." I gestured around us.

The rooftop area was pretty packed. Most everyone had broken off into couples or groups to talk and laugh. Bodies pressed close flirtatiously. Some people were even dancing.

Not me. With my toe, I'd probably somehow pitch myself off the roof.

Then again, a lawsuit might set me up for life. Forrester had the cash to spare. Assuming Luna didn't tell anyone how much questionable rum I'd consumed like a dumbass beforehand.

"He didn't stay in school long enough to learn how to count very well," I added, chewing on a piece of cucumber since it was there. "I said a couple. Max three."

"Seems like he tacked a zero onto the end of that number," she said drily.

It wasn't quite that bad, but Lucky was on my shit list, regardless. Especially since he had some tiny little thing on his lap as he fed her from a skewer of tropical fruit. I didn't know if she was another neighbor or where she'd come from. Maybe he'd brought a date. Why not, since he'd invited half of Crescent Cove anyway?

"I wanted her to find someone. You know, since she couldn't find me."

Bess nodded with sympathy for my plight, although I wasn't sure she knew who or what I was talking about. "That was kind of you."

"I thought so. Maybe not. I think I've lost my game."

She stopped assembling her own mini sandwich with an assortment of vegetables to lean forward, her brow furrowed. "Like a handheld device?"

My laugh sounded rusty. "No, like you know, my ability with women. I used to be extremely popular."

"Oh. Naturally."

"I'm not going to say I had to beat them off with sticks or anything, but it was pretty close."

She nibbled her sandwich delicately. "I can see that."

"You can?" I hated the desperation in my voice. I'd probably regret this conversation tomorrow when I sobered up—because my current state could not be my real personality now, nope, nuh-uh—but right now, I appreciated any crumb an attractive woman threw my way. "If I could dance, you'd be impressed with my moves too."

"Oh, would I now?"

I jerked a shoulder. "Just saying. I have them."

"I would think nothing less of you."

"Luna left, didn't she?" I asked moodily, swinging my gaze around the rooftop in a wide arc that almost levered my head right off my neck.

"No, I don't think so." Bess shifted around to check. "She was dancing with Kylie a little while ago. Then Justin, Kylie's beau, came up here and then they disappeared. Not sure where Luna got off to. Knowing her, she went to replenish the refreshments."

"You think so?" I swiveled in my chair to look behind me just as Lucky climbed up on a chair and shouted about changing the playlist. His bouncy, fruit-loving friend was nowhere in sight.

A minute later, hip hop music boomed out of unseen speakers, the kind of stuff fitting for a club. That wasn't Lucky's preferred genre usually, but he hopped down to bump 'n grind with yet another woman, this one with long dark hair and a giggle piercing enough to make me rub my temple.

"Where did all of these people come from," I said under my breath to no one in particular.

Bess seemed similarly mystified. "Did he pass out flyers? I don't recognize most of them."

"You and me both. I know a few new tenants just moved in, like me. Hey, you live here too?" I cocked my head at Bess.

"I do." Her small smile was indulgent. She probably saw me as an equivalent to a dopey grandson, assuming she had one of those. "In fact, if local legend can be believed, I'm reasonably sure your niece was conceived in my apartment."

I'd made the mistake of taking a sip of something alcoholic. I choked and it spewed over the leftover vegetables on my plate as Bess handed me a cocktail napkin without blinking.

"Which one?" I forced out. "I have two." Then I held up a hand. "No, please. I'm already seasick." I frowned. "Is this roof moving?"

"No, I'm afraid it isn't." She leaned forward to press the inside of her wrist to my forehead. "You're not feverish. Must just be too much drink."

"I'm a teacher," I said indignantly. "I know my limits."

Too bad I never managed to abide by them lately.

"You have two nieces?"

I nodded, trying valiantly not to lay my head down in my plate.

"That's lovely. I have two granddaughters. My Asher has—"

"Wait, Asher Wainwright?" The dots connecting made my brain hurt. "The podcast dude? Today's show is about an ax murderer. Dammit, I missed it." I put my watch up to my ear.

"Pretty sure that's not how that works." She shook her head and started to rise, swirling the voluminous folds of brightly colored fabric that draped around her. "I'm going to find Luna, see if she has any suggestions for...this." She waved a hand at me and I couldn't even object at being a *this*. I'd have to climb up several levels to hit that status right now. "She's mentioned a hangover cure that could work for what ails you."

"I'm not hungover. I haven't made it to morning yet."

But Bess was looking around, a quizzical expression on her face. "Or you mentioned Lucky? The boisterous one?"

I snorted. "He's an asshole. But I don't need help. I'm good." I lurched to my feet and admired the stars revolving above my head. How cool. "I got it," I insisted, holding a hand out directly in front of me when Bess hurried around the table to offer me her support.

"Lucky can just come downstairs with you, make sure you get in okay. Where did he get off to?"

"Probably in that girl." I grimaced and clutched my head. "Sorry, Bess. Ma'am."

She sighed. "You think you're having a good day then you get *ma'am*-ed."

"Sorry, Mrs. Or Miss? Whatever. Sorry, lady. I gotta go. Thanks for the advice."

"I didn't give you any," she called after me as I focused intently on making it to the door of the roof.

Well, that explained why I didn't feel any more enlightened.

Through the miracle of gravity, I made my way down the stairs. I nearly fell into the wall when a pair of women started heading up the narrow staircase, but one of them offered a steadying hand and somehow slipped something in my pocket. I didn't know if it was a roofie or her phone number. Either seemed equally possible. She and her friend were gone before I could get my wits about me enough to ask.

I was tempted to shout after her, but at that moment, Christian Masterson appeared at the bottom of the stairs, his uniform hat set precisely on his head and his mouth in a grim line.

"Beck. Why am I not surprised you're part of this melee?"

I frowned. I wasn't at the peak of my wits right now, but I was pretty sure I was alone in the stairway—other than Christian himself of course. But looking around did not seem advisable right now, so I focused on the good officer's unsmiling face.

"It's Lucky's fault."

He nodded. "Also not surprising Roberts is involved." He took out a notebook. "We've received numerous noise complaints. As well as," he cleared his throat, "a report of a large male exposing himself as he urinated over the side of the roof."

I shouldn't have laughed. It wasn't funny. Or it wasn't that funny. But hell if I didn't have to grab my stomach as I barreled into the wall yet again.

Christian, however, was not amused.

"That wasn't you, was it?"

I grew serious immediately. Even toasted off my ass, I remembered just fine that I was employed by a Catholic elementary school, and Sister Tobias would not be amused by such antics from her educators. "Absolutely not. I'm more than the average eight inches, but I wouldn't say—" I was pretty sure I giggled at Christian's look of disgust. "Okay, fine, I can't say I'm not large, but I didn't pee off the roof. I don't even have to go."

"Thank you for that needless explanation. A yes or no would've sufficed." He started to push past me then stopped on the stair above me. "You live in this building?"

I nodded, the movement seeming sluggish even to me. Obviously, I'd have to sleep this off. I was a hot mess, as the kids would say.

God, I was getting old. Not even thirty yet, and I couldn't handle my drink. *Again.*

"Okay. Think you can get to your apartment on your own steam?"

"Of course." I stepped off the last step and fell into the door forehead-first at the bottom of the stairs.

"Right. You seem in great shape." Shaking his head, Christian blew out a breath and snapped his notebook shut before ascending the last few steps to the roof.

Once he'd gone, I took a deep breath and opened the door to the hallway. I could do this. A few more feet, and I'd be at my apartment.

I shambled up the hall, cocking one eye open to watch the passing numbers. Just a few more doors and I'd be able to fall into my bed and sleep it off. And when I woke up, I would ensure there wasn't any more alcohol in my apartment. Not even one drop.

I tried one door and found it locked. Not mine. I'd left mine open. Crescent Cove was safe. Pretty safe, other than the risk of getting peed on if you passed by the Forrester Apartment building at the wrong time.

Giggling again to myself, I leaned against the wall until my feet worked. My damn toe ached like a bitch. I was sure it was absence of Luna. Like that was a physical condition.

Hey, if I could make it outside, maybe I could serenade her at her window. That was in a movie once, and the heroine had probably banged that dude senseless. Chicks loved sappy romantic gestures.

Then again, if I even managed to get it up at this point, that'd be romantic enough.

I continued on down the hall and turned another doorknob once I was reasonably sure I was in the right spot. This door swung open easily, and I smiled in triumph.

Bingo.

And Christian had wondered if I could handle finding my apartment. *Pfft.* I hadn't had any issue.

I stumbled inside, immediately assaulted by a cool water scent that made me sigh. Smelled so good. So soothing. That would appeal to all the hordes of women I wouldn't be having sex with because of my ninja swimmers.

Bummer for them.

I bumped into something and frowned. That wasn't where my couch was. Or was it? I'd moved things around more than once since moving in. Since when had I been so indecisive? I needed to put stuff in one place and keep it there.

A shaft of moonlight through the wide windows illuminated a table with a vase of some green fern-y stuff. I frowned again. Did I have flowers? I didn't think so. But I continued on, lured by the intriguing items strewn upon the floor of the open plan apartment so like my own. I followed them to the bedroom with its large dark blue bed, finally stopping by the foot to pick up a lacy bra dangling from the post. That definitely wasn't mine. I checked the tag.

38 DD. Damn. I had good taste.

Hmm. I turned my head and took in the space. I noted a few girly touches like candles and glittery gems in piles or circles on top of pieces of furniture that could've come from my sister-in-law's and my brother's vintage shop. Then my gaze zeroed in on one particular artifact, one that I couldn't forget in this lifetime or any other.

Luna's gleaming silver stripper pole.

Shit, wrong apartment. What the hell was I doing here? New

building or not, how did I screw up so badly? We were right across from each other, but this clearly wasn't my place.

I frowned as I stared at her bed and rubbed my aching temple. Bedding was piled high, with enough pillows that it probably felt like sleeping on a cloud. Not that I cared about such things when a woodpecker wasn't trying to drill his way out of my skull. But right now, I wanted to dive in and sleep for a century.

At least for a dozen hours or so.

I gathered a handful of her silky sheets and breathed deep. Her bed smelled like a mixture of wildflowers and the ocean. All beachy and floral and sexy as hell. The combination shouldn't have made me lightheaded, but none of my reactions to this woman made sense.

Then again, the alcohol was probably helping. I was never drinking again.

Nope.

I glanced over my shoulder then back at the bed. Maybe I could just take a little nap? Luna wasn't even here, and besides, it was the neighborly thing to do to offer comfort if possible. I was clearly ailing.

Once I'd had a nap, I'd be on my way, with my head full of things that I shouldn't know.

Like her choice in bras. And her cup size. And what it was like to sleep in her bed, even if she didn't happen to be there at the time.

"Just a few minutes, I promise," I muttered, slipping between the cool sheets. I groaned so loudly at the feel of her pillows beneath my aching head that I went still, fearing I'd somehow alert her wherever she'd gone. I didn't think I was physically capable of getting up and leaving at this point.

All I wanted was some time alone in her luxurious, sweetly fragranced bed. Please God. Just long enough to make the stabbing in my brain stop.

This time, it wasn't even caused by a homicidal neighbor. Although it just might be when Luna found me in her apartment.

I grabbed for the item I'd dropped in my haste to lay down and brought it to my nose. And smiled at the scent of Luna on my face as I closed my eyes and prayed for oblivion.

SIX

 Luna

I climbed the stairs to my apartment. I'd be glad when the renovations were done and the elevator would be in working order. The stairs didn't bother me for the most part—mostly just on grocery days.

Right now, this sore body would have taken the elevator gladly.

I had not intended to sleep on Ryan's couch last night. I'd escaped the impromptu roof party to rescue my bestie. This heat wave was doing a number on everyone—including Ryan's car. It had only made it a few blocks before overheating.

Instead of dragging her back to the chaos of the roof, we'd decided watching *This Means War* with a bottle of wine was a way better use of our time.

I'd lost count of how many times we'd watched that movie. But it was a comfort and the friendship in the movie matched our own. Funnily enough my new neighbor and his burly best friend reminded me a little of the male counterpoints in the movie.

With more hair.

There was definitely an air of competition between them, layered with an obvious love that few guys liked to show. I was waiting for

Lucky to grab Caleb by the face and say, "I love you, man," much like the guys in the movie.

Maybe I'd get the chance with another party. I had a feeling it would be a recurring thing based on how quickly people arrived. There was little to do in the Cove after eight o'clock. Oh, there were a few restaurants like the Haunt, the Cove, the Mason Jar, and the Spinning Wheel that catered to the younger people in town—but when it came to summer there was nothing quite as good as a rooftop.

Especially when those places required spending a bit more money than the average twenty-something had at hand.

Speaking of...Responsibility weighed on me as I got down the hall. I really shouldn't have left cleanup to Tabitha and Bess. Normally I enjoyed a bunch of happy people and I even got off on the energy exchange most of the time. However, I'd had a full week of heavy readings and the heat had kicked my ass.

Even now, the hallway was oppressive at nine in the damn morning. I just wanted a shower and to sit under my overhead fan with the air conditioning on blast.

"Come to mama." I sighed and glanced down the hall. "After I check the roof."

Dutifully, I took a quick run up the stairs and found nothing amiss. The chairs were set back in their respective quadrants. There was even a new hammock set up that I didn't recognize. "Bless you, Bess and Tabitha."

I could have kicked up my heels cartoon style as I got back down to my floor. I dug into my rainbow hemp bag for my keys, ignoring my buzzing phone. Ryan had sent me on my way this morning with thanks and a croissant. The only other person who would contact me right now would be looking for an "emergency" reading.

Because tarot readings were not an emergency no matter what some of my regular clients thought, I ignored my phone. I gripped my doorknob and was about to insert my key when the door opened freely. I frowned.

Had I forgotten to lock it last night? I'd been in and out with all the food prep for the small party. Maybe the SOS call from Ryan had me running out without double checking.

I frowned at the sandal in the middle of my floor.

And because I'd been on my own since I was seventeen, I grabbed the retractable baton I kept in the drawer of my kitchen island. I snapped it out and peered around my space.

It didn't look like anything had been stolen. More like someone had lumbered their way through Hulk-style. A few of my crystal towers were toppled over and a package of incense cones lay crushed on my rug.

I scanned the room as I blindly rummaged into my bag for my phone, prepared to call for reinforcements. Luckily the Chief's station was a short trip from my building. There were advantages to being located on Main Street.

I held the baton facing down and away from me as I quietly crept through the main space. It was an open floorpan that was cut up by my furniture and, of course, the stripper pole I'd installed. Nothing seemed amiss beyond an orphaned sandal. My altar was the same way I left it yesterday. The swing I'd hung with August's assistance was still, the little crystal sun catcher above it sparkling in the morning sun.

The room didn't feel wrong per say, but it definitely was full of energy that was not my own. I moved further into the adjoining hall that led to the bathroom and bedroom. The first thing I saw was a man splayed out face first on my bed.

Naked.

Well, mostly naked.

I tightened my fingers on my baton.

Khaki colored shorts were pooled next to the bed and a blue checkered shirt was twisted around his waist as if he'd only gotten it half off before crashing into my bed.

My bed.

What in the goddess?

Was he...a snore answered the question before I could even ask it.

59

One of the man's feet was dangling off the edge of the bed since he was laying diagonally. I frowned at the tattered bandage on the toe.

"Caleb?"

He just kept snoring on.

I resisted the urge to slap his bare foot with the baton. The thin tip would make him sorry he was alive—especially if I went for a particular part of the sole of his foot. I was an accomplished reflexology student. I knew where to hit where it would hurt for days.

Unfortunately, I used my powers for good, not evil.

And he'd been bumbling along adorably last night about his toe while trying to flirt with me. I was secure enough in my own self-worth to know when a man was into me. Even if I'd felt a tiny twinge about it since Tabitha had seemed interested enough to invite him to our little get together.

At least until a bevy of beefcakes had landed on our rooftop. And more than a few of the firemen had been giving her some attention. I seemed to remember she'd been very chatty with a certain new deputy in town as well. Their auras had been full on glow so she couldn't have been too into Caleb. More like a lonely soul open for any and all opportunities.

Something I wish I'd still had. It had been a damn long time since any man had made me interested in doing more than flirting. But this one...

Mostly naked in my bed at the moment which should be more annoying than it was—but he'd been very hard to ignore.

And those very tanned shoulders with a smattering of freckles as the only ink on him were very nice and change up for the guys I usually went for. As were the tapered muscles that led to a very nice butt.

I collapsed the baton then slipped it in my bag before I tossed it onto my chair covered in laundry I'd yet to put away. At least it was clean.

I eased around the bed to find him hugging my favorite pillow. The one that always helped to cool me down since I was a hot sleeper.

Looked like he was of a similar sort.

Or he was just an overheated drunk.

One of his knees was hiked up so he was frog splashed across my entire bed. It wasn't exactly a small bed, but Caleb Beck was a pretty sizable guy—and a fit one.

I can't say I minded that one little bit.

Was the Universe giving me a little present today? *Ahh, Luna you've been working extra hard and you haven't taken time to have any fun.*

I frowned. Was something under his cheek?

I covered my mouth against a laugh. My purple bra cup was cradling his cheek like a lover.

I shook my head. The not-so-little pervert even had a sweet smile on his face.

And just showed that the Universe had a sense of humor. Have a little gift, but it comes with a bit of a clown package.

Figured.

He'd been in a bad way last night. Surprisingly since he'd only had a few shots of rum—and a fairly lame alcohol content at that. Nothing that should have put him on his face. Unless he'd kept on drinking after I'd been called away.

His hair metal friend had been the life of the party. I caught a few cases of beer coming in as I was going down the stairs. And to be honest, I hadn't minded. Summer was for rooftop get togethers and I was pretty sure Ryan would have enjoyed a few of the firemen that had shown up.

But the moment the car thing happened that had been it. All we wanted was her projector, which made any wall in her place fair game, and some popcorn and wine fueled goodness to decompress. And waiting for a tow just sucked the party out of a girl.

Leaving just enough time for a certain intruder to enjoy my bed.

I crouched in front of his face and lightly tapped his arm peeking from the pillow—*my* pillow. Now it was going to smell like him. It remained to be seen if his bergamot scent would annoy me or not. "Excuse me, Goldilocks. I think you got lost."

Nothing.

I tapped his nose. "Hello."

61

He groaned and his ridiculously long lashes fluttered. Why was it that guys got all the good lashes?

But then those celadon colored eyes met mine. Instead of looking startled, he gave me a slow smile. "Hello, beautiful."

I couldn't help but smile back, damn him. "Did you get lost?"

He sighed and his eyes started to drift closed again. "No, I'm in the most perfect bed. It smells like the ocean and Luna." He sighed. "Perfect."

I pressed my lips together against a laugh and an audible aww. He really was far too adorable for his own good. I should probably be running for the hills.

"You know, getting an invitation to my bed is preferable, right?"

His eyes opened again, this time alert and shocked. "Oh, shit." He hopped off my bed and crashed to his knees since his shirt had clamped his arms into a weird position. Like one of those TikTok videos where you saw just how much a man's center of gravity could land him on his face.

I laughed again.

He popped up on his feet and looked around my room. "Oh, shit."

"Articulate, too."

He flushed. It was pretty impressive too. From his deliciously sculpted chest all the way up his neck and then it bloomed across his cheeks in scarlet slashes. "Shit. I'm so sorry. I, uh…" He glanced down at himself, his shirt dangling from his wrist. He tried to put it on, but failed miserably.

I took pity on him and came around the bed once more. I held up my hand for him to stop flailing with his shirt. Instead of helping him dress, I snapped it off his wrist.

He stared down at me, his chest heaving a little in panic. A guy's worst nightmare, I imagined. His aura went from a roiling dark chaos to a softly glowing orange. I laid my hand on his chest and dropped my shields.

The ones that I kept up to keep people out. To protect myself and my energy. Being a healer meant that I needed those boundaries so people wouldn't siphon it all away from me. It also meant that I could block out those little tingles that showed attraction and want.

I realized that gave mixed signals to a guy sometimes.

Right now I didn't really want to be mystical.

I just wanted to let the sweet and sexy teacher in a little.

His chest expanded with a deep breath and he turned to face me fully. He was almost a foot taller than me—most people were taller than me to be honest, but I liked the breadth of him. Big enough to get me excited, but not too big to make me nervous for my safety.

He'd been off center with me since we met, but now he seemed to know just how to approach me. I was pretty sure some of my boundaries were to blame. I went on my toes to kiss him and he leaned his head back.

I blinked.

Had I read him wrong?

I glanced down at his very happy boxer shorts.

He gently put his hands on my shoulders. "I want to kiss you more than anything, but I cannot make our first kiss full of foul dragon hangover breath."

I laughed and nodded toward the bathroom. "There's an extra toothbrush in the medicine cabinet."

He pointed at me. "Stay right there."

I couldn't stop smiling. "I'll be right here."

He zipped off into the hallway to the bathroom and I immediately rushed around my bedroom. Luckily I was the kind of girl to have girl junk all over and not just in the bathroom. I'd used my backup toothbrush at Ryan's house, but not much else.

I quickly shoved a comb through my crazy curls and spritzed some of my own concoctions of essential oils and floral scent in my hair and down the front of me. I had one of those ridiculously unflattering but super comfortable shelf tank tops on that did nothing to lift the girls, but I didn't exactly have time to swap out clothing.

While the water was running, I decided to check my face instead.

Yikes.

Pale and colorless, my lashes were practically non existent without makeup, but I didn't want to look like a raccoon post fucking either. You know, if things went beyond a kiss.

Because the way the air was humming and...well, how I was humming—definitely more than a kiss was happening.

Probably.

I was pretty sure.

"You're perfect."

I looked up and caught him in the mirror. His face was freshly scrubbed and his curls were slicked back as if he'd ducked his head under the sink. I dropped my makeup brush. "I don't know about that."

He stalked across the small space and looped his arm around my waist to turn me around to face him, then drew me up on my toes and covered my mouth.

Startled, I couldn't do anything else but hang on. I'd started out giving him the high sign and of course he took it to the next level. His mouth was firm, the tickle of his beard was just right, and his arms made me feel amazingly safe.

I pressed myself to him and opened to his swipe of tongue.

Then he took that little opening and flattened me up against the wall next to my bedside table. The macrame wall hanging dug into the back of my head and something else fell to the floor, but I didn't care.

I just wanted more.

I lifted my knee up on his hip and he took the initiative to hoist me up, wrapping my other leg around him before he pinned me to the wall. His boxers were even happier and I'd been impressed on the first check-in. The kiss was wild as a tempest. I didn't have time to breathe or pull back. And for once, I didn't want to.

The sun slanted through the windows of my room turning him into a gilded warrior. Fanciful, but the way he looked at me between kisses fit the definition. I was the spoils of our little war. One he didn't even know we'd been in.

I'd thought I could ignore this. Believed that it would be easier to keep him out, but then he'd been right here in my damn room and it felt so right. So freaking good. Like a gift.

He hiked me up a little higher and nudged down the low scooped tank I was wearing with his beardy chin. He watched me for a reaction and when I nodded, he swiped his tongue over the tip of my breast before drawing on the tip. It was just on the edge of pain, but then he released it and swirled around the tip lightly.

"Goddess," I panted out and gripped his shoulder.

"Caleb."

I gave him a throaty laugh that morphed into a groan as he ground the shaft of his definitely happy cock against my center then went for my other breast. He hummed around me and licked and flicked, bit and nibbled.

He didn't leave anything untouched.

"I can't get enough of your skin." He dragged his beard up my neck to my ear. "You taste like the ocean."

I tightened my legs around him. It wasn't even ten in the morning and we were heading for ninety degrees outside. "Is that because I'm sweaty?"

"No." He leaned back a little to lock his gaze with mine. "Everything about you and your apartment feels and smells like cool water. It's why I ended up in here."

"Not for me?" I teased.

"Everything is for you."

My eyebrows headed for the ceiling.

He pressed a quick kiss against my mouth. "That was supposed to be way less creepy. I just mean something about you makes me think of cool, calm waters. Comfort."

I wiggled my decidedly uncool self against his hot cock. "Comfort, hmm?"

"Last night I was hot and drunk—but not drunk if you know what I mean. I barely had anything to drink. But the antibiotics I'm on made me queasy."

I rolled my eyes. "You know you can't drink when you take those, right?"

"You can't?"

I sighed. "No. It makes you loopy and sideways on alcohol." I scraped my nails along his neck. "Even big strong men."

He flushed again, but also leaned into the scrape of my nails. He nipped at my chin. "Yeah, well, I was feeling crappy and just bounced down the hallway like a pinball. Then I was here. I must have locked my door."

He tucked one arm under my ass and backed up to swing around so he could sit down on the edge of my bed. But instead of letting me off of him, he gripped my hips so I'd stay straddled over him.

Now I was the one with the upper hand. I straightened and lightly rolled my hips against his. "So, you decided my apartment was the best place for you to lay your weary head?"

He hissed out a breath, lifting his hips as if to fit us together. His puzzle piece was definitely looking to lock us in place. "Not bright, I know. I was just going to lay there for a moment."

"Quite a few moments, Goldilocks."

He grinned up at me and flicked his tongue under my chin before he tasted his way along my jawline to my ear. "But your bed was just right." He bit down on my lobe, his teeth clicking over the tiny star earrings that climbed up the shell of my ear.

Then he flipped me onto my back on the bed.

I let out a yelp and bowed up in a fit of giggles as he pushed up my shirt to get to my belly. His beard was just long enough to tickle. He nibbled his way over my ribs to my belly button and tucked his tongue under the navel ring I'd gotten as a rebellious teen.

When he pulled lightly, it seemed to be attached to a gossamer string attached to my clit. It throbbed in reaction, making me reach for one of the scrolling bars of my iron headboard.

A wolfish flash of teeth made me gulp down another gasp. He dug his hands under my ass and flipped my shorts and panties off in one fell swoop, tossing them over his shoulder. When I thought he'd go right for my pussy, he stopped for a moment and kissed my ankle before whipping off each daisy sandal to follow my shorts.

Disoriented with the odd bits of sweetness in the seduction, I could only hold onto the headboard. He splayed his long fingers over my lower belly before he tunneled his thumb through my slit to expertly find my clit and pressed down in little fluttery pulses.

I blew out a calming breath, trying to get my bearings, then he lowered his mouth to drink from me.

His other hand slid up my body to push at my shirt. His green eyes flashed as he came up for air long enough to say, "Off."

I struggled to get it over my head, shoving pillows out of the way. My dreamcatcher swayed above us, and the clink of bells and crystals were the only sounds beyond my ridiculously wet pussy. I should've been a touch embarrassed, but I was too busy enjoying his very talented tongue.

He hummed out a growl as he replaced his thumb with his lips and tongue. He dragged his damp thumb up my sweat-sheened skin to my breast. He pulled and pinched as I arched up against his mouth.

I held onto the headboard. It was really all I could do. The tempest was back and he was pitching me into the heart of the storm. I dug my heels into my mattress when the rasp of his tongue tossed me into a screaming free fall.

He clamped a hand over my middle and held me down, demanding more.

My eyes flew open and I dug my nails into his forearm as I came apart in a kaleidoscope of colors. We both glowed hot and I slammed my eyes shut against the pure white light of perfection.

His name was a litany. A prayer. A chant.

I didn't even know at this point.

I just wanted to bask in it forever.

Then he was gone.

My brain went offline as I tried to recover. Suddenly, he was back, pulling me up from my starfished position on my bed. What was oxygen? I surely didn't know right now. I was living in the land of orgasmic bliss, and I really wanted to buy some property on it.

He draped my legs over his thighs, then dragged me upright to straddle him.

I wrapped my arms around his shoulders. "Hi there."

He nibbled on my swollen lips and grinned. "Hi."

"Wow."

He laughed and kissed my neck. "I almost came just from listening to you say my name." Pride tipped up the corner of his mouth. "Many times."

Now it was me with the full body flush. "I wasn't expecting all that."

"Me neither, truthfully. But fuck, you're so goddamn beautiful." He pressed his dick against my belly, the length of it reaching up between us. "And I want inside you so bad."

I crisscrossed my arms behind his neck. "What are you waiting for?"

He held up a condom.

I snatched it out of his hand. "Goldilocks came prepared."

He winced. "Not really. I keep one in my wallet, but for a guy, it's mostly a beacon of hope."

I laughed and ripped it open. "Well, let's get that beacon suited up for a little party of two."

He gripped my thighs. "You are freaking incredible."

I shimmied back enough to get my hand on his considerable length. "You're just saying that because I'm naked and very willing."

"No. I mean, yes, that's a very good point. But that's not all—"

I leaned forward and cut him off with a quick kiss. "Let's just have fun with this. You're single and I'm single. It's the summer and—"

He cupped my face. "And we're really good at this."

My fingers stilled over the hot, silky tip of his cock. "We haven't even had sex yet."

"Well, get that condom on so I can show you what I already know."

I rolled the latex down his length, then he laid me back on the bed. We detangled legs before he climbed over me and slowly lowered himself so he could slide inside of me. His stormy gray-green eyes flashed something akin to wonder before he met my mouth in a hot, hard kiss.

I lifted my legs up and around him and accepted him inside of me. The quick rush of energy buzzed through me as I took each thrust like an offering.

Heat and bliss.

Pleasure soaked connection.

A promise I wasn't sure I was looking for, but stole anyway.

I raked my nails down his sweat-slicked back as we chased our way out of the storm and to the sun. Arching under him, I clamped down on him as he flung back his head and groaned out my name. I rode the edge of his strained release and found one more of my own.

He collapsed on me and I held him there when he murmured an apology.

The overwhelming mix of emotions that followed sex flattened me. I always took on a piece of my partner, no matter how good my shields were. But I'd opened myself to Caleb and couldn't quite turn it off. Instead of running for the hills like most men, his quiet contentment poured into me.

He finally leaned back a bit. "I need to take care of this."

I nodded and shifted to let him up. I pulled the sheet over me as I curled onto my side. Muscles I hadn't used in a damn long time were deliciously stretched and abused.

He came back and sat on the edge of the bed, lightly tugging on my shoulder until I looked at him. He held up a washcloth.

I shook my head. "I'm just going to take a shower."

"Okay." He slid the cloth over my neck and skimmed along the edge of the tangle of short chains I wore. He nudged the sheet down to drag the cooling cloth over my breasts before dipping his head to taste the tip of one.

I groaned, my skin oversensitive.

He seemed to understand without me telling him that it was too much. He rolled me over onto my belly and straddled me.

"Caleb…"

"Shh." He dragged the cotton over my back and gently wiped me down before pressing a light kiss between my shoulder blades. "Let me cook you breakfast."

"Breakfast?"

"It's my specialty."

I stacked my arms under my head. "I bet it is."

"It's the least I can do."

"It's not porridge, is it?"

He laughed. "No. That Goldilocks thing is going to be drilled into the ground, isn't it?"

I grinned. "Yep."

"Come to my place. You probably don't have the stuff I need."

I looked over my shoulder. "Planned this all along, teach?"

"Nah. I'm just really good at one thing, so I always have it on hand."

"All right." My stomach growled at the thought. "Obviously, that sounds good. Let me take a shower and I'll be over."

He hopped off my bed. "Great." He swiped his clothes off the floor and headed out.

"Caleb," I called after him.

He came back in. "Yeah?"

Goddess, he was adorable. His curls were back and shagged around his angular face. And he was unapologetically naked. To be truthful, he should have no qualms about it. He took care of himself and I enjoyed looking at him.

"Put your clothes on. I'm the only one who's going to see you naked for however long we do this."

I wasn't sure what made me say that. Exclusivity wasn't exactly my style. I didn't exactly bed hop, but he didn't owe me anything.

Instead, he gave me a wide smile. "I like the sound of that."

Then he was gone.

I tugged my pillow under my head—the one that now smelled like a mixture of Caleb and me.

Goddess save me, I liked the sound of it too.

SEVEN

A RECENT MOVE WAS A BLESSING IN DISGUISE. MY PLACE WAS STILL pristine since I'd cleaned everything before putting my stuff into it. It had been in good shape when I moved in—Forrester was no joke on the classy digs—but it was still a construction zone and a fine layer of dust had been on everything.

I rushed through my apartment, stripping off my cargos as I went. I hadn't bothered dressing since I was right across from Luna's place. At least I'd made sure the coast was clear first. I wasn't sure how Luna felt about letting others know we were getting naked together.

She seemed cool about it, but post-orgasmic bliss was a precarious place. It could go very wrong, very fast.

I tossed my dirty laundry in my basket and rushed into the shower. Being the middle child had made me a pro at the seven-minute shower. Because there was hell to pay if I'd stolen all the hot water before my sister got her chance in the bathroom.

My antibiotics must have been kicking in because my toe barely hurt, but it was still nasty enough to require a Band-Aid. Evidently, the only Band-Aids I had were pink princess ones—thanks, Rhiannon—but it would have to do.

It was too fucking hot since my apartment was front facing, and the sun was blasting in my windows. I knew it would be awesome in the winter, but right now, I was sweating even before I hung up my towel. Lightweight shorts for the win. I brought a T-shirt out with me for after I finished cooking.

I wasn't a complete animal.

My fridge was severely lacking since the grocery fairies hadn't arrived overnight, but I did have the fixings for eggs Benedict. I hadn't been lying about that. My sister had also gifted me with an air fryer as a housewarming gift which left me and my multi-tasking skills at an all-time high.

I was just adding ingredients to my blender for the sauce when there was a knock on my door.

I draped my towel over my shoulder and rushed over, opening without looking who it was. My first mistake.

"I smell bacon," Lucky said as he came in and shut the door. He slammed a twelve-pack of beer on the counter. "I figured I could—"

"Nope. Out." I turned down the heat on the eggs poaching. "You gotta go."

"Why?" Lucky's face fell. "I was just checking in on you. Figured we could watch some golf."

"Luna's coming over for a late breakfast and…well, she's better than your smelly ass."

Affronted, Lucky crossed his arms. "I took a shower."

"Still, I'll take the wildflower and water-scented Luna over you."

"Wildflower? Dude. How do you even know what that smells like to name it?"

"Haven't you ever gone on a picnic or something? Fields of flowers, you know." God, I sounded crazy.

"No. The only picnic smells I know are grilling burgers and dogs. Maybe some veggies for the chicks."

I rolled my eyes. "Nice."

Lucky leaned a hip on the kitchen island. "What the hell is going on? Are you…oh."

"What?" I hurried back to the stove to save the eggs from being overcooked.

"You moved pretty quick."

"Moved?" I lifted the pan off the heat, then rushed back over to my hollandaise sauce.

"Not even a week and you're cooking breakfast? Last night you looked like death warmed over rice."

"Last night you were drinking enough for three people. How did you even know?"

"I notice stuff." His voice was cool.

I pulsed the blender so everything mixed evenly. "Look, it was a weird thing, but Luna and I hit it off." Minus clothes, but I wasn't mentioning that part. "Now I want to keep impressing her, if you don't mind."

"I see how it is." He grabbed his half case. "Catch ya later."

"Dammit." I had to add the melted butter to the sauce before it split. I'd apologize and bring Lucky his favorite beer tomorrow.

Another knock came just as I was pouring the melted butter in. "Come in."

Hopefully, this time it was the woman I was cooking for and not my brother or dear God, my mother.

Luna peeked her head around the door. Her pale blond hair was pinned up in the puffy pigtails she wore most days. They gave me inappropriate thoughts immediately. There was something about the messy cuteness of them that always made my chest tight.

"Hey. Did I take too long?"

"Not at all. Right on time."

"Smells amazing."

I grinned. "I forgot to ask if you were okay with meat."

"Carnivore to the core." She slipped inside and closed the door gently and I got a full view of her from the back.

Fuck.

She had on short white denim shorts and the daisy tattoo I'd caught a glimpse of last night was in full view on the back of her thigh. Her shirt was short, showing off a solid two inches of her lightly tanned skin. Something glittered at the small of her back, but then fell down under her shorts as she turned.

The blender pulsed on high and I quickly fumbled for the button to turn it back down.

Luna grinned and came in with a carafe of some sort of juice. "Whatcha making?" She set it down on my kitchen island.

"Uh." I quickly looked down at my sauce and stopped the blender. It was definitely done. "Eggs Benedict."

"I've never had it." She shoved her hands in her pockets and I got another flash of that glittery something. A chain around her middle?

Fuck. She was going to kill me.

"Where are your glasses?"

I cleared my throat. "Next to the microwave—left."

She peered down at what I was making with a raised brow, then went to the microwave and opened a cupboard. She had to go up on her toes and the only reason I kept my damn hands to myself was because I had to get this just right or it would taste like crap.

But Jesus, her ass. I just wanted to crowd all up against her and touch her skin.

She turned around with two heavy mason jars. "I took you for the cheap glasses from Target kind of guy."

"First of all, Target is definitely not cheap."

She giggled. "That's true."

"And secondly, that's because of Ivy. She got me addicted to smoothies and those suckers screw right onto my blender."

"Oh. Guess I'll have to try one of those too. Can I help?"

"I'm good. You could grab us some plates though. Other side of the microwave."

"Got it." She looked over her shoulder. "Is that just so you can check out my ass again?"

"Definitely."

She grinned. "I'm enjoying the half naked chef myself. Though aren't you afraid of bacon splatter?"

"Air fryer."

"Miracle invention."

"That's a fact." I walked to her and reached around her to put the

English muffins in the toaster. My arm coasted along her waist. The shirt she was wearing was as silky as her skin.

She stared up at me, nibbling on her lower lip.

"You're stunning."

Her smile spread. "A shower works wonders for the both of us." She ticked her nail down my belly, making me tighten the abs I actively worked on thanks to a rowing machine at the gym.

Close up, she hadn't bothered with makeup from what I could tell —women had lots of tricks of the trade there though. But there was something sparkly on her skin, and I swallowed at the large gap in her shirt.

She'd only fastened the bottom two buttons of the very brief top. A trio of gold necklaces hugged her at the neck, then hung a little lower and finally, a triangle of some sort of brown stone literally made an arrow down to her very unencumbered breasts.

I slid my hand across her waist and under the cropped shirt. Her skin was petal soft along her belly and warm where I feathered my thumb under the fullest part of her breast. She stared at my mouth, licking her lips. Her nipples tightened under the silky fabric, raising against the material with every stroke of my thumb.

The toaster popped behind her.

She jumped a little and laughed. "Breakfast is served, I guess." She slid away from me and went around the island.

I gripped the counter and blew out a slow breath before grabbing the muffins. My cock was trying to break free of my damn shorts.

Slow your roll, son.

I turned to find her climbing on one of the stools that made my island a quickie eating nook. That shirt was going to kill me. Every time she moved, I got a peek of her stupendous breasts.

She trailed her fingertip along the lip of her glass, gold rings glittering from every finger. A few even adorned her fingers at the middle bend so I couldn't help but stare at them, imagining them curled around my dick again.

I'd never had a woman take me in hand with such confidence. And she'd damn near killed me when she rolled the condom down my length without even a blip of hesitation. She'd known what she wanted, and fuck, I was glad it was me.

When I met her gaze, she gave me another one of those half smiles. Secretive, seductive, and a whole lot of playfulness. I leaned into the emotion. It was a rare post-sex situation where the woman wasn't looking for something more or to dissect the act.

I forced my shoulders to relax and took this for what it was. Sexy fun with a woman who was endlessly fascinating. And I was not going to fuck it up.

"Hey Siri, play my Sunday playlist."

She smiled wider as Siri actually followed my first directive, and INXS blasted out of the speakers I'd synced up in my apartment. I did a little shimmy back to the air fryer and was rewarded with one of her warm laughs. Perfectly crisp bacon was ready. And I couldn't resist popping a piece in my mouth.

I turned with one for her. "Madame."

She leaned forward and a hint of rosy nipple dragged my attention away, but I managed to resist the urge to hop the counter and have a taste. She opened her mouth for the half broken piece, and I placed it on her tongue like an offering at church.

Her lids lowered as she chewed. "Delicious."

"Fuck."

A bit of grease glossed her lip, and she swiped it away with her thumb. "Feed me first."

"Right." I plated the eggs over the bacon and buttery English muffin, then the sauce and a sprinkle of parsley on two plates. I fanned out a few strawberries I'd cut up that my sister-in-law had left the other day.

I definitely needed to go grocery shopping if I was going to cook to impress her again. Maybe hit up one of those MasterClass tutorials from the membership my mother had given me for Christmas.

I nodded to the actual table I had set for us.

"Fancy." She slid off the stool, her bare feet sparkling with more adornments both on her toes and ankles. She was like a pocket of glittery sunshine in my apartment.

I set the plates down and held out a chair for her. Still holding her glass, she went on her tiptoes to give me a quick kiss. "Thanks."

I swallowed at the quick jerk inside my chest. Not my dick— though that was still more than interested. No, this was a far more dangerous thump. "You're welcome."

I sat down next to her and laughed as she lowered her face so she could look at it from the side. "Feels too fancy to eat."

I reached over and slid my knife through the pile of food to destroy the magazine-worthy display.

She pouted. "If I was the type to take a photo to share with the world, it would have been sharable."

"And now it's edible."

I sliced through my own and popped a bite into my mouth.

She followed suit and made a low moan. "Oh, wow." Then she dug in and requested another muffin to mop up the rest of the sauce.

We laughed through the meal as I filled her in on the rooftop party. "It definitely wasn't as fun as I'd hoped."

She tore off a piece of an English muffin. "You mean when you convinced poor Tabitha to invite you?"

I winced. "Caught that, did you?"

"Maybe." She took a sip of her juice. "It was inspired to invite the fire department though."

I rolled my eyes. "Yeah, that was not the plan."

"Lucky?"

"Guessed it in one." And because she had a good idea with the extra bread, I returned to the kitchen to make another English muffin and brought out the rest of the sauce.

She took the sauce bowl from me. "This is like crack."

"I won't tell you how many calories are in there."

"Don't worry, we'll work it off." She winked at me, and my dick went back to fully hard.

"You're not like any woman I've ever been with."

"I do like being an original."

I leaned over to steal some of the sauce she'd filched.

She twisted until the bowl was out of reach. "Nope."

"Greedy."

"You have no idea."

"Is that right?"

Her laugh slipped away as she flicked open the two buttons that kept her shirt together. "I like getting what I want."

I gripped the edge of the table when she slid her shirt open to reveal one breast. "Isn't that every woman?"

She dabbed her fingertip into the sauce and trailed it over her tight nipple. "Maybe. But I bet you haven't tasted this sauce off all the women you've made this for." She stood as she licked the creamy hollandaise off the pad of her finger. Then she tucked my hair over my ear. "Do you usually make it as a parting gift?"

My gaze fell to her breast. "Sometimes."

"Is this a one and done, Caleb? It's okay with me if it is."

"No. There's nothing about us that's one and done, Luna." I leaned in and flicked my tongue over the salty tip, watching as her bright blue eyes went dark with pleasure. I drew her closer, tucking my hands into the pocket of her shorts to anchor her between my legs.

I used my beard and lips to caress every square inch of her beautiful breasts. She swayed as I took my time to learn her. To watch her eyes dilate when I nipped a little too hard and then go slumberous as I gentled. All the while she played with my hair until we were both practically purring.

I wanted to take my time with her.

Instead of sprinting for my own orgasm, I wanted to watch her go over again.

She shrugged off the shirt and it pooled at our feet. I slid my hands free from her shorts to unbutton them until they followed suit. She wore a pale pink scrap of panties, but instead of removing them too, I spun her around.

"Christ, you're beautiful." I raked my fingers lightly down her smooth back to the lush curve of her ass. The panties were almost not worth wearing. It hid nothing, but accented everything. She rocked lightly to the music, her hips keeping rhythm with the beat.

What I thought had been a single chain was actually a double layer of gold with little pink crystals dangling from the clasp at her hip. I traced the curving line along her lower back then skipped to the lace string of her panties.

I drew my thumb down the cleft of her ass and reached between her thighs. "Are you wet for me again?"

She looked over her shoulder. "Maybe I'm still wet from this morning."

"Is that so?" I dumped her into my lap.

She yelped out a surprised laugh.

I buried my nose into the stray curls along her ear. "How bendy are you?"

"I do have a stripper pole in my apartment." She rubbed her ass against my cock. "What do you think?"

I slid my hand around her middle, the chain teasing my forearm as I coasted my two middle fingers down the damp lace between her thighs. "Open wider."

She draped her knee over each of my thighs. "Like that?"

"Wider."

"I can't reach the floor, Caleb."

"I've got you." I kissed my way over the skin of her shoulder before scraping my beard back along the way I came.

"Sure your chair can handle this? We could go to your bedroom," she said on a groan as I tucked my fingers under the lace into her silky heat.

"We'll get there."

Maybe.

I wasn't sure about that, especially since she kept grinding on my dick. She was flowing over my fingers and I strove to hear that soft whimper she made right before my name had tumbled out of her mouth. I could manage to hold out against just about anything to hear that again.

I kissed her throat and concentrated on unlocking all her secrets with my hands and memorizing the little noises she made. With my other hand, I tugged and plucked at her nipples, cupping her breasts gently between the firmer caresses she seemed to crave.

Her back arched and I opened my thighs to spread her farther.

I wanted it all. Knew instinctively the tiny bite of the stretch would make her hum all the more.

"Luna."

She was past conversation. Sun streamed into the apartment. The golden beams cut across her body, highlighting the shimmer of her skin, the dark blush of her nipples I'd caused, and the lace cutting into my knuckles as I thrust into her again and again.

Her soft cries turned to strangled gasps. I held her down and demanded more.

My dick screamed to get inside of her, to ease my own pain, but I didn't have a condom on me.

I'd have my turn.

I might die first, but she'd come for me, dammit.

She cried out to some name I didn't know, but it had an inflection that I recognized. Nirvana. God. That place where you weren't exactly in your own body. She shook and clamped her hand over mine. Her fingers slid between mine until we were both stroking the soft flesh of her pussy.

"Fuck, Luna."

Her other hand came up and gripped my hair as she practically levitated off my lap. Her body bowed and every muscle tightened while she shook.

Then a moment later, she simply dropped back onto me with a shiver. She turned her face until our lips met in a messy kiss that was more sighs than technique.

I sat up and shifted her so her legs were together, then hoisted her up in a princess carry.

Her sleepy blue eyes sparkled as she quickly looped her arm around my neck. "Now that was some brunch."

No 'I'm too heavy. Don't do that.' She just embraced the moment and allowed me to carry her. "Just wait until dinner."

She tipped her head against my shoulder. "I think you tried to kill me."

"Nah. I still have plans for you."

"Maybe give me a couple minutes?" She yawned. "I'll be ready for round three in a few."

Disappointment made my dick want to whimper, but she was too cute for words.

I headed for my room. While I could probably rouse her to get a little something for myself, I resigned myself to some downtime.

Gently, I set her on the navy sheets of my king-sized bed. She instantly curled onto her side and tucked a pillow into her chest. "I'll just be a second. A few minutes maybe," she mumbled.

I kicked off my shorts and crawled in next to her.

She settled back against my chest and pulled my arm around her waist. "Just a lil' nap."

I shoved a pillow under my head and prepared to wait out her nap. Surprisingly, I followed her into slumber just as quickly, wearing a smile.

Magical Luna properties apparently worked even when she was in my bed.

EIGHT

 Luna

I ROLLED OVER AND BUMPED INTO A WARM AND VERY SOLID BODY. CALEB was on his back, his arm flung above his head at an angle he'd probably regret when he woke.

My first instinct was to slip out of the bed and head back to my own place.

How many times had I done the disappearing act?

I really didn't want to figure out that number. Instead, I wondered what the next steps might be if I actually stuck around for the first time since I was... Wow.

Yeah, that was a memory lane I definitely wasn't going down.

Pushing that aside, I perused the very nicely made man lying beside me. The man who'd made sure I had been well taken care of this morning and post brunch. Of course most guys were on their best behavior for the first few rounds.

Either that or they were just selfish pricks from the jump and not worth my time. Caleb was...different.

He had player written all over him. The charming grin and effortless hotness factor had given him a leg up. I'd known men like him all my life, but when he was around me, he seemed to trip over himself in ways that confounded him.

There was a difference between guys who were normally goofy and inept introverts and those who were generally comfortable in their skin.

Caleb was definitely aware of the checkmarks in his good column. He was a teacher, so he was smart and good with kids, charming, and had the All American Dude label practically stamped on his forehead.

All the things that would make him comfortable to be around, but not the kind of guy I usually let in my bed.

Our worlds would never have collided if not for the hallway between our apartments.

Was that fate interfering? The universe liked to fuck with me as much as it had saved me.

"That's a lot of thinky thoughts going on."

I peeked at him over the pillow I'd commandeered. He still had his arm above his head and his eyes were closed. "A woman's prerogative."

He grinned and rolled onto his side to face me. "Looking for an exit strategy?"

"Reviewed and discarded."

His sun-bleached eyebrow arched. "Noted."

I tucked my hand under my cheek. "We're not dating, and we're not exactly one-night-stand level here."

"We're our own thing." He leaned in and brushed his nose along mine, then rolled me onto my back. "Whatever it is, I like it."

I slid my leg along his and opened for him. There was something delicious about a man's weight when the intimacy was easy. Maybe that was my problem. I didn't want to keep my shields up around him.

That was dangerous.

His cock lengthened, the blunt tip pressing against my belly. I reached between us and familiarized myself with the shape of him. The last time had been quick and mindless. He'd had me on the edge before I could even catch up. But now, I could take the time to make him crazy.

He was warm and smooth with a flared head that made me want to take a taste. I started to inch down and he stopped me.

"I would really love to watch that pretty mouth around me, but I'm still ready from before."

I nipped his chin. "You had a hard-on the whole time we slept?"

"I dreamed of sinking into you."

My fingers paused around the base of him. "You dreamed of me?"

He lowered his mouth to mine instead of answering. And then it was just the warm, late afternoon light haloing around his head as he pushed himself into my hand with a groan.

No talking. Just action.

I was pretty sure he had the right idea. I wasn't usually an overthinker by nature and it was throwing me off.

No more of that.

I licked my way up his neck, swirling my tongue around his Adam's apple. The scruff of his beard rasped against my lips, making them buzz.

With my other hand, I gripped his very bitable ass. His stormy eyes met mine. They were heavy-lidded and intent. The soft orangey glow of his aura flowed into me.

I rode on the high of it.

Happiness without any angst or trauma.

He lived solely in the moment and dragged me along with him, cupping the back of my head and angled me so we lined up from mouth to hips. My breasts brushed over his lightly furred chest, raising the tips until they ached for a touch.

Our hips moved in tandem to each stroke of my hand. Easy and unhurried—we had nowhere to be. I sighed, drawing in his breath and recycling it through my body back into his.

His eyes went wide as the unconscious energy exchange filtered into him, ramping up the pleasure. The tip of him was damp against my belly as his arm flexed into the mattress to hold us in the moment.

"Luna."

I smiled into his kiss as my name became a prayer on his lips.

He braced himself on his forearm, digging his arm under my neck so he could reach into the bedside drawer. "I need to fu—I need to get inside of you."

I nodded and we fumbled between us to get the condom on. Both of us shaking a little as the moment became larger than it had started out being.

I lifted my knee up and around his other forearm as he shifted us over to the middle of the bed. He seemed to understand that I needed all of him in one fluid thrust.

My breath hissed out as he stretched me to capacity. I arched my back even as he pinned me to the mattress. He leaned back, rising up on his knees to spread me open using long, achingly slow strokes.

I looked down between us to see how his cock glided in and out of me.

For a moment, I wondered what it would feel like without the barrier. I pushed that thought out as quickly as it came. I propped myself on my elbows and cupped my breast, tugging at one nipple then the other as he watched me.

He closed his hand over mine, then coasted up to my neck and held the back of my head as the slow strokes went deeper and harder. The angle made the room fuzz around the edges as I went from slow burn to orgasm before I was ready.

I choked out a scream only to have Caleb right there with me. He slammed his mouth over mine and swallowed each cry as I twined around him, locking him inside me. I pulsed around him, the release skipping from one to another raging orgasm as I shuddered under him.

He stiffened over me, burying his face into my shoulder with a scrape of teeth and finally, a heady groan that made my toes curl.

I lightly trailed my fingers down his sweaty back as our racing hearts synced up then steadied. He didn't move for a few more minutes, and talking seemed like it would break whatever this spell was.

Finally, he rolled us so that I was sprawled across his chest. "I'm not ready to move yet, even if the massacre under the sheets says I need another shower."

I giggled against his chest before peeking under the sheet. "A few minutes ago, I thought to myself…Luna, that's one of the most beautiful cocks you've ever had in your hand."

"Yeah?" His lips kicked up at the corner. He lifted the sheet. "Looks pretty sad right now in his wrinkly raincoat."

I rolled onto my back with a startled laugh. "No, you didn't just say that."

"I mean, there's nothing attractive about a condom. You know, except the lack of a baby or STDs."

I lifted the sheet once more. "We thank you for your service, sir."

He snorted and rolled up to a seated position. "I'm starving."

I tucked the sheet around me. "We literally just ate."

He leaned back and gave me a quick kiss. "I need a huge burger. Or maybe a steak." He groaned against my neck. "Loaded baked potato."

My stomach growled at the description. "Okay, I see you."

"I could take you to The Cove."

I wrinkled my nose. I didn't want to get dressed up and wait in line at the fancy bar and grill at the edge of town. "Why don't we barbecue up on the roof?"

"A woman after my own heart."

I curled my fingers through his damp curls. "Want me to run to the store?"

He slid off the bed and took care of the condom, hiding the evidence in his cupped hand. "Nah, why don't we go shopping together? We can find a bottle of wine too."

I tucked my knees up and looped my arms around them. "That sounds nice actually."

"So, you want to shower with me?"

"How about I run over to my place? Easier so I don't have to do my hair again."

He reached back and tugged one of my lopsided space buns. "Too late."

"I mean, wash it. Girl magic."

"Okay. Handily, you're right across the hall."

"Handy," I murmured. Handy for a lot of things, but it also could turn into shit if this went sideways.

He stood and hid his hand behind his back. "I'll come get you."

"And this time, it won't even be breaking and entering, Goldilocks."

Grinning, he dropped his chin to his chest. "Never living that down."

"Nope."

He sighed. "I guess I'll just have to make it up to you with a spectacular steak dinner."

"Feeding me twice in one day. I'm a spoiled girl."

"I plan on spoiling the hell out of you for the foreseeable future." A frown rolled over his features before he cleared his throat. "Sorry, was that weird?"

I tucked my chin on my knees. "I'm good with it."

Surprisingly, that was the truth. I liked this feeling. Maybe things between us just were going to be easy. There was nothing wrong with that, was there?

He stopped at the threshold of his room. "Me too."

I waited until I heard him start the shower before I padded into the living room to find my clothes. For a second, I thought about doing the dishes, but I decided I needed more time to get ready than he did.

I'd make it up to him.

I quickly dressed before I ducked my head out into the hall, my fingers holding my shirt together. I darted across the way into my apartment, then sprinted to my bedroom. I quizzed my Alexa about the weather and groaned at the absurd temperature even at almost five in the evening.

Late July meant sunset was still well after eight which meant I needed something cool and cute to wear. I dug into my closet and found a floaty leopard print skirt that would dance around my ankles and decided to go with a T-shirt to dress it down.

I took a ten-minute shower to wash off the sweat and sex and swapped out my fried space buns for two French braids. I took a few minutes to do up my eyes while I was drying in front of my standing fan.

Damn summer.

I loved it, but anything over ninety with matching humidity was just wrong. Part of the fun of a lake town. Super snow and super humidity from the water. But I was still happier here than I'd ever been anywhere else.

I'd escaped to Syracuse when I'd tried the college route, but that hadn't stuck. My brain wasn't wired for that kind of structure. Instead, I'd juggled jobs and roommates until the tarot practice had become something more. Finding Kinleigh had been my next step. Working in her shop evened me out. One was a healer position that was more rewarding than I deserved, and one gave me the freedom to meet people without them wanting anything from me except some retail therapy.

Best of both worlds.

I brushed on a layer of waterproof mascara to combat the sweat that would be in my future before I pulled on a cute cotton bra and panty set. The hot pink flowers on the cup showed through the white of my shirt a little.

I shrugged. Caleb would probably enjoy it.

After I shimmied into the skirt, I layered it all with a lemon and mint spray I'd put together during solstice. The rose quartz in the bottle infused the blend with a bit of happiness.

I swapped out the tiger's eye jewelry I had on for something more playful. Obviously, there was no grounding myself around this man today. Instead, I decided to lean into the rose quartz with a few rings and a pair of dangly earrings. It was too hot for necklaces.

"Luna," Caleb called from my living room.

"In here."

He came down the hallway. "Sorry, I had to tear apart my apartment for my wallet and still can't find it."

"On my end table," I called out to him. "I forgot to bring it over. I found it peeking out from under my bed."

"Lifesaver—damn."

I turned toward his voice. "What?"

He crossed to me and cupped my face. "You are so damn beautiful."

"Well, thanks."

I went up on my toes as he lowered his mouth to mine. The kiss was soft and sweet. He tasted of mint and sunshine. Somehow those flavors fit him.

Finally, we broke apart. I smiled, openly checking him out. "You don't look so bad yourself, teach."

His hair was still wet, but he'd cleaned up around his beard, leaving him with a beachy sexy vibe with his disheveled hair. He'd dressed in a lightweight plaid button down much like the one I'd stripped off him to start the day. A pair of olive cargo shorts and boat shoes spoke of comfort without being slick like some guys who were obsessed with labels.

Then again, labels probably weren't a thing on a teacher's salary.

He pocketed his wallet. "Ready?"

"Yes." I grabbed my rainbow bag and transferred the contents to a brown crocheted bag. "Okay, now I'm really ready."

He slid his hand along my lower back as he led me out of my room. "Do you still want to hit the grocery store, or just get something to eat on Main?"

"Grilling sounds perfect." I stopped at the closet near my front door and tucked a few reusable market bags into my tote.

He held the door open for me, and we naturally fell into step with each other in the hallway. Our hands brushed, and he laced his fingers with mine just as Tabitha came out of her apartment.

"Oh, hey, guys." She glanced down at our joined hands and her grin got wider. "Hey, guys..."

My lips twitched. "Tabitha."

"So, this is a thing?"

I tried to slide my hand away, but Caleb tightened his fingers. "Definitely."

She nibbled on her lip, and I braced myself. I knew she'd been sort of interested in Caleb. But then her aura glowed yellow. "You're so cute together."

Relief nearly made me sag. "Yeah, I let him hang out with me."

Caleb curled his arm around my waist and hauled me closer. "Oh, sure. That's the story?"

"You got it, Goldilocks."

He buried his head in the crook between my neck and my shoulder. "Never going away." He dragged me down the hall. "Come on, I'm starving."

I laughed and stomped after him, waving goodbye to Tabitha. We flew down the stairs and through the vestibule. I fumbled with my bag to find my sunglasses in defense against the late day sun threatening to sear my corneas.

He didn't let my hand go, and we laughed our way past the café. I was half tempted to turn him around and stop at Rolling Cones for an ice cream, but it would probably melt faster than I could eat it.

Instead, we took advantage of some sun tea set up outside of the Lakefront Grocery. We sipped on the mint tea—mine with extra ice—and picked out more food than we could possibly eat. Caleb was a natural flirt and teased me about choosing the most expensive cut of meat.

I liked what I liked.

I found myself curling my arms around him from the back as we waited in line at the butcher like we'd been together for a lifetime. People recognized him wherever we turned. He seemed to know everyone's name as well.

Attractive women, harried mothers with kids in tow, and even men seemed to be drawn to him. It took us twice as long to get through the store since every aisle seemed to contain someone from one of his classes.

A few people frowned at me, but Caleb seemed oblivious.

Finally, we got back to the front of the store with our basket. He hefted it up on the conveyor belt. "Sure we got everything?"

I peered into the plastic basket. "Veggies, crusty bread, fruit and cheese, steak of glory—yep."

He flashed a prepackaged tray of kabobs. "Highway robbery."

"Do you really want to buy all the things to make them? Then, you know, *make* them?"

"Point taken. Easy for the win." He tossed that and a pack of gum onto the checkout counter.

We haggled over who was paying, and in the end, I lost. Or won, depending on how one looked at it. He didn't let me carry anything but the fruit and bread when we finished checking out.

"Looking hot with your rainbow bags, teach."

He grinned over his shoulder at me. "I am secure in my manhood, thank you."

I watched him walk ahead of me. His deliciously firm backside was definitely a plus as far as I was concerned. "You betcha."

"Stop watching my ass."

I pulled down my sunglasses. "Nah, I'm good."

He walked faster. "Objectification? Really, Miss Hastings. You should be ashamed of yourself."

"Shame, shame." I sashayed after him, then laughed when he turned and hustled me down into the park by the gazebo so we were out of the way of foot traffic. He crowded me up against one of the trees and kissed me senseless before leading me back onto the sidewalk.

I was almost dizzy with laughter and hunger by the time we got to the wine bar. Lucky for us, everything was within a few blocks since it was hot enough to melt us and the food into a pile of goo.

We left with two bottles of summer wine and a growing awareness building between us again. He was charming and sweet, but he also knew how to make me come my brains out. It was a heady combination, and I found myself wanting to believe it could really be this easy with him.

Huffing our way across the street to our apartment building, we both fervently wished aloud that the elevator had been finally finished.

Alas, no.

We cooled down in his apartment for a few minutes as we prepared our food and broke into the wine.

I sipped from my glass, my butt back on the stool at his kitchen island as he doused the steaks with some concoction he called his secret rub.

"I have a secret rub too."

He looked up, his fingers covered in spices. "Is that right?"

I set my glass down and came around to stand beside him. "Herbs are kinda my jam, though I use them for spellwork and medicinal purposes. Like the stuff I gave you for your sunburn."

"And it worked better than anything I've gotten from a store."

"Glad it helped."

I knew I was testing him early with the witch stuff, but I wouldn't hide that part of myself. Not ever again.

That pale eyebrow shot up as he gave me a bit of side-eye. "Spellwork?"

"Offerings to Brigid for my own spiritual practice, spells for clients to manifest things as simple as finding a job, or getting through periods of grief."

He set the steaks aside and moved to the sink without saying a word. I could practically hear his brain working it all out.

I reached for my wine glass and took another healthy gulp, jolting when his arms came around me from behind. "I'd heard from a few people that you were into tarot cards. Kinleigh is a little into that stuff."

"Yeah, part of my business. I even do a podcast with my best friend Ryan."

"Huh. Wow. I had no idea. So, it's kind of a religion to you? The crystals and cards and all the plants I saw?"

After setting down my glass, I turned in his arms and laid my hands on his chest. "Very much so." That was enough sharing for today. "Ready to go up?"

"Definitely." He lowered his mouth to mine. "It makes you even more fascinating."

I wanted to believe he meant that.

So very much.

NINE

No one ever said being a teacher was glamorous.

A day of getting my classroom ready for the new school year wasn't exciting, but it needed to be done. I'd slacked a bit in June on my cleaning, knowing I'd step it up in the fall, and lo and behold, the fall was almost here.

Hadn't it just been July a minute ago? Now it was verging on September. The time was flying by at a truly scary rate.

Soon, my lazy afternoons spent with a certain someone would come to an end. I wouldn't be stopping by Kinleigh's anymore under the guise of shopping for eclectic furniture pieces no one truly believed I wanted.

What I really wanted was to see Luna.

As lame as it was, I kept up the pretense anyway. We were exalting in this whole "no labels" business.

All the flirting, all the fucking, none of the drama.

And she had a hell of a way with a staple gun.

"Is this good enough?" She inched up on her toes to hang the "Welcome Back, Students" banner over the top of the whiteboard. Except Luna was a little thing, so she couldn't reach very high.

Which meant I could crowd into her from behind to help her...stretch.

"How about this?" I asked against her ear, gripping her hips to hoist her up to hang one end of the banner. I'd already done the other side.

She laughed breathlessly as she stapled it into place. "Where are your hands, teach?" Her laughter turned husky. "Should you be touching me like this in a place of learning?"

"Absolutely. Fuck, are you wearing a string bikini under here?" Her denim mini skirt was very brief and showed a hell of a lot of curvy leg, ending in wedge heels with straps that wound up her calves.

I did not mind in the slightest.

"Maybe. I didn't know what you had in mind for my afternoon off."

"Oh, you can guess what I have in mind." Nuzzling her loose, beachy hair, I let her slide slowly down my body, dragging her right over the definite stirring in my khakis. "But I figured we could work before we play." I slipped my hand under the hem of her peach tank top on my way up to cupping her breast. "Why'd you have to wear a bra?"

"Because I don't want to be arrested, maybe?"

I nibbled down the side of her neck to her shoulder. "I'd save you. But if you want to play cops and bad, bad girls we can do that too."

A throat was cleared from the doorway. I knew that throat clearer. I heard that particular sound in my nightmares.

I went still. Were my lungs still functional? It felt as if I had a sudden, unexpected blockage. One that resulted from knowing I might be unemployed and unemployable once the principal of St. Agnes Academy put out the word to the administrators at nearby schools that Caleb Beck was a big ol' perv.

Fondling a very willing woman in a parochial school classroom while readying the space for innocent seven and eight-year-olds. Why, I never.

Luna peeked up at me from underneath her wavy hair. "Oh, thank you, Caleb. If you hadn't rescued my contact, I'd just be flailing around here like a blind person." She pretended to smack at her eye. "There, that's better. I can see now. I can't thank you enough." She turned and flung herself at me, hugging me around my arms currently glued to my sides.

Sheer panic at potential public shame did that to a man.

"Hi there," she added brightly, moving toward Sister Tobias and extending a hand. "I'm—"

Sister Tobias did not shake. She seemed riveted by the sparkling daisy charm dangling from Luna's belly button, nicely revealed due to the wandering hand that had pulled up her tank top.

Thanks, hand.

"Mr. Beck?" she asked in an exceptionally unfriendly tone rather than addressing Luna.

"Sister, you look lovely today."

She looked down her nose at me, which was a feat considering I was about a foot taller than she was. But she won on the menacing score. "You're one of the last ones to prepare your classroom. The ice cream social and picnic are coming up."

"I know, Sister. Why I wanted to get this done today."

"Done?" She glanced at my loaded desk.

"I just got started. Luna is happy to help"

"Luna Hastings," she tried again with a smile. "It's a pleasure to meet you. Caleb tells me Saint Agnes has some of the best test scores in the state. And your grade-to-grade student retention level is in the high eighties. That's wonderful."

I looked at her out of the corner of my eye. How did she know all that stuff? *I* didn't even know the retention percentages, so I definitely hadn't informed her.

Besides, I preferred much more physical activities for our time together than nerding out about facts and figures.

Sister Tobias, however, was not impressed and grunted out something as she crossed her arms, flapping the sleeves of her habit. Not all of the nuns at St. Agnes wore them, but Sister believed in always looking the part.

That could've been why her gaze dropped to my neon green

sandals. Hey, I'd been walking down at the lake this morning. I wasn't wearing good shoes to clomp around in mud and dog poop.

"You did double-check with sweet Ivy about her truck stopping by for the social?"

"Yes. Three times."

Sister Tobias had warned me that if my sister's truck wasn't there on time with the exact selection of ice cream treats she'd ordered, there would be hellfire to pay—and I would be the one paying it.

I was fairly certain Sister hated me, not unlike my own years in elementary school. I'd never been the teacher's pet. More like the teacher's worst spitball-throwing nightmare.

"Good, good. I hope she brings Rhiannon. She's just the most adorable child." Sister Tobias clapped her hands together.

"You're in luck. Ivy's bringing Rhi with her to help today."

"She is?" Luna asked out of the side of her mouth.

I was almost sure Luna had met my sister along the way, since Kinleigh was Ivy's best friend, but the first few times hanging out with your lover's family were often awkward. So, I'd figured on keeping it casual. Ivy got along with everyone, and her husband was a damn rockstar. Or he worked with them, so same difference. If anyone would like and appreciate Luna being a little left of center in some ways, my sister should. She accepted everyone just as they were in any case.

"Yes, Rhi's coming with Ivy as long as she can get coverage for the truck for a couple of hours. Oh, and assuming she can drag Rhi away from my mother. She has those two girls attached to her hips—Rhi on one side, Vivi on the other."

"It's nice that your mother's *other* children gave her grandchildren." Sister Tobias shot me a searing look and swished to the doorway. "Tell your sister to stop by on her way through. I have sweets for precious little Rhiannon."

With that, she flew away. Only metaphorically speaking, but man, was it apt.

"Ouch." Luna rubbed her chest. "Did she punch you or did it just feel that way?"

"She loves me. What are you talking about?" I looped an arm around her shoulders and kissed the top of her head. I contented myself with a quick peek down her tank top in case my jailer returned. "Where did you learn that stuff about the school? You really helped out in the clutch."

Her cheeks went rosy. "I did some research when you said you worked here. Just so I had some idea what your school might be like."

"Wait, you didn't pester me with endlessly annoying questions with answers you really don't care that much about, you just checked it out on your own? You are basically my ideal woman." I reached down to palm her ass under her mini skirt. Just one quick touch to hold me over. "And not only because you can quote statistics like a boss."

"No?" She slid her hand up my chest, flicking her tongue along her lower lip as she cast a glance at the door. My girl liked to take chances, just like I did. "I thought it was my flexibility."

"That definitely plays a part. Your thighs could crack a coconut—oh, shit."

She laughed until she heard the sound of a child crying. "Is that wailer your niece?"

"Survey says yes." I willed my newly intrigued cock back into submission before my family made it to the classroom. "She's a good kid, but she's temperamental sometimes. Her dad's Irish," I explained. "Born in Ireland. Both he and my sister have that ginger thing going on. I've heard it makes people snarly. Poor Rhiannon was cursed from the beginning."

"I heard that," Ivy said, nudging wider the partially cracked door so my niece could toddle inside the classroom on mostly steady feet. She was too busy crying to care about the new surroundings or even about me.

"Hey, Rhi-Rhi. How's my best girl?"

She took one look at me and howled before clinging to her mother's leg.

Ivy rested a hand on her head and sighed. "It's been a day. You don't even know. The next time Rory even jokes about knocking me up again I'm going to give him a home vasectomy." She seemed to notice Luna then, who had gone quiet and still. "Oh, hey, Luna, is it? Do you work here too?"

"Yes, it's Luna. Hi, Ivy. No, I don't. Actually, I think we met at Kinleigh's once or twice." Luna gave my sister an easy smile that didn't change the momentary squalling child-induced terror in her eyes.

I'd been there many times, and I was a teacher. At least the ones in my chosen age group didn't fling themselves on the ground and pound their hands and feet.

Usually.

"Oh, yes, that's right. I remember talking to you there. You have such amazing style. That off-the-shoulder top with the moon cutout in the center was so gorgeous. I debated looking for one like that but maybe with an ice cream cone instead. You know, for my truck Rolling Cones?"

Luna nodded, her pupils growing larger as Rhiannon continued to scream. Her mother just talked over her about ice cream shirts as if it was an ordinary day.

Bellowing child, what? I don't hear one.

Red-faced and soaking the collar of her Disney princess T-shirt with her copious tears, where? I don't see her.

It was probably a parental self-defense mechanism. I had to deal with cranky kids all school year, but I could send them home to their parents at the end of the day. When they were yours, you were screwed. Only choice was to ignore them or perish.

Maybe even ignore them *and* perish. Lord help my sister.

Crouching in front of Rhiannon, I produced a surefire crying quencher from my pocket and held it out to her—a red sucker.

She didn't even look at it. She just pressed her chubby face into my sister's leg and cried.

In the midst of her tears, I heard something that sounded suspiciously like "Dabnit." "What is she saying?"

Ivy sighed and stroked her little girl's wavy blondish-red hair. The hue seemed to change every few weeks. "Daddy. It's always worse after we leave him."

"Her father isn't here?" Luna asked, keeping her voice low.

"He comes back and forth. He's a producer with a lot of clients on the west coast. I keep wondering if maybe we'd be better off traveling with him. If having my ice cream truck here is hurting my daughter." She bent down to lift Rhiannon onto her hip. "Rhi, your Uncie Caleb has a sucker for you. Don't you want that?"

She knuckled her eyes and kept right on sobbing.

Luna stepped forward and laid her hand on Rhiannon's arm. Rhi turned her face into her mother's shoulder and peeked out from behind her hair, still crying.

"May I hold her? Just for a minute."

"By all means. Rhi, Luna's a new friend of Uncie Caleb." Ivy couldn't unload her fast enough. "If you yearn for more than a minute, that's acceptable too."

The odd phrasing made me blink until I remembered how Ivy had said Rhiannon was picking up more words from being around adults so she had to change things up to keep Rhiannon on her toes.

From what I could tell, Rhiannon was the one doing that to my sister.

Luna shifted Rhiannon in her arms. She was all arms and legs and usually preferred to not be lifted too much anymore, but when the waterworks started, all bets were off. "Hi, sweetie. I'm Luna. What's your name?"

Rhiannon glanced tentatively at her mom before saying in a whisper, "Rhiannon Ferguson."

"You know your whole name? Such a smart girl. And pretty too. Do you like Disney princesses?" Luna touched Rhi's T-shirt. "My favorite is Ariel. Who's yours?"

Rhiannon instantly brightened, the tears in her big blue eyes drying up. "Ariel too! I have her on my bed."

"Oh, you do? I'm so jealous. I had a bed like a car when I was your age. It had a steering wheel and you could press a button for the horn. I loved it so much."

Rhiannon pursed her rosebud pink lips. "Like a red one?"

"Yes. Mine was red. Kinda like your hair." Luna tugged Rhi's curls. "But you're blond too, like me."

"Daddy says straw-ber-ry." She sounded it out carefully and then her chin started to quiver.

Ivy and I exchanged a look. *Uh oh.*

"I love strawberries. Do you?" Luna grinned. "I have an idea. Your uncle needs to decorate his classroom because he has new kids just a bit bigger than you starting soon. But we need more decorations. Can you draw?"

Rhiannon's eyes grew wide. "Yes."

"Can you draw strawberries?"

She nodded vigorously as Luna grinned.

"Okay, let's go draw. We have some crayons right over here." She shifted Rhiannon onto her hip to carry her to the table where I'd started placing some bins with extra supplies for kids who didn't have them or for when we ran out.

Ivy stepped closer to me. "Man, she's a lifesaver, isn't she?"

I couldn't take my eyes off Luna where she'd crouched beside Rhiannon to help select crayon colors from the big box. Rhiannon was smiling so broadly now as she chattered about colors that other than her still red cheeks, it was impossible to tell she'd even been crying. "She is. I had no clue she was good with kids."

My sister hip-checked me. "Giving you ideas, mate?"

"You aren't from Ireland, so don't pull that *mate* crap on me. Rory is a bad influence on you."

"Well, sorry, but he is my husband. And don't try to stall." But before I could drum up an answer for her crazy question, she leaned her head against my arm until I wrapped mine around her shoulders. "She's so beautiful. Already growing so fast."

When she sniffed, I glanced down at her with incredulity and made sure my voice was pitched underneath Rhiannon's question if she should use red-red or pink-red for Ariel's hair. "She was just howling like a wolf in mating season. Now you're sad she's getting older? That's when the crying stops."

"No, it doesn't. That's when *we* start crying because she's starting to date. Her father isn't going to deal well with that. He's already discussing sending her to an all girls' school."

"Right. That causes chicks to end up in 'girls gone wild' shows. Doesn't he know anything?" I tapped my chin. "Then again, probably not. He didn't date much before you. Too much work makes Fergie a dull boy."

Ivy poked me in the gut and circled her fingers. "So, tell me about...*this*."

"About why you always have such jabby nails? I don't know, but you always wear those press-on ones and—" I laughed at her disgusted expression. "It's new." I made sure to keep my voice low.

Handily, Luna was on her knees next to Rhiannon, coloring and giggling while they worked on their joint masterpiece.

I would have to hang it in a place of honor. Maybe right on the door until my students' artwork filled the space.

"How new?"

"We're having fun."

My sister sighed. "I love you, but you're a dumbass."

I pulled on one of her long braids. "People today don't respect the lack of labels. Lu and I are cool with that. She's amazing, and I love spending time with her." This last part I said loudly enough for her to hear.

Luna tossed a look over her shoulder. "*Lu?* New nick. And um, yes. He's right. Labels are for nutritional info and jeans, not relationships."

Ivy smiled tightly and said under her breath, "Oh, God, you've met a female you."

I had to chuckle. "No, she's definitely not that. But we have an understanding."

Luna was about to chime in again when someone knocked on the doorjamb.

Mike London, third grade teacher extraordinaire, flashed us a grin. "Hey there, Beck. Back on the grind, huh?"

"Soon enough," I agreed, stepping around my sister to bump knuckles with Mike. His T-shirt showed the dust streaks that were common on classroom clean-up day. "Have a good summer?"

"Definitely. Lots of brews and bonfires and camping. It was freaking awesome. How about you? That break beard is intense." He ran his fingertips over his own neat scruff.

"Yeah, I'll be dealing with it soon. Time to bring myself back to civilization." I grinned and stepped back to encompass my sister. "You remember my baby sister Ivy."

"Hardly baby. Younger suffices. Hi, Mike." She smiled and gave him a little wave. "I bet your classroom is closer to done than this schlub's."

"Nice to see you, Ivy. And yeah, I'm getting there, but I started early today." His gaze slid over to Luna, who'd just risen to dust off her knees. "Well, hello. I'm Mike London, third grade teacher here. Who might you be?"

"I'm Luna. I work at Kinleigh and August's Attic among other things. Pleasure to meet you." She moved forward to shake Mike's outstretched hand, her smile dazzling.

He lingered far too long before moving back, and only Ivy hooking her fingers in my back pocket kept me from separating them.

Bodily.

"The pleasure is mine." Mike cocked his brow at me. "Or maybe not, huh?"

"No. Definitely not. Keep your pleasure to yourself." I walked over to Luna and looped an arm around her waist.

"Don't pee on her, for heaven's sake." Ivy shook her head. "How're you doing, pumpkin?"

"Good, thanks," I answered in a falsetto, making Luna laugh before she went back over to Rhiannon. My niece was ignoring all of us and happily coloring away.

Sometimes I wished I could give as few fucks as kids did. They were definitely smarter than adults. They didn't bother hiding their feelings.

Mike gave me a thumbs up when Luna turned away to grab another big piece of paper off the roll of scrap I kept on hand. Ivy sat down cross-legged on the floor and was just settling in with her own crayons when I decided to burst her bubble.

"Sister Tobias wants to see you."

"Okay. We'll stop in on our way out. She probably wants to talk ice cream again. I actually brought my itemized list of flavors for her to triple-check to ease her mind." She kept coloring.

So, the only one with a popped bubble at the moment was me, and it was directly related to Mike checking out my girlfriend's ass as she bent over the table to reach for more crayons.

She wasn't my girlfriend though. And she did have a superior ass—and all the rest of her.

"Nice job, my man," he said in an undertone.

"You seeing anyone?" Judging from his disturbingly lascivious smile in Lu's direction—that she was not privy to, since she was talking quietly to Ivy while they colored—I had to assume no, but Mike didn't suffer alone for long. He also hadn't suffered a social life slowdown in recent months during the Cove baby boom.

Either he liked playing with fire, triple-bagged, or had no swimmers in the tank.

"I was earlier in the summer, but it fell apart. She was here on vacation and we tried to make a long distance go of it and that didn't work out. I'm okay with being single though." He spread his arms with a smile. "More of me to go around that way."

"Uh huh." I couldn't keep the derision out of my tone.

"What's with the judgment? It wasn't so long ago you were singing the same tune. Gotta say that one might make me sing in a different key myself," he added, waggling his brows as Rhiannon picked the right moment to let out a loud giggle and fall over backwards.

"I don't judge anyone. Just so much stuff to do. You know how it is." I led him over to the door. I managed not to drag him there, but I thought about it. "Good luck with your classroom. I'm sure I'll see you at the picnic."

"Definitely. I hope to see Luna too," he said at a level meant to carry over to the women.

The tiniest one was currently trying to chew on a sienna crayon. Her mother successfully pried it out of her mouth and mimed wiping her brow.

Yeah, this parenthood nonsense was vexing. Who did this voluntarily and why?

Luna let out a breezy laugh. "Well, Mr. Beck hasn't seen fit to ask me yet, so I can't say if—"

"Come." My unintentionally suggestive demand had Mike grinning and Luna arching a brow. "Please. I'd love to have you."

"Oh, I just bet."

I ignored Mike and wondered why I'd returned to the inept state I'd been in upon first meeting Luna. I'd hoped we'd progressed past all of that, but nope. Wishful thinking.

"Sure. Depending on my schedule, I'd love to go with you. If it fits."

This time, I was the one who arched an eyebrow. "Oh, you know it fits, baby."

My sister heaved out a breath. "Know what doesn't fit? Me in this conversation. C'mon, Mike, walk Rhi and me down to the principal's office."

"Have you been bad?"

"Married," I reminded him.

He shrugged innocently.

"No!" Rhiannon declared, knocking over the box of 64 crayons and watching dispassionately as they rolled under desks and tables in every which direction. "Don't wanna."

Then she toddled over to me and held up her arms for me to swing her around as I always did if she wasn't having a breakdown. I did it a few times until we were both dizzy, and by then, Mike and Ivy had gone.

Laughing and out of breath, I set Rhi down and bent to take her little hand. "Wanna have some fun?"

"Fun! Fun!"

My niece was practically a genius, if I did say so myself.

I led her over to the sight words chart we'd hung up in a new spot on the wall. "Remember this? You're so good with these words, even though they're for kids so much older than you. You're my best smart girl, aren't you?"

She reached up to move a word from one clear pocket to another, making the sentence not make sense. But it didn't matter, since she was still a toddler and these words were way too advanced for her. "What's this one?" I pointed to the word for one of her favorite things. "Can you sound it out for me? C-ccc. A-aaa. R-rrr." I rolled my tongue to say r and she giggled, smacking her hand over her mouth. "Zoom zoom. Like Luna's bed."

"Car!"

"Good job. For that feat of magnificence, you get one of my prized possessions. Only the very smartest kids get one of these." I reached into my pocket and pulled out the tiny doll with red pigtails I'd picked up for her at a toy store.

The kid was a fiend for minuscule things, the smaller the better. She was obsessed with the dollhouse Ivy and Rory had put together for her, and this girl should fit at the small kitchen table her amazingly awesome Uncle Caleb had given her last Christmas.

Of course it had been built by her other amazingly awesome uncle August, but that didn't matter. I'd come up with the idea.

She squealed and grabbed the baby doll, clutching it to her chest. Then she eyed me slyly and pointed at another sight word I'd taught her before. "Sky."

I laughed. "Yes. Very good."

She held out her other hand and I laughed harder, ruffling her soft curls. "Dream on, sister. One per day. But I do still have this." I produced the sucker I'd tried to offer her earlier, and she grabbed it eagerly.

Still grinning, I looked up and realized Luna was watching us as she filled a bin with safety scissors and tape. Her gaze was surprisingly tender.

Instead of her expression filling me with my typical panic—*oh, God, she just saw me interacting with a small child, her ovaries must be on high alert!*—my grin just widened and my chest grew tighter in a not unpleasant way. I liked Luna seeing me in my element with kids, even if this one was below my typical age range. It proved there was more to my so-called playboy veneer than met the eye.

Besides, a guy only played the field before he met the one—

I choked as that nice warmth in my chest turned into an inferno crawling up my neck. Anytime now, I'd go up like a torch.

Had I grown a vagina? What the hell was happening?

It was this town. I should move far, far away. Turn exclusively to drinking and showering with spring water from Fiji. I couldn't even trust the Cove water to be safe to wash my dishes.

All it took was a few little drops, and the next thing you knew, you were wondering if Pampers or Huggies provided the most absorbency to protect delicate little tushies.

To my relief, no one saw me incinerating where I stood, since both Rhiannon and Luna had rushed to the window at the sound of manic quacking.

And it was not due to my singlemanhood flying south forever.

I followed them and leaned over to lift the window—one plus about being in an older building, we still had some of the hand-crank kind—and leaned out to see not one, not two, but a whole family of ducks trailing along the edge of the grass.

"I canna see. I canna see." Rhi jumped up and down, hanging on to the edge of the bookshelf in front of the window.

"Here you go, Ariel."

Rhi giggled at Luna's nickname for her as she lifted her up and leaned forward so she could stick her face against the screen. "Duck! Duck! Quack!"

I had to laugh as I ruffled Rhi's hair and pressed a kiss to the top of her head. "They're a whole family traveling together. Pretty cool, right?"

"Yes." Her laughter was delighted until the duck family verged toward the road, somehow knowing where to cross at the crosswalk.

Traffic stopped on both sides, but that didn't calm Rhi.

"Stop!" She held both little hands against the screen. "Stop! Now!"

"It's okay, sweetie. The cars know to stop for people, or um, ducks in the crosswalk. See how the cars aren't moving?"

"Nononono." She shook her head in a frantic motion that told me tears were on the way.

Not again.

Not today.

I took a deep breath and threw back my shoulders. I knew what I had to do.

"C'mere, Rhi-Rhi. We'll make sure the ducks are safe."

Her lips trembled and her eyes welled with tears as I took her from Luna.

"Where are you going?" she asked as I crossed the classroom.

"Outside to protect the ducks," I said over my shoulder. "You can wait here."

Or not, since she was dogging my heels.

Rhiannon's thumb crept toward her mouth as we went down the maze of halls to the exit. The three of us weaved through the people on the sidewalk. The ducks had attracted quite a crowd, and the birds weren't very speedy. There was a line of them moving in formation, but they hadn't made it far yet.

"Can you hold her?" I asked Luna once we made it to the front of the assembled group.

"Sure." She took her from me, her forehead wrinkled with confusion. "What are you doing?"

"Saving the day, babe." I gave into impulse and kissed her, and she let out a surprised, pleased noise.

Rhiannon shrieked and shoved her fingers between our lips, making us both laugh.

Cutest cockblock ever.

"Be right back."

I moved into the street in front of the line of cars and trucks respectfully waiting. I kept a good distance between the ducks and me, since I wasn't sure if the parents might be vicious if they sensed a potential threat to their ducklings.

This was a baby-friendly town in all ways.

In the center of the street, I shut my eyes and did a quick mental request for some karmic kindnesses for this act of public embarrassment.

Then I stuck out my arms in both directions as if I was directing traffic.

Shouts and applause broke out all around me. I glanced back at the curb and grinned at Luna holding up Rhi on her shoulders so she was taller than everyone else. My niece was giggling and cheering and pumping her little arms, and hell if I didn't feel 100 feet tall.

That was me, Caleb Beck, duck defender.

And I was something else too. I was a guy who couldn't get enough of making my girl—both of them—smile.

TEN

 Luna

I HOPPED UP AND DOWN TO GET THE STRETCHY SKIRT OVER MY HIPS. I had been spending way too many evenings eating all the dude food Caleb and Lucky had been making on the rooftop. We'd fallen into a pretty easy summer evening routine with a few of the people in the building.

Post-work we met on the rooftop with Tabitha and Lucky. Sometimes August and Kin stopped over, but the parent thing wasn't easy to work around. We didn't mind when they brought Vivi with them, but I was pretty sure Caleb's older brother had grown out of the beers on the rooftop evenings. Especially with a little one who was getting more and more mobile—aka getting into trouble constantly.

Personally, I was pretty sure he and Kin liked their time alone together too.

I definitely understood that. It was getting so I didn't exactly want to share Caleb with his best bro Lucky. I wasn't sure what to do with that feeling. It had been a few weeks since the Goldilocks incident, and we'd been locked and loaded with the sexy times every night since.

I glanced over at my phone as it buzzed on my dresser.

Am I bringing wine? Or is this tequila night?

That was the question. I sent back a quick reply for him to go with the harder stuff. I was feeling a little reckless tonight.

I blamed him completely. He knew just how to get my motor revved, and I didn't want to think too closely about how excited I got seeing his name on my phone. I'd pushed back my podcast with Ryan twice just because I'd been in a perpetual state of postcoital bliss.

And tonight, I was looking for a repeat performance.

Not that Ryan was all that concerned about our usual schedule. She was filling in for April, the third in our little triad, at April's office assistant job this week. And to be honest, April had been just as MIA lately.

Was this what growing older included? Growing apart from my friends?

Nope, that would not happen to me. I added a reminder on my phone to contact the girls tomorrow and make sure everyone was okay. Especially after the call I'd gotten last evening from Ryan's new temporary boss—while he was in her bedroom.

Yeah. It was like that.

If Caleb hadn't been so overwhelming, I would've called her first thing today to get the full scoop. Okay, maybe not first thing. I had a feeling Ryan was doing some naked overtime in her new position.

Literally and figuratively.

There was much to discuss on both sides. But right now, I had some entertaining to do.

I padded into the living room and picked up a few random items that had cluttered up my small living room. I lifted Caleb's shirt to my nose and took a nice big whiff of his spicy scent. It instantly flushed my skin with that familiar buzz.

I was quickly becoming addicted to his aura being part of my space. And tonight, I was going to drive him a little crazy.

I pulled his favorite chair from the far side of the room to directly in front of my pole. Finally, some of the heat had broken today. I set the overhead fan to low, closed the drapes over my windows, and draped a few of my silk scarves over my lamps.

The room took on a pink and purple hazy glow.

I curled my hand around the pole to make sure it was slick enough for me to work with, then did a few stretches.

I'd been working my way up to the advanced class online. Pole dancing wasn't exactly the kind of thing one would find in the small town of Crescent Cove. Maybe in nearby Syracuse, but that probably included a darker element than I was looking for.

I flicked through my playlist as I pushed myself for a wider split on the floor. Stretching was one of my favorite things to do, but it took a damn long time to get my body to comply sometimes.

Making Caleb lose his mind was on the agenda tonight, and I wouldn't even need tequila to start the party.

I sent off a text to tell Caleb just to come inside as I put my warmup song on. Beyonce's "Crazy In Love" was the best song to do the long slow swivels on the pole. When I danced for myself, I didn't usually bother with shoes, but I thought the extra effort would pay off.

I tied on the five inch Mary Janes I'd found online during a late night shopping session. I loved the paisley purple skin on the glossy black heels. I'd never be able to walk around town in the stupid things, but a little murderous pole action?

Yes, sir.

The sexy tones of the piano and Queen Bey's breathy voice helped me slip into character. I bent my knee around the pole and put myself into a light spin. Slowly, deliberately, and with a shit-ton more effort than it looked like to anyone watching, I climbed up so I could do a backbend and brace myself with the pole.

Just as I inched to the top of the pole and flipped, the door opened. I forced myself not to look at him. I kept myself in the zone as I tightened my hold on the pole and lightly spun upside down, bending my hips and waist around the steel as my muscles warmed.

I did a slow spin and finally touched the ground before I glanced up.

Caleb stood in the middle of the kitchen, his mouth slack.

Somehow I managed not to laugh. I did a slow walk around the pole, the click of my insane heels so loud as the song ended. I did a backbend and glossed my lips with the tip of my tongue.

"Hey, babe."

Caleb dropped his bag. "Fuck."

"Thought you might like to see one of my routines." I nodded to the chair. "Would you like a front row seat?"

"Absolutely. I'm the luckiest fucking man." He left the bag where it landed and started toward me.

"Bring the tequila and salt."

"I'm a dead man," he muttered as he spun around and dug into the bag.

"Limes?" I asked as the song changed to a decidedly naughtier one.

"Dead man," he said again as he craned his neck to keep watching.

I laughed and undulated my hips through a backbend before I did one of my fast flips. The pole shuddered, but his reaction was worth it as I grabbed my heel with one hand and clamped my arm and knee around the pole with the other.

My muscles strained as I stared at the mandala I'd pinned up around the pole on the ceiling. The wild kaleidoscope of colors blended as I sped up and slowly spiraled toward the floor.

Just before my knees touched the hardwood, I extended one leg and heard something hit the floor in the distance. I laughed and gently brought myself into a handstand then lightly did a backbend and stood up.

I'd worked up a nice sheen of sweat.

I walked slowly into the kitchen where he'd lined up shot glasses. I trailed my fingers down over his T-shirt then over to his arm. I lifted his wrist to my mouth and licked him. "Salt?"

Caleb blinked. "Salt?"

"Salt."

"Right." He grabbed the salt shaker and shook it over his wrist.

I lifted one of the shot glasses with a wink and tucked a wedge of lime between his teeth. "Cheers." I tossed it back, licked the salt off his wrist, then stole the lime and strutted my way back to the pole.

Caleb followed me with the bottle and dropped into the chair. "Have you done this before?"

Lightly, I trailed my fingertips over the pole as I lowered to my knees. "I've been dancing for a few years."

He opened his legs and his eyes went heavy-lidded in response as I slowly crawled his way. The song changed to a raunchy Nickelback song. I took the bottle from him and dipped my finger in to coat it then dripped the tequila on his lips. I licked it off his lower lip and inched away when he tried to deepen the kiss.

This was way too fun.

I returned to the pole and did a quick hop up to the middle, clamping my hand near my chest and high above my head. I tucked my knee around the pole to spin in a wide arc. As the song came to a close, I pushed out my tits.

"Hello?"

Was that...? Holy shit.

My Alexa speaker overrode my playlist, and my best friend's voice boomed through the room.

"Hello?" I squeaked out my reply.

"Lu?" Ryan asked.

"Yeah. Just a second." I waved at Caleb, who shook his head at me.

"No," he mouthed. He gestured for me to call her back.

I quickly rushed over to him and kissed him. "You know that saying bros before hoes?" I whispered against his mouth. "Same applies for girls. Out you go."

"Are you serious?" He looked down at his straining hard-on.

"Did I interrupt something?" Ryan questioned.

"What? No. Nothing. I was just dancing." I shooed him out of the seat. "I'll make it up to you," I purred before brushing my knuckles down the impressive erection he was sporting.

"You fucking better," he growled against my ear. He palmed my ass and gripped hard enough that I wavered for a split second.

"Oh," Ryan said. "Sorry. I'd call back, but it's kind of important."

The tone of her voice told me there was no way I could tell her to call back. "Yeah, totally. No problem at all, girl." There was a touch of regret sitting in my chest as the door closed behind Caleb. "Okay, you have my undivided attention."

"Was someone there? Oh, man, were you…"

"Nope. All good. Nothing to see here. Was just my neighbor."

I winced at the blurted half-confession. I still hadn't told Ry about Caleb. I kept assuming things would just fizzle out, but somehow they only got more tangled between us. Not the bad kind of tangled. More like the twisted sheets and long summer days kind.

"I thought you were dancing."

"I was." *Abort!* "Anyway, it's not important. You sound stressed, girl. What's up?"

Man, I sounded like a flake, but she seemed too distracted to notice. I sidestepped the kitchen island and almost turned my ankle.

Being a seductive pole dancer was dangerous work.

"Hurricane Rainbow showed up."

I bent over to undo my Mary Janes with a wince. Well, that explained Ryan's frazzled tone. My bestie never enjoyed her motherly visits. That was one thing we had in common. Luckily, mine didn't actually want to see me.

"Oh, shit. Are you okay?" I stepped out of the heels with a sigh, then went to the fridge. This was not the conversation to have with Patron Silver swimming through my veins. At least Caleb had brought the good stuff this time.

A smile twitched on my lips. No more questionable coconut rum.

I grabbed my pitcher of filtered water and filled a glass. "How much did she want this time?"

"Oh, if it was only just money." I heard a clunk through the speaker. "So much other stuff is going on."

I paused with the glass at my lips. "Do you want me to come over?"

"No. I'm heading out with Rainbow."

"Wait, what?" I took a big swallow of water so I wouldn't start swearing. What the hell was going on? Ryan would never go anywhere willingly with her mother. Mostly because it usually cost her too much money. "What do you mean you're leaving?"

"She wants to do this road trip thing, and I kinda need to get out of here."

I snapped the glass down on the countertop. "What the heck is going on? I knew something was up, but I figured you'd come talk to me when you were ready."

I stared at the ceiling. Goddess, I was a shitty friend.

"Yeah, well, I'm not ready. For any of it."

I opened the fridge and took out a stem of grapes and leftover watermelon. I desperately needed something in my stomach besides tequila. "You're not making sense."

"I know." She blew out a breath. "I did something."

I put the grapes down. "Like bank robbery? Murder?" I lowered my voice in case the neighbors could hear. "Do I need to bring my shovel? Go buy supplies in cash three counties over?"

She was my best bish. I would totally bury a body for her. In a hot second.

Ryan's laugh came through the speaker. "No, there's no body."

"Remember that little white fox I used to draw on everything?"

"Of course. I still have it on my journal. I paid some kid on Etsy to make me stickers of it. You're welcome."

She laughed. "You did not."

I popped a grape in my mouth. "I sure did. I hoarded them in my keepsake box. My bestie's artwork is priceless."

"Aww." Ryan sniffed a little. "That's the sweetest thing anyone has ever done for me."

"That's what best friends do, girl."

She sighed. "Well, I did something stupid last night. I actually posted one of my comics on a story. You know those quick twenty-four hour things. I figured it would just go away, and no one would really notice."

I took my fruit and water over to my couch and curled into the corner next to my speaker. "You know the universe doesn't work like that."

She let out a strangled laugh. "That is the truth."

117

"So, did you blow up the internet?" I picked out a fat triangle of watermelon.

"Kind of. Penn Masterson reposted it to his bazillion followers, then he sort of slid into my DMs."

She kept babbling about names and people I didn't really know, but finally, the name clicked in. Masterson was sort of a big deal around here. Although he lived in New York City, Penn had a sister and a bunch of brothers who lived in town. That bunch included Christian, our favorite cop, who kept crashing our rooftop parties—and not in the fun way. I'd overheard people talking about Penn at Kinleigh's store, and I was familiar with one of his graphic novels.

"No way! So, that dude you made me read—Penn Masterson—he contacted you? The famous dude?"

"Yes." Her voice was a squeak. Very unlike Ry.

"This is amazing!" My girl was going to be freaking famous.

"No, it's really not. I'm not ready. I can't do this."

"Of course you can. You're a kickass goddess who can do freaking anything. Let me come over, and we can talk about this." I started to heft my tired butt off my couch. "We can throw some cards and drink lots of wine. I'll be a buffer between you and Rainbow."

I'd done it plenty of times. I liked her mother, to be truthful, but I knew she could be a bit much for Ryan.

"Thanks. I think I just need to get out of here. Go think about it. Maybe go through my drawings and fix them up."

I rolled my eyes. The curse of the perfectionist best friend. I could practically hear her brain moving a mile a minute. I also knew when she was in supreme avoidance. That was the trouble with knowing one another so well—and why I hadn't really wanted to talk about my stuff either.

"Okay, I get that. But is there something else going on? What did PMS do?" I stood up. "I'll kill him."

Her laugh came through the speaker. A more natural one that made me feel better.

"He didn't do anything. I mean, we did a lot of stuff, but none of it was bad. Exactly."

I picked up my plate. I didn't really believe her. And sometimes I needed to see her face to face to get her to really talk. I heard a few electronic dings.

"Ry? My spidey sense is vibrating like my rabbit, girl. What's going on?"

"I need to figure some stuff out. Then I promise I'll talk about it."

"Seriously, so I need to get my shovel?" I brought my plate into the kitchen, then grabbed my keys.

"No. But I think we both need to have a little discussion."

I put down my keys and leaned on my counter. I hadn't exactly been hiding Caleb, but I'd been enjoying our private bubble. "Looks like we both have some tea to spill."

"With all the wine. I don't think tea will cover it."

I went back to my living room and pulled the silk scarves off my lamps. "Are you sure you can do this trip with Hurricane Rainbow alone?"

"No," she said with a laugh. "But I think I need to. I need to ground myself. I'm a freaking mess about everything."

I stepped in front of the speaker and crossed my arms. "I hate this. You should let me come over."

"Rainbow is gassing up the Rainbow Mobile, and we're heading out."

I knew she'd made up her mind, dammit. "Make sure you at least text me while you're on the road, so I can make sure you're all right."

"Yeah. I will."

It was a rare moment that my girl's voice wavered. Instantly, I took all her twisted emotions inside of me. Being an empath sucked sometimes. "Take care of you."

"Take care of you," she answered automatically.

And then she was gone.

I sighed. The urge to dance for Caleb had disappeared. But I didn't really want to be alone either.

Grabbing my phone, I went across the hall and knocked on the door.

Caleb answered with interest in his eyes, but he quickly banked it under concern. "Hey. Everything okay?"

I shrugged. "She's okay. Just going through some stuff."

He cupped my cheek and gave me a soft kiss. "Chinese food and some *Lucifer*?"

"You don't mind?"

He laughed and backed up to let me in. "Not at all."

He was a good man. Probably too good for me, but I really wanted him to hold me. I wasn't used to leaning on someone, but maybe I'd give it a spin.

Giving and receiving comfort was part of being friends with benefits, right? Or it could be. No harm, no foul.

It wasn't as if we were already getting in too deep.

ELEVEN

 Luna

"Are you sure about this?"

"About what?"

I looked over my shoulder at the crap-ton of cars in the parking lot of St. Agnes Academy. Ivy and her ice cream truck had a line winding around the parked cars as if she was selling tickets to a One Direction reunion.

I sort of wanted a Bomb Pop, but I didn't want to end up wearing it as it melted. I pulled at my cropped T-shirt. Maybe I should have gone with a longer top.

"I mean, we haven't really done the whole boyfriend-girlfriend thing."

"Is that what we are?" He gave me an arched brow as he laced our fingers together.

"Asshat."

His smile got wider. "You look beautiful. And you're way more interesting than I am. I'm going to be the one in the background, refilling soda cups."

"Stop."

"What are you worried about? You can command a room at ten paces." He hefted the soft-sided cooler we'd filled with a fruit and veggie platter, since he'd asked me to come to this shindig with him on relatively short notice.

Not just any picnic. The one with all the teachers and their families, for goddess's sake. "I know. I just haven't really hung out with any of your people except Lucky."

"Well, Lucky is my best friend. But I definitely wouldn't take him here. He'd make all the nuns faint."

"Nuns? A fleet of penguins will be here?"

"You met Sister Tobias. It's no big deal. The school is a mix of nuns and laypeople."

"Laypeople," I muttered.

This was definitely not my current world. Not even my old world.

Which I absolutely wasn't thinking about today.

He released my fingers to wrap his arm around my shoulder and pressed a kiss to my temple. "Don't worry, the nuns don't drag people around by the ear anymore. At least not when anyone can see them."

He waved to a woman with three dogs and a child—all on leashes.

Another man and woman came rushing across the grass. A boy of indeterminate age was racing ahead of them.

"Dammit, Wes, slow the hell down!"

"You cannot say *dammit* and *hell* at the same time at a Catholic picnic, Dare!" A red-haired woman punched the guy in the shoulder.

"We're not in friggin' church," her companion muttered. He was big and broad and scowly.

The little boy seated on the man's shoulders giggled. "Daddy said a swear."

"He sure did." Suddenly, the redhead waved at us.

As they approached, we slowed down.

"Hey, Caleb," she said cheerfully.

"Beck," the man said with a near growl.

Caleb didn't seem afraid of him. He gave him a cheeky smile even though the dude seemed as if he could put Caleb into a deep freeze with the power of his gaze.

"Don't mind my husband," the redhead said.

I shook hands with her. "I'm Luna."

"I'm Kelsey. I've seen you around at the store, but I don't think we've ever been able to chat." She nodded to the small boy riding on her husband's shoulders. "This is Sean, the reason why I'm forever rushing." She nodded ahead. "That's Wes, our pre-teen and the bane of our existence."

The man grunted.

"And the delight next to me is my husband Dare."

I looked between Caleb and Dare. Had to be a story there.

"I'm a teacher here with Caleb," Kelsey volunteered before I could ask.

I bumped Caleb. "Is that right? Are all of your fellow teachers so pretty?"

Caleb nuzzled my neck. "Nope. None as pretty as Kelsey here."

Dare growled.

"I can't help it if I hit on your wife, Dare. I didn't know you were in the picture. Besides, Kel only has eyes for you. Even before you got your head out of your ass."

"Caleb," I said with a laugh.

"Caleb has a bit—" Kelsey seemed to have swallowed her tongue. "You know what? Never mind. We all change."

"Oh, do we?" I looked up at Caleb, who was a spectacular shade of scarlet.

"Okay, that's it. We're done here." Dare nudged Kelsey along. "See ya around, Beck."

"So, am I going to get that story?" I asked as we started walking again.

Caleb ran his fingertip along his collar. Suddenly, he looked flushed. "Nope. No story to tell."

"Hmm." It was going to be an interesting day.

We followed Dare and Kelsey at a distance. They were really in a hurry to find their other kid.

I glanced up at Caleb. "How long have you been teaching?"

"Half a dozen years. Think my seventh anniversary is coming up."

"Wow. I've never had a job that long in my life."

"Really?"

"The tarot cards and podcast are my longest gig."

"Longer doesn't necessarily mean better."

"Says who?" I waggled my brows. "I saw Rylee Kramer has a yoga place next to the coffee shop. I was wondering if she needs a new part-time yoga instructor. Or maybe I could do a class focused on working the stripper pole."

A woman with a toddler shot me a look and started walking faster past us.

Caleb chuckled. "Ignore her. She thinks *The Golden Girls* are scandalous."

"Blanche is my hero."

"As well she should be," he said with a grin.

A few other women gave me a wide berth. I tugged at my shirt. Maybe I shouldn't have worn my celestial skirt. But it was pretty and had stars and the symbols for the zodiac.

Ugh. No, this was me. I didn't dress to fit in anymore. I dressed for me.

Period.

I straightened my shoulders and matched my much shorter stride with Caleb's.

"Hey, where's the fire?" He unwound his arm from me and lagged behind.

"I'm just anxious to get—"

Dammit, that wasn't the right way to go about this.

"Get it over with? Isn't that my line?" He drew me to a stop. "Hey."

I huffed out a breath. "It's not that. Exactly. I just forgot for a minute."

He took both of my hands and shook them out a little. "What does that mean?"

I glanced down at my baby doll T-shirt that coasted a good inch above my low slung skirt. I'd put in a matching crystal and moon dangle in my bellybutton ring. I'd even worn my belly chain again because I knew he liked it.

And because I did too. I liked feeling sexy and didn't shy away from my particular style for anyone.

I looked around the field along the side of the school. Dozens of families dotted the green grass with large blankets set out for picnicking. Tents offered cover against the sun to protect the food and the younger children.

What blew my mind—and gave me severe flashbacks—were all the pretty sundresses in similar florals, sedate shorts here and there, and khakis as far as the eye could see. Even the man right in front of me was wearing the corporate beige.

He had on perfectly pressed khaki shorts with bright white sneakers and a golf shirt. He fit in with all of the people here.

Me? Not so much.

"I'm me, Caleb," I said softly.

He smiled. "I'm well aware of that. In fact, that's exactly why I like being around you. You're so very uniquely you."

I looked down at my daisy sandals. I hated feeling off-balance. I'd worked hard to ensure I stayed centered and never forgot who I was.

Never again.

He dropped the cooler next to us and slipped an arm around my back. "There's a reason why I've never brought someone to one of these school functions."

I met his gaze. "Because you're an eternal bachelor?"

He dropped a kiss on my frowning lips. "No. Well, I have been. Mostly because seeing everyone pair off in the Cove pretty much equals baby in three seconds."

I curled my fingers into his shirt. Babies weren't something I thought of every minute of the day, but I'd always figured it would happen someday, if it was meant to. "Babies are pretty much the thing in a small town. That's why people live here."

"Yeah. And I get it. Rhiannon is the love of my life."

I tried to shove down the ball of heat in my belly. Seeing him with his niece in his classroom the other day had been a whole new experience.

"I like what we have going on right now."

"Me too." I smiled. "I didn't mean to get heavy. I just…"

This whole scene reminded me of a different life. One that I didn't ever want to go back to.

I went up on my toes. The sun was shining, and I had a hot guy I liked to spend time with. That was what mattered.

"I just felt out of place," I admitted.

He glanced around, then he slid down his hand to cup my ass. "You're with me. That's the only place that matters. Besides, all the Target summer wardrobe action is mostly because people here are afraid of Sister Tobias."

"Well, she is a little scary."

"A lot scary. Besides, I like these skirts you wear sometimes. Gives me easy access."

"Says the man worried about a nun on the premises."

"Doesn't mean I don't want to get under these things every chance I can." He kissed me again. This time, the kiss was softer and longer. "I'm the luckiest man here. You'll make every husband, dad, and priest think impure thoughts."

"Priest, huh?" I raised my hands to his shoulders. "Would they splash holy water on a witch in their midst?"

"Witch?"

My eyes widened at the voice a few feet away. *Oh, shit.*

Caleb glanced down at the kid, who had to be around seven years old. "She's kidding, Charlie."

I stiffened.

Absently, Caleb drew circles over my lower back. "Where's your mom?"

The little boy pointed toward the big tent.

"Think your mom would be happy you ran off?"

The boy wiped his nose, then he swiped it on his pants. "I want to hear more about the witch."

I stepped back from Caleb and crouched so I was at the kid's height. "It's just a different religion. No scarier than yours." I tugged on the little boy's ear. "I just believe in the trees and the earth and giving back as much as I take from the universe."

"God made the universe." But his face was very uncertain.

126

Minefield alert.

"Everyone's idea of God is different."

"Like my friend Anna who's Jewish?"

Well, that was easier than explaining my religion. "Exactly. Being different is far more interesting, wouldn't you say?"

"Sure." He gave me a gap-toothed smile. "Bye."

And then he was off.

I glanced up at Caleb. I couldn't read exactly what was going on with him, but we were saved by the bell.

Or airhorn.

"Attention teachers, make sure you check in at the blue tent."

"Guess that's my cue." He held out his hand to me.

I let him help me up, and we crossed the field to the dark blue tent. Evidently, there were going to be some games for the kids and every teacher had to donate half an hour.

Caleb got to handle the lawn bowling. He rolled his eyes when he was handed a small disk that looked like something you would get from a restaurant when your table was ready.

"When this buzzes, report to the east lawn, Mr. Beck."

"Yes, Sister Linda."

I couldn't tell what was going on with her, but she wouldn't look at me. And she was wearing sunglasses so I definitely couldn't read her. Sister Linda's aura was even on lockdown. She had pretty impressive shields.

Caleb tucked the disk into his pocket and took my hand.

"Do you need a drink or anything, Sister?" I asked.

"I'm fine, thank you." She laced her fingers together on top of her notebook. "Run along. Mr. London, I see you over there. Come here and sign up for your time slot."

I glanced over my shoulder. "Hey, Mike."

Caleb threw an arm around my neck, drawing me closer. "London."

Mike grinned widely. "Miss Hastings, you look ethereal. Dump this chump and come away with me. I'll treat you like a queen."

I was close enough to Caleb's chest to hear the feral growl.

"Back off, London."

I pinched Caleb's side before he strangled me. "Glad to see a familiar face."

"I'll save you a seat at my picnic table." Mike patted Caleb on the arm. "I'll even let you sit with us."

I dragged Caleb away with a laugh. For someone who wasn't into labels, he sure didn't like any other males flitting around me. And for that matter, I wasn't overly excited about how a few of the women leered at his bite-worthy butt.

He made a few introductions as we walked past the various tents. We dropped off our offering to the food gods and got a couple of frosty bottles of flavored water. There were no adult beverages at this particular shindig.

I had a feeling if Lucky had joined us, he would've smuggled in some and been a hit. Especially considering most of the dads looked bored as hell.

We spent the next hour chitchatting with Kelsey and Dare and a sweet younger teacher named Sister Sarah.

Most people were nice enough. Some gave me a good deal of side-eye, but I thought that was more for the belly ring than the skirt.

Caleb came up behind me and kissed the nape of my neck. "Want to go for a little walk? I've got an hour before I have to referee ten-year-olds."

I tossed my bottle into the recycler. These people were no joke when it came to organizing. All the bottles would be returned for money that went into the playground fund.

They had raffle tickets at every table. I could only imagine what they did at actual student events. This was just teachers and their own families before school even started.

Caleb linked his fingers with mine. "You've been quiet."

I shrugged. "This place is very impressive."

He tipped his head. "It's just a school. They're good kids. Some of them are certainly in the entitled set, but for the most part, these are just families who want their kids to get the best education possible."

"I bet the tuition here is more than a state college."

He lifted a shoulder. "Probably. But we have lots of scholarships for people with lower incomes who really want their kids to go here."

"I'm sure."

"I didn't take you for an anti-establishment type."

"No? The witch? Really?"

He laughed. "Yeah, but you don't really talk about it."

"We don't do a lot of talking." I bumped him with my hip.

He twirled me out and back in. "We usually have more important things to do with our lips."

I let him draw me in for a light kiss. We were a bit away from the action, on a path that meandered around the school grounds. Benches with name plates were stationed between each large oak tree.

Would the trees have plaques too?

Planted by The Carters in 1942.

"It's a beautiful campus."

"Yeah. The grounds are super manicured right now, as they always are this time of year. Have to tidy up before the families come to see what they pay for. Next week, we have our meet the teacher nights."

I skipped out of his sphere, the light summer breeze lifting my skirt around my knees. "I bet all the moms love you." I walked backwards. "'Mr. Beck, I think my daughter needs extra tutoring.'"

His lips slid into a half smile. "I don't mess around with parents."

"No? Just the teachers? Scandalizing the nuns with your wicked smile and those delicious shoulders."

"Are you objectifying me?"

I shrugged. "Maybe."

"I can't say a few moms haven't flirted, but I definitely don't go there."

"Even the single moms?"

"Especially the single moms. They're on the hunt hardcore here. They've heard about the mystical properties of Crescent Cove and want to expand their families. As well as get a ring on that finger." He flashed his left ring finger.

"You really think they're that..." I trailed off, unsure what to call it. "*Deceptive* doesn't feel like a nice word."

He shoved his hands in his pockets. "Some women have one thing in mind."

"Not all women." I tugged him closer by the pocket of his shorts.

"No. And that's why I love spending time with you. You enjoy the no strings thing too."

My chest twinged. "As long as my bed is the only one you're in."

"Forever?" His eyebrow went up as he caught me closer.

"For right now." Though the idea of forever didn't seem quite as scary when we were alone.

I curled my arms around his neck and swayed against him. Sunshine and the scent of fresh cut grass surrounded us.

A few bees bounced from bloom to bloom on the hearty mums planted along the path. The light laughter of kids in the field doing some sort of relay race drifted down to us.

A quick buzzing went off between us. Caleb jumped and I laughed.

I stuck my hand in his pocket. "Think we could bring that home with us?"

"I think we can find something a little more interesting."

"Guess we might have to check out that bonus drawer I have," I said over my shoulder as I took off toward the tents.

"Wait. What bonus drawer?" he called after me.

I turned with a smile. "Maybe you'll find out tonight."

He caught up with me and lifted me up. "You better believe it."

"Mr. Beck! Over here, please! Please put Miss Hastings down." Sister Tobias waved him over.

"Busted," I said, trying not to laugh.

"I don't want to put you down though." Caleb's strong arms kept me hooked against his hip.

A man with curly dark blond hair stood next to Sister Tobias. He turned quickly and my heart stuttered to a stop.

"Caleb." I gripped his arm.

"Maybe you can help me referee. They'll probably be too interested in seeing a pretty girl to try to knock down the pins."

No. No, this was not happening.

Not here. Not now.

130

"Lu?" Caleb frowned at me. "What's wrong?"

"Crap." I turned around, but there was no way to escape.

"What?"

"You gotta go do the thing." I headed over to the food tent and wished it was full of alcohol. All of the booze. Maybe a lake of it for good measure.

"Luna," Caleb called after me with an exasperated grunt as he chased me up the hill.

"Luna, is that you?"

My shoulders hunched at the sound of his voice. One I hadn't heard in years. "Shit. Shit." I spun around to face him with one hand on my hip. With the other, I pushed my windblown curls out of my eyes. "Hey. How's it going?"

"How's it going? That's all you're going to say after three years?"

God, his eyes were still the same. Squinty and so blue.

Blue like my own.

I tipped my head back to stare at him straight on. "How's tricks, Xavier? Is that better?"

"Luna?"

Caleb from the back and my past standing there big as life from the front. I had nowhere to go. I was tempted to bend at the waist and just breathe from between my knees, but that would show weakness. And I was definitely not showing weakness in front of my brother.

"Who's this guy?" Caleb's hand went to my lower back. The heat of his skin made my skin sing.

"Mr. Beck!" Sister Tobias called again.

"Just a moment, Sister." Caleb's voice carried. But Sister Tobias was not happy in the least. She went off in a huff.

"Go, Caleb. I can handle this."

"*Handle* this?" Xavier's eyebrow spiked and he shook his head. "Some things never change." He held out his hand to Caleb. "Nice to meet you. I'm Xavier."

When Caleb didn't reach for his hand, I sighed.

"Caleb—"

"Xavier Hastings," my brother said tightly. As if that would mean anything to Caleb, for fuck's sake.

"Hastings?" Caleb turned me to face him. "Who is this guy?"

The accusation in his eyes made my hands fist. Of course he immediately thought the wrong thing. Because that was just what I needed on top of it all. "He's my *brother*, Caleb."

"Brother?" His shoulders relaxed. "Oh." He raked his fingers through his hair. "Sorry, man. I had no idea she had a brother."

"I'm sure you didn't." Xavier dipped his hands in the pockets of his Ralph Lauren pants. His beloved Bulgari watch peeked from the nearly white fabric. His hair was longer than the last time I'd seen him. The curls floated in the breeze in that carefree way that only a four-hundred-dollar haircut could.

Everything about my brother screamed wealth and prestige. He was the perfect Hastings heir, unlike me.

He unhooked his sunglasses from the pocket of his shirt and set them over his eyes. As usual, I couldn't read my brother. It had been that way since...

Well, for a damn long time. And I didn't really want to rehash how long it had been since I'd seen him. Or anyone in my family, for that matter.

"Caleb needs to get—"

"I'm sure they can get along without me." Caleb spread his hand along the small of my back. "Hastings. I don't think I saw a teacher with that name on the roster."

Xavier laughed. "Definitely not. I don't mold young minds in any way."

"No, just ruined them," I muttered.

My brother stiffened. "Come on, Lu. That's not fair."

"Isn't it though?" I patted Caleb's chest. "My brother usually shows up to grab a little PR spotlight. This doesn't seem like one of your pet projects, X."

"Just because I don't mold young minds doesn't mean I don't want to support them. Father makes a large annual donation to ensure

Crescent Cove has a good school when one of us eventually gives him a grandchild."

I laughed, the sound hollow and harsh. "You?"

"Maybe you."

I crossed my arms over my chest. "Oh, but I'm not part of that world anymore. You made sure of that, didn't you?" I stalked up the hill and away from him again.

Just like he'd walked away from me three years ago.

Caleb quickly caught up to me. "Want to tell me what that was about?"

"Nope." I kept walking.

"Luna."

I stopped. "We don't do the heavy stuff, right? Let's keep it that way, huh?"

At his shocked face, I spun on my heel. The strap of my sandal slipped and I swore. I yanked them off and bent to grab them.

Were there bees around my head? There was certainly something buzzing in my ears. Actually, it felt like everything was humming all the way down to the soles of my feet.

"That's not fair."

"We agreed not to talk about deep stuff." Sort of. Goddess, I just needed to get away from him for a second. I didn't want to do something stupid like cry in front of him.

"We never said that. We just…don't."

He was correct there. Instinctively, we never discussed heavy things. It was easier to talk about surface stuff like movies, our mutual love of steak, and orgasms. Oh, and to enjoy summer like two semi-young people. "And that works for us."

"Yeah, but you're upset. I'm not an asshole, Lu."

I threw down my sandals. I could feel eyes on me, and I still couldn't stop myself from marching over to Caleb. "Yes, I'm upset. It's just family stuff. My family isn't like yours."

"Obviously not."

I gritted my teeth. My emotions were fuzzing out of control. Everyone in the park was just a color. Friendly colors, happy colors, some more anxious like the sweet Sister Sarah. But there were no faces. I dragged in a deep breath and tried to calm down.

"Just go. I need a few minutes, all right?"

Why wouldn't he listen?

"Luna?" His voice gentled. "It's okay. Relax."

I waved him off and plopped down on the ground. I closed my eyes and pressed my hands and my feet into the grass to ground myself. I hadn't had one of these episodes since I was a teenager, when hormones and my gift for reading auras had collided into a bright, beautiful mess.

My parents hadn't understood what was wrong with me. As a child, I'd been happy and just thought the colors were part of life. That everyone could see them.

I'd learned quickly that wasn't the truth and to not tell my mother about the strange glowing colors I saw around people. Telling her about my father's darker auras scared the crap out of her. He wasn't a happy man, and the energy around him always felt heavy. He rarely slipped into the blues and greens that I saw around most people.

I was different, and they hated it. In fact, they'd been in complete denial about me. So, as a teen, I'd taught myself how to use shields and how to protect myself from all the energy that came at me. I'd gotten so good at building my shields that my gifts had gone away for years.

Until...

My eyes burned. Until everything exploded.

I felt a hand on my shoulder. Some of Caleb's innate calm actually helped soothe the chaos rioting inside me.

"Lu, you're scaring me."

"I'm okay. I just need to calm down."

"Okay." He sat next to me quietly for all of two minutes. "Can I do anything?"

The blades of grass under my fingers came into focus. I could feel the pulse of the earth under me as I grounded myself in my body. I pictured all the flying emotions settling like sand after a dust storm. "You're doing it."

"I'm not doing anything," he murmured.

I smiled, but I was afraid to open my eyes. Not that Caleb wasn't a lovely shade of greenish-blue, but I just wasn't ready to face the world again yet. "You didn't leave me. Even when I told you to."

"I'm stubborn that way. Ask my sister." He tucked his chin on my shoulder. "Do I need to kick that Xavier dude's ass?"

"No." My lips twitched. "I'll keep that card for future use though."

"Deal."

I leaned my head against his. "I'm sorry I freaked."

"Do you want to talk about it?"

"Not really. Is that okay?" The warm, spicy scent of him mixed with fabric softener smoothed the rest of the edges away.

"I care about you, Lu. I hope you know that." He covered my hand in the grass. "But if you don't want to talk about what happened, that's okay by me."

I relaxed a bit more. "It's not a huge deal."

It was to me, but I wasn't prepared to open that trap door just yet. I wasn't only protecting myself. I also didn't want to put more on his shoulders than a casual relationship warranted.

Even if we were feeling less casual with every passing moment.

He snapped a blade of grass between his fingers. "Sure about that?"

Swallowing hard, I made myself look at him. Really look. If I'd seen any judgment or trepidation there, I would've closed down. But there was just concern—and affection. "My family just doesn't understand me."

"Do any of our families ever really get us?"

I laughed. If only he knew. "I like being the black sheep."

"Rainbow sheep? I don't think I've ever actually seen you in black."

I punched him in the shoulder. "Jerk."

He leaned in and pressed his lips to mine. "Think we can get up now? Pretty sure everyone's staring at us."

"Let them stare," I said and kissed him a little deeper.

TWELVE

 Luna

THE REST OF THE PICNIC WAS UNEVENTFUL. SURE, I RECEIVED A COUPLE odd looks and overheard the occasional hushed "witchy" comment I assumed was directed at me, but overall, the balance of the day was pleasant.

Especially the way it ended with Caleb and I parking down by the lake for some stargazing.

And other things.

Best of all, my brother never made another appearance. I didn't know where he'd gotten off to so quickly, but I was grateful for the reprieve.

Even more grateful that I hadn't had to visit Caleb's work again since.

I knew I would again eventually if this thing between us continued. But I didn't mind having some time to regroup.

It had been a few weeks now. Caleb had started school and we'd settled into a new routine. Gone were the afternoons of him visiting me at the shop, but we made up for it by spending evenings together. Almost every evening. And we weren't even naked all the time.

Just most of it.

But in between, we did what other couples did. We watched reruns on TV and went for walks or bike rides. We even occasionally attempted couples' yoga, which had been a laugh and a half. For all Caleb's stamina in the sack, his flexibility was sorely lacking. But he'd tried.

Several nights ago, he'd come home late after a meeting with a parent. He'd strolled in with takeout for dinner and a bouquet of fresh daisies.

And I'd given him a vibrating cock ring for dessert, which was actually a present for both of us.

I released a long, slow breath as I rubbed the twinge in my lower back. Maybe I needed to up those yoga sessions, because whew, I was out of shape.

But I knew that wasn't true. I did something physical nearly every day—athletic sex life notwithstanding. Plus, with my couple of jobs and busy social life, I always stayed active.

Yet somehow all of a sudden, I couldn't seem to move furniture or rearrange displays at Kinleigh's without getting out of breath or wanting to curl up in the corner on a hassock to take a nap.

"Need some help? Let me get that for you."

I looked up at August, Caleb's older brother. He had on a rather impressive toolbelt and sawdust in his hair. He'd just been building a custom crib in his workshop, but he'd taken a break to come down to the shop to kiss his wife and cuddle his baby. They were so adorable together, all three of them.

For unknown reasons, I'd teared up at baby Vivian giggling happily in her swing. Something about a child's laughter made me so emotional. I mean, not before *ever*, but today? Everything was hitting me weird. I was even tearing up looking at the hand-painted roses on this end table I absolutely could not lift without my back screaming.

I smiled at August. "Oh, thank you. I just couldn't do it for some reason. Did you see this? The blooms are so intricate. I can't believe what craftsmanship the artisan put into this piece." Sniffling, I traced my purple nail along the delicate yellow folds of the flower on the drawer.

"Uh, thanks. The artisan was me." August laughed self-consciously and brushed dust off the shoulders of his shirt. "Where do you want me to put it?"

"Over there would be perfect." I pointed to the opposite side of the new fringe circular rug I'd just arranged in the seating area. "I figured it was something that came in on consignment. I should've known it was yours. Gotta say I'm amazed you still have time to make stuff for the shop with all your custom orders for Ladybug Treasures."

"You know what? I think I'm going to move this one somewhere else entirely." August hefted the end table and carried it across the store to set it down near the front door.

I frowned, hands on my hips, as a pair of women came in. One of them clasped her hands over it, clearly in love.

I'd seen it first. Not that I needed it for my place. I had an apartment full of stuff already.

When August slapped a big *sold* sign on the end table, tears prickled once again. I couldn't say I was surprised it'd sold so quickly. It was just the right size to tuck near a sofa. Like mine. It would look so great in that spot next to Sir Anthony, my ficus.

Discreetly, I whisked my fingers under my eyes. I'd find another piece.

I whirled to pick up a pair of candlesticks to put on the carved coffee table with feet shaped into high heels. Odd, but charming.

"I thought you should have it."

I glanced up, still misty, as August approached. "What?"

"You clearly loved the end table. So, consider it a bonus for doing good work." August grinned. "I'm only partly giving it to you because you've made my brother a lot more bearable to be around lately. Whatever you're doing, keep it up."

I couldn't help teasing him. "He makes sure I do."

His ears tinged red like Caleb's did sometimes. "Okay, moving on."

I laughed and moved forward to give him a big hug. "Thanks. I adore it and I know exactly where I'll put it. Oh, and he makes me happy too."

"That's good to hear. If that changes, let me know. I'll put a snake in his bed." August smiled widely. "He's hated them since we were kids. I put this toy black mamba under his pillow once when he was six and—"

"He jumped so hard he fell off the bed and peed his pants," Ivy finished, coming around the divider that blocked off this section from the vintage clothing area.

"No way." I cupped a hand over my mouth to hold back the laughter. "You're kidding."

"He really hates them," August confirmed. "He won't go camping because he lives in fear of coming across one in the underbrush. I think one got into his shoe the summer he went to Camp Happy Face."

"Camp Happy Face?" I giggled.

This information would be good to have for later bribery purposes.

"Yep. So, naturally, Aug had to make his life hell at every opportunity." Ivy came up to her older brother, and he drew her into his side just as I'd seen Caleb do with her.

And if a hint of envy swam through my belly, who could blame me? I'd been close to my older brother too once upon a time.

So long ago.

"Well, it's my actual job. I was put on this planet to torment my siblings."

"You are exceptionally talented at it. And at trying to scare off my boyfriend."

"Uh oh, do you have a boyfriend now? Does your husband know?"

Ivy shook her head. "Jerk."

She had on the retro sixties' style denim jacket we'd just gotten in on consignment this morning. It fit her so well, nipping in perfectly at her trim waist. I'd meant to try on the jacket myself, but I'd gotten sidetracked.

Surprise. That was me to a T lately. I couldn't focus on anything. The auras I saw were way more intense. And there was that whole napping preoccupation. I hadn't succumbed yet, but I didn't know how much longer I could be strong.

Maybe I could sneak across the street for an extra long break. Extra caffeine definitely wasn't getting the job done.

I forced back a yawn and smiled at Ivy. "You look amazing in that. Are you going to get it?"

"You don't think it's too tight?" Ivy headed over to a cheval glass mirror and twisted around to see how she looked from the side.

"Absolutely not. What size is it?"

"Eight."

"It fits like a dream on you." I couldn't resist running a hand down the distressed sleeve.

Working at Kinleigh's was dangerous for my wallet. I liked too much of what she sold. Her funky, eclectic aesthetic was right up my alley.

"I bet it would on you too. Here, try it on." She was already shrugging it off.

August cleared his throat. "This is my cue to go."

He split in a hurry, just as Caleb did when I started talking about clothes.

I backed away. "No, really. I can't keep taking the merchandise from paying customers." I released a helpless laugh as she blew back her red curls so like her daughter's and helped me into it. "I suppose trying it on doesn't hurt, and it is my size—" I broke off, frowning, as I pulled on the jacket.

It didn't close.

I tugged harder. The sides grew closer together, but not as much as they should have. My breasts strained against the denim as if I was trying to squeeze into a size too small.

My bras *had* seemed snugger lately. I'd been eating extra snacks on breaks, and before bed, I'd enjoyed a bit more chocolate-covered popcorn than usual. Still, nothing that should have me busting through sizes.

"Oh, this must be odd sizing." Ivy yanked at the hem, as if that would help. "But man, I'm jealous of your figure. I bet you never had to stuff your bra with socks like I did before I finally developed."

"No, but I'm not usually this chesty. This is...whoa." Now that I was looking more closely in the mirror, I realized my V-neck top was almost pornographic if I bent down even a centimeter.

Had it always been that way, and I'd just been oblivious?

"Oh, no."

I glanced at Ivy. Though she was pale to begin with, her cheeks had gone translucent. "It's okay. I'm not going to have a meltdown. Just need to cut back on the wine consumption with my bestie Ryan. She isn't in turmoil anymore now that's she worked everything out with Preston. She's in luuuurve. Lucky bish." I feigned a breezy laugh.

Ivy was nodding so much that she reminded me of one of those bobble-head dolls. "Right. Love is nice. Boobs are nice too. I should buy a push-up bra. After babies, things start heading south, not that you need to know that. Hey, look at these pockets."

She started unbuttoning the lapel pocket, but I reached up to still her hand with my now freezing fingers. The AC was pumping in here, but it was a warm late September day. Not that I could feel anything other than the ice slicking down my spine.

"I need to sit."

"Sure, sure. Here." Ivy rushed to grab a straight-backed chair and pulled it over to me rather than nudging me toward the chair.

It was a smart move, since the second I sat, a wave of dizziness poured over me. I bent to put my head between my knees.

Caleb's sister crouched at my side and rubbed my arm, making soft, comforting noises while my rioting stomach decided now was a fine time to act up. A metallic flavor filled my mouth as I hurtled up from the chair and ran across the shop, passing the changing rooms to reach the bathroom in the back.

On the way, I went by our sweet new sales associate, Brynn Bowman, who'd just started an hour ago. Not even. She had the misfortune to be wheeling a rack of discarded clothes from the changing room at that very moment, and I had no choice but to shove the thing out of my way on my flight to the sink.

I couldn't even chance yelling back an apology. Not if I wanted to keep Kinleigh's spotless floors clean.

Please, goddess, just let me get to the sink.

The last thing I heard before I flung myself at the bathroom door was Brynn shrieking.

Shit.

I raced into the one-stall bathroom—thank heavens it was empty —and tossed every crumb in my stomach into the tiny basin.

It seemed to go on forever. When I was finally done, I turned on the faucet and let the cold water run over my hands before I soaped them thoroughly.

I looked up in the mirror to see Ivy standing behind me, her big blue eyes miserable.

Because she knew what it meant.

I grabbed a sheaf of paper towels from the dispenser on the wall and wiped my face and dried my hands. "Good thing I have mints in my bag." My voice was too loud in the echoing space. The low music carrying from the speakers in the main part of the store filtered into the room, somehow a counterpoint to my false cheer.

Ivy certainly wasn't speaking. Why would she? It wasn't like there was anything to say.

I tossed out the towels and gave her a bright smile. "Guess I'll just go grab a water and those mints—" My gaze dropped to the jacket's pretty embroidered pocket, now stained. "Oh, no. Oh, God. What did I do?" My throat closed off as the words clogged there, my pseudo-happiness draining away.

"It's just wet. Just water. Here, honey." Ivy hurried around me to the sink to blot another towel and returned to clean up the spot.

All I could do was watch her. And sniffle like an idiot.

"I'm not a crier."

"Of course you're not. Here we go. See? Water just splashed it when you wiped your face. All clear." She showed me the towel and then threw it in the bin. "And even better..." She pried a halfway flattened box of Chiclets gum out of her pocket. "My baby loves these. I mean, Rhi. She's not a baby anymore."

I smiled mistily as she shook two into my palm. "She'll always be your baby. And she's small yet."

"She is, and she will be, yeah. My husband is in denial she's growing up. He can't believe she's potty training. I told him that's likely going to be a multi-year process, so he doesn't have to worry. His little girl is still little." She laughed uneasily. "I'm babbling. Sorry. Bad habit."

"You're sweet." I popped the gum into my mouth and chewed until the lingering taste from being sick faded.

"Here, why don't you lean on me a bit and we'll go in back, sit down on that fabulous settee Kin keeps making noises about moving into stock but never will? It's nice and comfortable."

I let her lead me out of the bathroom. Right then, I didn't trust my legs to keep me upright. It wasn't entirely due to my physical... condition either. The white noise buzzing in my ears and mad hummingbird wings flapping in my belly from nerves weren't helping matters.

We hurried into the back room, and I collapsed on the settee in relief. Until my head spun and I had to bend over again to get my wind back.

Ivy rubbed my shoulder. "Maybe you should see a doctor? Just in case."

"No. No doctor yet." I knew what I had, and it didn't require a prescription.

"Okay." She sat next to me, still rubbing. "Then do you want me to call someone? Like Ryan? She's your bestie, right?"

I straightened again and shook my head. Miracle of all miracles, it didn't fly off my shoulders and land in the planter in the corner.

"She's not your bestie?"

"She is, but that love business is keeping her busy."

"Not too busy for her best friend. Besides, she needs to come up for air and sustenance sometimes. Trust me, I know."

"Well, you're in a long distance relationship a lot of the year, right? That keeps everything fresh."

"Fresh, maybe, but it's really freaking hard when your kid wants her father and you can't give her that simple thing."

"No, but there's FaceTime. And she has you." I gripped her hand and gave her knuckles a quick rub.

She exhaled and then pasted on a smile of her own. "We aren't talking about me right now, but nice try."

I shrugged innocently.

"What about Caleb?"

Like a switch had been flipped, I heard his voice in my head.

"Some women have one thing in mind."

That wasn't me. At all. And I wasn't used to asking for help, even if he shared this responsibility as much as I did. Imagining what his face would look like when I told him just made me want to put it off forever.

"No. No way."

Ivy's face softened. "He's probably still at school. He always sticks around for any kids who need help with homework or if they want to talk."

There was absolutely no reason for my eyes to well up. "Yeah."

Ivy swallowed audibly. "Look, I know he has this whole 'parental hands-off' vibe, but I think he's just intimidated by the prospect."

"He's not the only one. Only difference is he doesn't have a womb."

"Unless there's something he neglected to tell us, no. But..." That *but* hung in the air between us. "Anyone can see how he is with kids. He has a gift with them. Relates to them in a way most of us can't."

I dashed at the deluge now dripping off my chin. "Sure that's not because he has a similar maturity level?" I held up a hand before she could speak. "Sorry, not fair. For one, he's your brother. You shouldn't be put in the middle. And secondly, he hasn't done anything wrong. Nothing has to change."

"You should take a test."

"I don't need to."

Alarm contorted her features. "No, you can't do that. He deserves to know. How can you assume he won't step up? He's a good guy, I swear he is. If it'll make it easier, I can come with you to tell him. You *have* to tell him," she pleaded, turning her hand over to fiercely grip mine. "It would kill him not to know."

"I never said I wouldn't—oh, no, you think I meant..." Rapidly, I shook my head. "No. Of course I'll tell him."

Someday. When I grew some lady balls or when I busted through the seams of my dress, either or.

She narrowed her eyes. "You don't need a test, but you swear you're not thinking of not going...along with it?"

"I don't need one because I know. I think I've been in some denial, but now I'm not." I released a slow, steady breath, cocking my head as her energy took on a cool blue hue from the pulsing red it had been just a second before. Auras lately had been getting stronger and stronger for me. Yet I'd tried not to notice, like the other changes I'd resisted seeing. "You were so worried you were going to lose your niece or nephew."

"My niece or nephew." She closed her eyes before opening them again and focusing on mine. "God, yes, I was. I didn't know what you were thinking."

"Not that. Never that."

"Good. I'm glad." She yanked out her phone and glanced at it. "Shit."

"What's wrong?"

"Just time to pick up Rhi. Though my mom won't want to give her up. She loves being a Nana way more than she liked dealing with us kids when we were small."

I tried to keep my smile in place, but my lips quivered. "Mine won't ever know what that's like."

"What?"

"Having a grandmother to dote on him or her. My mother—we aren't close."

Understatement of the millennium. We hadn't talked in years. There was no indication that would change anytime soon. Not unless I gave up the parts of myself that made me *me* and I wouldn't do that for anyone.

"Oh, sweetie." Ivy slid closer to me on the settee and slung her arm around my shoulders, squeezing hard as she tipped her head against mine. "You're not just gaining a...Caleb, you're getting the whole Beck family. My mom will love your baby every bit as much as her other grandkids. You don't have to worry about that, I promise."

146

Her words set off a soft pink glow in my chest. Not for me, but for the baby. I'd grown used to making my own family. I had April and Ryan and now she had Preston, which was another branch. Maybe someday I'd even have X in my life again, assuming we ever managed to make it through a conversation.

Or if I ever dared to trust him again.

Knowing I had a child on the way changed things. I wanted him or her to have loved ones to count on. Even so, I wasn't going to build myself up with false hopes.

No matter what, I was a realist. I always trusted the universe to provide what was for my highest good.

That didn't mean I didn't ever delude myself. At least it never lasted long.

"We're supposed to be having dinner tomorrow night with Ry and Preston. Can you come?" This time, my smile was genuine. "I'd really love it if you were there."

Ivy frowned. "Oh, I would, but Rory's coming home tomorrow, and I can't guarantee what time he'll be getting in."

"If you'd rather catch up alone, I totally understand. But if you want to join us, you're welcome whenever you can make it. Rhiannon too," I added, hoping everyone else agreed.

Ryan loved kids—from a distance—and I didn't know how Preston felt about them, but an adult dinner was a bit different than one including children. But I appreciated Ivy being there for me today, and I wanted to spend more time with her.

Besides, Rhi was adorable. Especially when she wasn't sobbing.

Ivy brightened as she rose. "You know, maybe we can. Let me see what Rory says, and I'll let you know."

I stood too. Thankfully, the earth felt a lot more solid beneath my feet than it had just a short while ago. My stomach had settled, and I wasn't nearly as dizzy. Of course that might've been because my panic had finally receded.

For the time being anyway. I hadn't begun to fully process everything. I just couldn't yet. Right now, I was just trying to get through each minute. To come to terms with my new reality. Only then could I think about my next steps.

We walked out into the main part of the store into chaos.

Clothes were spread all over the floor and the rack that had held them had toppled on its side. Brynn was sitting amidst the mess, gathering accessories, tops, and skirts. Kinleigh crouched near her to help pick up while another employee manned the register. A long line of customers had already formed and more than a few of them seemed disgruntled.

I hurried over to join Kinleigh and Brynn. "Oh my gosh, I'm so sorry. I was sick. I didn't mean for this to happen. I'll help Brynn. Go on and assist your customers, Kin." I bent over near the biggest pile of unsorted clothes, but as soon as I did, a pink hue pulsed around Brynn.

"Hang on there." Ivy rushed over to steady me again, and I wobbled before I sank onto my ass on the floor.

I glanced up in time to see Ivy and Kinleigh exchange a look. One that said so much. Besties could convey a whole conversation without words.

Seeing mine tomorrow night without letting on what was happening with me was going to be a challenge. But she wasn't the only one I'd have to convince my world hadn't turned upside down.

There was also Caleb.

THIRTEEN

"ARE YOU SURE YOU DON'T WANT TO TAKE MY MOMMA OUT, MR. BECK?"

I gazed down at little Tommy Molloy and tried to keep from grinning. "Well, Tommy, I'm sorry, but I have a girlfriend. But that's awfully nice of you to want to set up your mom."

"She needs to go on a date. She and my dad are diz-vorced."

"Diz-vorced?"

Tommy pushed his glasses up his nose and nodded. "For like a really long time."

"That so?" I thought his mother had just told me about the divorce recently, but time had no meaning lately.

Everything was moving in fast forward. It wouldn't be that long until first quarter report cards were due, which would mean the joy of parent-teacher conferences. Then not long after that would be Halloween and our classroom party, which would herald in a season of more holidays, numerous chorale concerts, and insanity.

On top of that, my relationship with Luna seemed to be accelerating too. Neither of us said anything. We weren't into labels or designations. We hadn't discussed her being my girlfriend, but I'd told Tommy how I felt. I didn't know what else to call her. We spent the bulk of our free time together. Slept together almost every night—

literally. Sometimes at my place, sometimes at hers. We'd wake up and make breakfast together or I would make our meal while she did yoga or did one of her routines with her blessedly wonderful pole.

We felt solid. Like a real couple. As if we were becoming...more.

More than I'd ever had before, that was for certain. And I liked it. Telling Tommy what I hadn't said to anyone else yet—including Luna —seemed right. So much, in fact, that I couldn't keep from grinning as the little towheaded boy told me how his dad had moved out "forever ago", so now would be a good time for another guy to become the "man of the house."

"But aren't you the man of the house now? You have a little sister, don't you?"

"Yes. Tina." Tommy screwed up his face. "She won't pick up her toys but still marks off the chart so she gets a dollar. No fair."

"I have a younger sister too. She's actually one of my best friends. It'll be different when you're older. You'll see."

Tommy gazed up at me as if I'd just said the tooth fairy was really Santa Claus. "Tina steals food."

"She's just a baby now. You wait." I tapped my chin. "You know, if your mom gets remarried, you might get another sister."

The horror that crossed Tommy's face had me swallowing a laugh. He hightailed it out of the room without even saying goodbye.

Apparently, the fear of another little sister was enough to kill even his basic manners.

Shaking my head with a smile, I packed up my soft-sided briefcase with the homework I had to check over. I made sure I had my lucky pen, since the kids were always trying to borrow it.

A text from Luna made me grin on my way to the bathroom before I headed out.

I was in the area so I'm coming up. Or is that you'll be coming up?

When you're involved, babe, that's a definite. See you soon. I missed you.

I frowned as I took care of business in the bathroom and washed up. How could you miss someone you'd just seen this morning? And last night? And rinse and repeat for all the previous days for the last several weeks? The nights we didn't spend together were few and far between. As it was, I hadn't hung out with my best friend in a while, and it wasn't for his lack of trying.

As he was trying again right now, texting me while I dried my hands. I checked my phone with a wince.

Okay, asshole, I'm about to tack a photo of your face up at the post office and offer a reward for sightings.

I'm around. You know what the start of school is like.

School started weeks ago, and hello, Friday night beer fest? Where was your ass? Not at The Spinning Wheel, that's for sure.

I scratched my neck. That had been the night Luna and I had gone for a picnic down by the lake—and finished with a romp in the Hamiltons' boat house. Hey, it was convenient, and Seth was a friend. Surely he'd understand the call of nature.

And the demands of a really hard dick after seeing the see-through thong Luna had on under her pretty floral sundress.

I had something come up.

Uh-huh. I can guess what.

In lieu of an answer that sounded smug, I sent him a winky face.

Whatever, man, you can't ghost another dude. It's just not done.

I'm not ghosting you.

You know, never mind. Just enjoy Luna and forget all about me.

My thumbs blurred over the screen as I stepped out of the bathroom and glimpsed Luna at the opposite end of the hall, looking like a damn vision in her kicky skirt and denim jacket. I typed faster.

I was going to ask you to dinner tonight at The Hummingbird's Nest. Can you make it?

This probably wasn't the best idea, and I hadn't run it by Luna in any case. Our small intimate dinner with her best friend and her new dude was about to be blown to hell.

A long pause during which I waved to Luna—and scowled when Mike London sauntered out of his classroom and immediately began chatting up my girl.

Hurry the fuck up, Lucky.

Ok. What time?

Six?

He sent me a thumbs up sign, so I decided not to mention the whole date thing. You could never be sure who he might show up with. Sometimes he brought multiples. Once or twice, he'd even asked the server to take a break and join us.

With Lucky, anything went. Often.

Luna walked away from Mike and strolled toward me, her smile bright. She was like a damn ray of sunshine with her blond curls escaping from her updo. Big glittery moon earrings swung from her ears and matched the pendant that dipped teasingly low between her breasts in her lemon-colored top.

I started to smile back—it was almost impossible not to—but her expression seemed glassy. A pretty veneer that didn't match what was beneath.

"What's wrong?" I demanded, meeting her in the middle of the hall.

Her easy smile dipped for a moment before she shored it up again as she leaned up on her tiptoes and slung her arms around my neck. She pressed her mouth to mine in an entirely school-inappropriate kiss, her lips almost frantic. Her tongue slipped in to wrap around mine when I would've spoken, and I let out a sound that was half groan and half growl.

I might be frustrated that she was trying to distract me through sensuous means, but my cock had no issue with the circumstances.

Still, I gripped her upper arms and gently drew her away from me as footsteps sounded behind me.

In a different world, it would've been a fellow teacher or maybe the custodian. But that would've been too easy.

"Mr. Beck, this is not a club of ill repute." She stopped beside us and fixed us with a stern expression. "Kindly take your physical consortium out of this building at once."

Physical consortium? That was a new usage. Leave it to Sister.

"It's my fault. I'm sorry." Luna jumped away from me as if my touch had scalded her skin. "I'll leave."

She rushed down the hall before I had time to make sense of what happened. What the hell?

Sister sniffed. "I've received reports about you before, Mr. Beck."

I bristled, staring after Luna. I had to figure out what was going on with her, but what could I do? This was my boss.

Heaven help me.

"What kind of reports?"

"That you're a consummate flirt. Which is fine in its place."

"Is that so?"

"Some of our single parents find a friendly smile puts them at ease."

I crossed my arms. "And makes them open their wallet?"

She didn't blink. "But displays such as what I witnessed, when children are still running these halls—"

"Most of the children are gone. In any case, I'm sure most of them have seen a kiss before and not fallen over in shock."

"Their parents are one thing," she said stiffly. "But you're not in a committed—"

"That's where you're wrong. Luna and I are extremely committed. We aren't seeing other people. There's no other woman on this planet I would rather be with than her."

At the clatter at the end of the hall, I turned my head. I wasn't at all surprised Luna had returned. But she didn't seem overjoyed at what I'd said. In fact, she looked...tormented.

"Can we have a moment alone?" Her voice sounded raw.

Sister glanced between us before slowly shaking her head. "Not on school grounds is all I ask, Caleb." Her tone softened. "I'm not an ogre. I do understand young love."

I expected a denial to leap from my lips. Even if she was my boss, *love* wasn't a word I allowed to be tossed around casually in regards to me. I was always brutally honest with the women I dated—or with anyone else who made assumptions about the nature of a relationship I was in. No matter what.

But with Luna, I didn't want to argue. I didn't want to dismiss the possibility. And not because she was listening either.

I fucking loved her and I didn't care who knew.

Even her.

"You're better than me then, since I've never been in love before." I swallowed hard while Luna stared at me as if she was temporarily struck mute. Ocean eyes wide, mouth trembling open. "But I'm absolutely in love with Luna."

Sister sighed. Unless I was mistaken, the sound was slightly wistful. "Then as Beyonce said, you better put a ring on it." It was my turn to stare as she swished down the hall in the opposite direction from Luna.

I headed toward my girl as she turned away and bowed her head. For a terrifying second, I thought she was crying, but when I reached her and gripped her shoulder to shift her toward me, she was laughing.

Damn near hysterically.

"You don't love me. It's too soon. But that was a convincing performance for Sister." She wiped away the tears of mirth gathering on her cheeks. "You really had me going there, gotta say."

I frowned. I couldn't say I'd ever imagined telling a woman I loved her, but if I had, this would not have been the reaction I would've hoped for. "I wasn't kidding."

"No, no, seriously, you can stop now. She's gone. Besides—"

"Luna." My voice never wavered as I took hold of her arms and waited until she gazed at me. "I love you. For real." I reached up to run my thumb over her lower lip as it quivered. "Realer than anything I've ever felt before."

"Is realer an actual word?"

"Yes. Are you stalling so you don't have to answer me?"

"Did you ask a question?"

She had a point. "No. Just usually when you say those words to someone, they say it back."

Her pupils grew even larger, but she said nothing. Her silence landed a blow to my chest as acute as if she'd physically struck me.

But I still made myself smile, for my ego if nothing else. "I get that people feel stuff at different rates. Several women have been in love with me before and—"

"Oh, whoop ti do for you."

I blinked. "I was just saying I've had women love me when I didn't feel the same. So, maybe that's the thing with you. And if so, we can still..." I trailed off and frowned as I stepped back.

What could we do if she wasn't in love with me? Still hang out together? Still have sex? Still pretend we were building something, just as long as I ignored that pesky missing love thing?

I supposed I could wait. What choice did I have? It wasn't as if I could turn off my feelings. Maybe she'd eventually develop some for me.

I rubbed the sudden throb in my forehead. "Karma is a bitch."

"What?" she asked shakily.

For her part, she did not look or sound as euphoric as I would have had our positions in this conversation been reversed. But I already loved her, so hearing her say she loved me first would not send me into the throes of depression.

Which meant one thing.

She was an empathetic woman. She wouldn't crow about having to let me down easy. But she clearly wasn't bicycling down the same love lane I was riding in.

My tires were deflating more by the minute.

"You heard me. I just said I've been with women who claimed to love me, and I didn't feel it back. Now I feel it and *you* don't."

"I never said that."

"Do you?"

"I never said that," she repeated.

"Now it's so much clearer. I thought witches believed in harming none."

She clutched her stomach. "Sorry, I'm just overwhelmed right now."

"*You're* overwhelmed? I just poured my heart out to you. I practically set my feelings to a Celine Dion ballad, and you basically said 'that's nice.'"

"I did nothing of the sort. Jesus, Goldilocks, stop being dramatic."

"You have not *seen* drama yet." I didn't think I stomped my foot, but in the rush of emotions currently coursing through my bloodstream like a bad college LSD trip—not that I knew anything about those—I couldn't be certain. "I have feelings too, Lu, and they can be crushed. I'm more than a sexual object."

"Caleb," she whispered, darting a glance down the hall. "You're going to get fired. Knock it off."

"Says the woman who stuck her tongue down my throat and gave me an erection and made me fall in love with her, all while I was at work. And then didn't even have the decency to love me back." My voice was perfectly low and level.

Possibly.

She rolled her eyes. "You know what? I was trying to make it easier for you."

"Oh, right. I see that now. It always helps a guy to know his girl doesn't love him. Next, you'll tell me you were faking those four Os last night to spare my feelings."

"Three. Don't flatter yourself."

156

"It was four and you know it."

"No more than three and a quarter. Anyway, that's irrelevant."

"Says who? Do you want to leave me with nothing?"

"There are things you don't know, things that may change your supposed undying love for me."

"I never used the word undying," I muttered.

Although I was concerned it actually was, and then what? I'd be well and truly screwed if she couldn't even admit I'd given her four legitimate orgasms last night—no quarters here, thank you—never mind love me back.

God, love had already made me a sap.

She continued on, ignoring me entirely. "But you're being such an ass that I'm not going to bother. It wasn't just my doing. I didn't get myself pregnant, dammit."

"It wasn't my doing either, this whole loving you thing. I didn't ask for it. It was your own fault for being so irresistible. And for fitting against me perfectly every time I wrap my arms around you. And for always knowing the exact right thing to say when I've had an exhausting day at work. You're always just exactly what I need. You have been since the very first day I laid eyes on you."

"Caleb. Did you hear me?" she asked gently, her eyes suspiciously wet all over again.

She didn't seem so shaky anymore. In fact, she seemed like a tower of strength standing there in front of me, so starkly beautiful with her steady gaze and her shoulders thrown back. Whatever I said, whatever I did, she would be just fine.

Damn if her rock-solid sense of self didn't make me love her even more.

As for the rest, my mind was on hyperdrive. I didn't think I'd hear anything but those words in my head for the next nine months. Well, less than that now.

I didn't get myself pregnant, dammit.

Holy shit.

"I heard you." I paced away from her to the opposite wall and back. About ten times.

She didn't say a word, just let me pace while my vision blurred with…sweat.

Yeah. That was a good one.

I tipped back my head to stare at the ceiling. The ice that had formed around my heart when she hadn't said "I love you" back cracked apart as if blasted by the sun. "It fucking worked. I wondered if it would. If it could be real."

"What?"

I went to her and gripped her cool hands in my much larger, warmer ones. Rubbing them so that she could feel every bit of the intensity inside me. So much that I wasn't sure I could contain it. "For almost a year, I wouldn't sleep with anyone. I wouldn't take the chance. The Cove, man. There's something mystical here. Unexplainable."

"You're in shock. Maybe you should sit down. I'll get you a glass of water. I need one too." She tried to pull away from me.

But I held fast.

"You meet this beautiful, smart, funny as hell woman one day, and then the next thing you know, she goes and changes your whole world. Makes you see things you never could've imagined. Or could ever think might be yours." I tried to swallow despite the fist around my throat. "First, I fell in love with you. And that wasn't enough. Now you're saying…" I took a breath. "Now you're saying you're giving me —us—someone else to love too."

She started to speak but then frantically swiped at her cheeks and shook her head. "You don't know what you're saying. You're probably hungry. This is a lot. Let's go to dinner."

"Go to dinner? We can't do that. We have plans to make."

"Plans? What plans?" She finally succeeded in yanking her hands out of my hold.

"You just said that you're—" I gestured wildly at her stomach before my gaze drifted slightly north. And lingered while all the moisture in my mouth dried up. My woman was smoking hot. "That's why your tits look so huge."

"Do you know where you are?" She smacked my arm. "You can't be talking about or looking at my breasts here."

"I can when I planted that baby in you."

"Oh, no, you don't. You are not going caveman on me."

I crossed my arms. I could go caveman if I wanted to when my sperm had emerged victorious.

Granted, in a town like the Cove, it wasn't as much of a feat. But my swimmers had carved a renegade path through two layers of birth control. That deserved some celebration. Maybe a small party with streamers and pointy hats.

Luna arched a brow. "Maybe I'm not."

A bolt of ice shot down my spine. "What do you mean?"

"I haven't actually taken a test. Maybe I'm just gaining weight. What about that?"

"Just in your tits? Not likely. Besides, you have to know if there's… a thing inside you."

"A *thing?* Now you're calling our baby a thing?"

"It's not a thing, it's a fetus. I'm just saying, I'd damn well know if I was carrying one around. It's not like an extra bean burrito, for God's sake."

"No, right now, it's so much smaller than that." She rubbed at her dripping nose. "I wasn't prepared for any of this. You're just supposed to be a summer fling. I'm happy with my life. I didn't want it to change."

Some part of me wanted to demand her to admit I was the best thing to ever happen to her, as she was for me. But from somewhere down deep, a sense of calm rolled over me as I stepped forward to wrap my arms around her.

"We were meant, Lu. You know it as surely as I do."

She sniffled against my chest, but she didn't argue.

"And maybe this was just the universe making sure we didn't screw it up."

"I wouldn't have screwed it up." She drilled her pointy nail into my biceps. "You're the screwer-upper."

"No arguments there."

"You're the one who gets drunk on bad rum and mixes it with antibiotics and sneaks into my bed to impregnate me so I can't even get on my freaking pole anymore without a backache." She jabbed again. "*You* did that. You made me bust out of my bras, and you aren't even sorry."

My lips twitched as I took a long, leisurely look at the body part in question. Poetic speech or not, I wasn't entirely sure it wouldn't be my last one, since apparently, pregnant women were erratic and emotional.

Dear God, she was actually pregnant.

With my baby.

I was going to be a father to an actual human child I couldn't send home with someone else while I kicked back with a cold beverage.

I wavered a bit on my feet, and this time, she gripped my arms to support me. "You okay?"

"Yeah. I am. I'm just...a baby."

"Yeah." She bit her lip. "I can't believe we're discussing this here. Can we please go before Sister Tobias brands us fornicating heathens?"

"Well, we are. At least on the fornicating part. Heathen is a title I'm still working to earn." I slung an arm around her shoulders as we made our way down the hall, stumbling like people who'd had too much to drink.

Or had engaged in way too much sex and had way too many orgasms until boom, egg meets sperm and holy eggs Benedict.

I hadn't brought my briefcase with me, but I'd come in early tomorrow to check over the kids' homework. My thoughts were too consumed with *my* kid just now.

Mine.

Ours.

How freaking amazing. Assuming I didn't drop dead from sheer, mind-numbing terror.

"Think of it this way," I suggested as we walked through the now mostly empty hallways.

Thank God for that, or else someone would overhear us and I'd be on the unemployment line just as we needed money for Pampers.

Back to the eternal Pampers or Huggies debate. Ivy had used cloth diapers early on, I was pretty sure. I would have to ask which she recommended.

I was officially spinning out into a mindfuck of Baby-O-Rama proportions.

"What?" Luna asked, a little wobbly herself as we finally stepped out into the sunshine.

"At least we didn't discuss our lovechild in the actual church." She giggled until I turned her toward me and lifted her hand to my mouth, kissing her knuckles. "Because that's what he or she is. For real," I said hoarsely.

"Realer?"

"The realest." I kissed her forehead. "I love you."

"Even now that you know?" Her voice was barely a whisper.

I forced myself to look directly into her beautiful sea-tinged eyes. "Somehow even more."

FOURTEEN

 Luna

The incessant ding of my text messages finally dragged me back from my faceplant on my bed.

This pregnancy thing was no joke. Dear goddess. It had been a little over a week since I'd told Caleb about the baby, and morning sickness had come to my village in a huge way.

I peeled my face off of the book I'd been reading. I'd barely gotten to page twenty before I passed out like a drunk frat boy at three in the morning.

Oh, but it was one in the afternoon here in the land of reality. And I was becoming a narcoleptic.

I reached down to the floor where my phone was and lifted it to see if anything was pressing.

Five messages from Caleb.

He'd checked in with me each hour. I'd managed to reply to one before I passed out. I quickly sent him a reply that I'd taken a nap before he sent one of our neighbors to check in on me.

Again.

Another three dings and a flood of messages made me groan. I'd expected him to move to another state after my news, not turn into Mr. Attentive from a Disney afternoon sitcom.

I glanced at the top of my phone with a groan. My calendar notification reminded me I had a client in twenty minutes.

At least I'd get a few minutes reprieve from Caleb. He was overwhelming the hell out of me, and I needed a freaking minute. Especially since this morning sickness thing was trying to take me out of commission.

I sent off a quick reply.

Have a client. My phone will be off for a bit.

How's the nausea?

He just had to mention it. I closed my eyes against the first wave of cold sweats prickling my skin.

My wind chimes alert trilled from my speaker. I set up the reminder to give me time to ground and center before I interacted with a new energy.

Too bad the baby wasn't into it.

I rolled onto my side as the wash of nausea had me covering my mouth.

Oh, no, not again.

I stumbled off the couch and ran for the bathroom, skidding on my knees to the bowl right before everything, including air from the last twenty years of my life, came up and out.

Holding on to the toilet, I prayed to every goddess I knew. Finally, the retching faded to dry heaves, and I sat back on my feet.

I didn't even know what I had in me that could actually be thrown up at this point. I hadn't eaten since dinner last night. Well, okay, I'd had goldfish crackers.

It was the only thing that didn't make me immediately want to throw up. I guess that was off the menu too.

I reached up for the sink by the commode and hauled myself to my feet. I swayed a little and winced when I caught a glimpse of myself in the mirror. Dark circles and glue-white skin.

Oh, yeah, that was super cute for a video call.

Instead of looking at the horror story that was my face, I dunked my mouth under the faucet and rinsed away the sickness. After brushing my teeth and using copious amounts of mouthwash, I felt a bit better.

My hair was another story. Yikes. With very little help, I could have been an extra on *The Walking Dead*. If I'd had another half hour, I would have jumped in the shower. Dry shampoo wasn't going to cut it. Not with the sweats that came before and after the dry heaves.

I padded into my bedroom and found a cute rainbow head scarf I wore in between hairdresser appointments. I was a natural blond, but with the super sunny summer we'd had, my hair had lightened to an almost platinum hue.

To Dye For would definitely be getting my business soon.

I paused as I tucked the silk behind my ear to hide my hair. Was hair dye bad for moms-to-be? I picked up my phone and made a note on my rapidly growing questions list.

Between Caleb's intense research each night and my own spiral of near hysteria, my Notes app looked like I was writing a new and improved version of *What to Expect When You're Expecting*.

After dusting on a bit of powder and some blush, I looked less like a corpse. I pulled on one of the kaftans Bess had bought me when she'd graduated from level one of my impromptu tarot class. The psychedelic rainbows and drunk sunflowers would distract the eye from the morning sickness chic thing I had going on.

I headed into the living room. Another wave of nausea had me bracing myself on the arm of the couch. Lucky me. I just needed some electrolytes. And since Pedialyte was my new best friend, we had a little date while I reviewed my notes for my client.

A love reading.

Just great. Exactly what I needed to be doing right now. I couldn't even get my own brain in order on the subject, and I was supposed to give advice?

"Not about you, Lu," I muttered to myself as I went over to my tarot deck wall and took out a few decks that called to me. And because Madeline, my client, was about as grounded as a hot air balloon, I snagged my *Truth Bomb* deck to help her check herself before she wrecked herself over whatever new guy she was contacting me to discuss.

Setting up my camera and backdrop took a few more minutes than it usually did because the room kept tilting. Finally, I gave up on making everything pretty and sat down, put my headphones on, then logged into Zoom.

Forty minutes wasn't too bad. I could do anything for an hour.

Madeline's sweet face came up on the screen. So earnest and full of that rosy glow of love. Her aura glowed hot pink. She didn't need me to tell her she was in love today, that was for sure.

"Oh, Luna. Are you okay?"

So much for the makeup helping.

"Just feeling a little under the weather."

"Oh." Her wide smile dimmed. "I'm so sorry. Do you want to reschedule?"

Yes. So much yes. "No, that's okay."

She frowned. "If you're sure."

My hand trembled as I reached for my favorite gentle tarot deck. Shuffling required a bit more dexterity than I was currently capable of, so I went with a messy spread across my table. "So, tell me what we're talking about today."

That was all she needed to hear. Her aura went bright and fluttery like Monarch butterflies in the spring. His name was Patrick and he was too perfect to live on this earth. The way she described him, the dude was going to sprout angel wings.

I surreptitiously floated my hands over the cards and flipped one. I'd been doing this long enough not to let my face betray the card. Seven of Swords wasn't the best one to pull when thinking about a guy. Nor was the next card, Knight of Wands. Both hinted that Patrick might've been a player.

"So, how long have you been seeing one another?"

"Four months. We have spent every Thursday together. That's his night off. He works on the road a lot."

I bet he did.

I pulled out my favorite oracle deck and groaned at the Spy card.

Okay, cards, I get it.

"I'm really glad you've found a guy who makes you so happy, Madeline."

"Do you think we have a future together?"

"Do you think you do?" Most of the time, when people came to me it was because they already had a bad feeling.

She looked down at her hands. She was gripping a startlingly large hunk of rose quartz. "I really like him, Luna."

I curled my fingers into my palm before stretching my fingers out again. My hand heated over a card. I flipped over the Four of Cups followed by the Star and Ace of Cups. Her hopeful nature and giving heart always got her into trouble, but she really shouldn't settle for half measures.

"I'd be careful. Keep things slow and steady."

She leaned forward. "Is it something bad?"

I left the cards that I'd pulled and gathered up the rest. I set them down and took a quick drink against the flood of moisture in my mouth.

Come on. Hold on just a few minutes longer.

With unsteady fingers, I reached for the rollerball of lemon oil and ginger I'd mixed last night.

I slid it over my wrist and waved it near my nose.

Slowly, the nausea settled. I drew in a deep breath. My hand was much steadier as I overhand shuffled and pushed away my own maladies. I didn't want to put my fucked-up energy into the cards.

When I turned over Three of Swords and a reversed Knight of Cups, I looked up.

"That's not a good face."

I was usually better at schooling my expression and giving a positive spin to even the worst cards. "Tell you what. I think some of my energy is messing up this reading. I'm really sorry. Would you mind if we rescheduled? I'll throw in an extra ten minutes for free."

"Oh, that's okay. Are you sure it's just not really bad cards for me?" Her lower lip quivered.

"I think you should search your heart. If you're worried, there's a reason."

A huge tear dripped down her cheek. "Why do I always end up with these kinds of men?"

I leaned forward and gave her a soft smile. "Because you have an amazing, gentle, and open heart. And you're beyond beautiful." I watched her aura fluctuate between the pink of hopeful love and a more muted green.

Ever since the hill at the picnic with Caleb, I'd had more and more trouble with auras. They were stronger and harder to control. I had a feeling it was a lovely part of being pregnant.

I'd heard of witches with augmented gifts because of their pregnancies. Whether it was taking on the gifts of the child for a while, or just the chaos of hormones, there would be some fun times to come.

"I feel like this guy may not be giving you the whole story. I don't know what that means yet, but I think you need to have a heart to heart with Patrick to see if you're on the same page."

I shuffled all the cards again, then cut the deck into three and flipped the middle. The Star came up again. I flipped it around to show her. "There's always hope. If that means there is hope for you and Patrick, or that you'll find the right guy soon, I just don't know."

She dashed away another tear. "You always know what to say. Even when you're so sick. Is it the flu?"

I gave her a wry smile. "Baby flu."

"Oh, Luna!" Her eyes flooded again. "Congratulations. That's amazing."

It felt weird to tell someone. Well, other than Caleb and his sister. But for the first time, it seemed like something wondrous and not just fear-inducing. "Thanks. I'm one of the lucky women with an enduring relationship with my bathroom, unfortunately."

"Oh." Her huge dark eyes flooded with tears and empathy. "How awful. Get yourself some mints. It always helped my sister-in-law."

"I will." I had a large order to fill at Moonstone and Obsidian. And I'd ask Georgia for a little help as well. She was used to tending to women with all sorts of ailments. I couldn't be the first pregnant woman who needed assistance in this area.

"I'm really sorry I had to cut this short."

She held up a hand. "It's all right. I just hope you start feeling better."

Relief made my shoulders loosen. I hadn't even known the muscles were bunched up with tension. "Patrick doesn't deserve you, Mads."

She gave me a watery smile. "He probably doesn't. Just send me a note when you're feeling more yourself."

"I will."

I ended the video chat and slumped back in my chair.

Then the nausea returned. No amount of lemon oil was going to stop it. I bolted from my chair, but tripped over the cord for my microphone and landed hard on my hip.

A string of inventive words for what I was going to do to Caleb's man parts ended in a dry heave.

Someone knocked. "Luna?"

"Go away," I yelled at the door.

It was a male voice, but I was too busy trying to get off the floor before I had an extra mess to clean up. I gave up and started crawling to the bathroom.

My foot hooked on the cord to the speaker on the end table beside the couch as the room swam. Everything came down with bang. The lampshade bounced off my butt, and my lamp rolled under my desk.

Another bang sounded from the front of my apartment. Something slammed into my door. Then the doorjamb splintered before the door bounced off the wall.

Great. Someone was breaking in as I was crawling to the bathroom to puke up my Pedialyte. Or knowing my luck it was Caleb. Right now, I wanted to turn him into a eunuch for doing this to me.

I'd thought his cock was beautiful. Well, the fruits of that beautiful cock were going to kill me dead.

"Jesus."

I knew that voice. Caleb would have been a better choice. "Oh, no.

169

How did you find me?" I asked the floor as I pressed my forehead into the hardwood.

"Lu." Xavier knelt beside me and placed his warm hand on my back. "Do I need to call an ambulance? 911?"

"No. Goddess, no. I just need to go into the bathroom." I hated asking for help more than anything on this earth.

My brother's strong arms slid around my waist. Gently, he turned me until I was cradled against his chest. Since when did my brother have this kind of muscle power?

"Which way?"

I pointed limply.

His eyebrows snapped together. "Are you sure we shouldn't go to the hospital?"

"No. It's just..."

The baby flu. I really couldn't keep calling it that.

He set me down carefully. "Do you want me to, uh, go in there with you?"

I pushed him back and slammed the door in his face just in time to lose the rest of my Pedialyte and whatever acid was trying to shoot hellfire up my esophagus.

"Can I do anything? Crackers? Ginger ale? Hazmat suit?" he asked through the door.

"Go away."

I heard him pace down the hallway before returning. His voice was a low murmur. I didn't really care since my cheek was currently pressed to the tiles of my floor. It was so lovely and cool.

"No, I don't know when I'll be back in the office. Just cancel the rest of my meetings."

Meetings? My brother? Was I moving into the hallucination portion of my symptoms?

"Go back to work," I tried to shout through the door. "Work, ha. Since when," I mumbled.

"I heard that."

I flipped off the closed door.

"Is it safe to come in?"

"No." I moved my cheek to another tile. Ahhh. Coolness. I could just sleep here.

"I'm coming in."

"Haven't you witnessed enough puke?"

"It was far worse after Jackson's Memorial Day bash. You drank enough purple punch to fill the lake."

"Ugh. Don't remind me." That was the first and last day I drank grain alcohol in my life. "You're the one who made the punch."

"I didn't tell you to drink all of it." He opened the door and hauled me off the floor, then stood me in front of the pedestal sink. "You look like shit, Lu."

"Thank you. I match how I feel." And then I had to grab the sink for a whole new reason. My brother had a faint blue glow around him. It was dark and a little murky, but it was new. In all the years I'd had my abilities, I'd never once been able to read my brother.

I reached back and held his hand for a second. "I'm fine, X. I promise. This will pass."

He met my gaze in the mirror. Eyes so much like mine stared right back at me. "Is this a nine-month affliction?"

I looked away and turned on the sink.

"I take it that's a yes. Do I need to kill the teacher?"

"Takes two to tango. You should know. You get around quite a bit."

"Yes, but I'm safe."

"So were we." *Ish.* Sometimes we got a little careless in the heat of the moment, but we always came to our senses. And I was on birth control. "Evidently, the universe had other plans."

"Oh, don't start with that shit again." He backed out of my small bathroom and headed down the hall.

"Some things never change," I said to my very scary reflection. My scarf was twisted and I looked like I'd been on a three-day bender. But I'd also learned that sometimes I didn't have all the answers in this life.

I slid my hand over my still-flat stomach. This demon spawn was a gift.

Even if it came with an unnatural love for kicking all the food and drink out of my body. And this extra sparkly version of reading auras.

I brushed my teeth again and rummaged around in my basket of samples. Makeup wasn't worth the effort, but I wiped down my sweaty face with some toner and used a mint-scented moisturizer.

That seemed to steady me a bit.

I followed my brother's voice into the living room. He was back on the phone. And now that I wasn't yakking up my toes, I noticed he was wearing a three-piece suit. His wild blond curls were tamed back from his face. His navy suit had the lightest tone on tone pinstripe to it. He'd opened the jacket, showing off a brown belt that matched his shoes exactly.

It might not be a rich boy casual outfit like I was used to, but this was definitely a blast from the past. He still knew how to put himself together. I was sure he would've gone into fashion if he wasn't a Hastings.

Apparently, he'd been roped into the family business. Wheeling and dealing in the financial sector seemed to have finally rubbed off on him.

He turned and saw me, then quickly told whomever was on the other end of the line that he'd be busy for the next few hours.

"No you won't."

"Thanks, Devon." He slid his phone into his pocket.

"What are you doing here, Xavier?"

"I came to talk."

"Why?"

"Because you're my sister."

I eased back on my couch. And when everything seemed to stay where it was supposed to, I relaxed. "Since when?"

"You're the one who walked, Lu."

I stared down at my chipped purple polish. "Mom wanted me gone, so I got gone."

He tipped his head back. "She never said that."

"She wanted me to be a different person." I blew out an annoyed breath. "You know I was dying in that house."

"Do you always have to be so dramatic?"

I stiffened. "Look, I appreciate you helping me, but you can go."

He crossed his arms over his surprisingly expansive chest. When the hell had that happened? "I'm not going anywhere."

"Haven't you done enough?" I gestured to my doorway. "Speaking of dramatic."

"I heard you in here, and things falling over." He raked a hand through his hair and a few curls dared to spring out of his neat hairstyle. And that little thing actually made me feel much better. That was more like the X I knew and used to love.

I looked down at my nails again. "Yeah. I just need to rest."

"I don't think you should be alone. Where's your...whatever the teacher is."

"The teacher's name is Caleb."

"Yeah, well, where is he?"

I crossed my arms. "None of your business."

"You told him, right?"

My hands fell to my sides. "Of course I told him."

"Good, because he deserves to know."

I frowned. That sounded oddly specific.

He raked both hands through his hair and his curls started popping everywhere. It took about five years off of him, reminding me of the big brother I'd always loved and looked up to. "What about that girl you used to hang with? The Amazon with the killer legs."

I laughed. "Ryan?"

"Yeah." He tugged at his collar as he stopped pacing. "She was insanely hot."

"Still is. And you still couldn't handle her. Though she does seem to go for the suit types these days."

One eyebrow rose. "Oh, yeah?"

"Taken."

"Figures."

I laughed. Goddess, it was easy to fall back into rhythm with him. But he was still Xavier Hastings, golden boy. And I was still Luna, the outcast weirdo. He hadn't backed me up when I needed him. My mother had made the ultimatum based on our father's directive.

I was to go to college and stop with the occult nonsense.

Occult.

As if they understood any part of me.

When I declined, I was cut off. No pretty credit cards or bank accounts with the Hastings money. If I wanted to be so frighteningly 'unusual', as they'd put it, then I'd do it without any help from them.

Xavier had just stood there. He hadn't even looked at me.

I'd left and that was that.

He sat down next to me. "I came to talk."

"I'm not really in any condition to do the chitchat thing."

"No, I don't suppose you are. But I'm not leaving you like this."

"Since when? You've been really good at letting me deal with my own problems for years."

"I tried to contact you. Over and over again."

I fussed with my sleeve. "Would it have changed anything?"

"It might have."

"You had your chance to stop me."

He gripped my hand. "Look, I know I fucked up. But you weren't the only one who received an ultimatum."

I wanted to rail against him. Ultimatum or not, he should have taken my side. I would've taken his. Instead, he'd left me swinging in the wind alone.

Early on, I'd learned not to count on anyone. Was I just supposed to forget all of that now?

My eyes burned as I stared at the tie-dye swirl on my kaftan. "It was always me and you against them."

"No. You only saw it that way. They're not perfect, but they just wanted what was best for you."

"Best for me?" My head jerked up to meet his gaze. "A closet full of twin sets like our mother?"

"Come on." He squeezed my hand. "She didn't wear twin sets. It was more like Chanel suits in pink. Lots of pink."

I shuddered. "So much pink. But not the good kind." I pointed at the hot pink in the kaftan. "That's the good kind of pink."

"Yeah, if you're twelve."

"Twenty-seven, thanks."

He turned my hand over and laced his fingers with mine. "We can help you monetarily. With whatever you want to do."

I tamped down the offense brewing in my gut. Or it could be acid heading for higher ground once more. The Hastings always wanted to throw money at a problem to make it go away. "I don't need your money, X. I've been taking care of myself for years."

He bristled and pulled his hand away.

I turned toward him. "I could use my brother though."

He wound his arm around my neck and dragged me against him. "But you really need a shower."

I punched him in the belly. "Ow."

"Serves you right for punching me." He set his chin on top of my head. "Are you sure you don't want to come home with me? I have an awesome housekeeper."

"I'm sure she'd love to take care of a stranger."

"I pay her handsomely."

"I bet you do." With our family money. The golden boy was exactly what my father had groomed him to be. "I just need to get out of here for a little while and think."

I hadn't even realized I was going to say that until it came out. Instantly, my chest felt less tight. Maybe that was what I'd needed all along.

"Then come back with me."

"No. But I'm going to call Ry." She had a small apartment, but we'd slept on the same bed a few dozen times. It was no big deal.

I started to rise, but he held up a hand. "What are you doing? If you get up, you'll probably fall on your face."

He wasn't wrong. I sighed. "Can you get my phone? It's over on my desk."

He retrieved it and held it out of reach. "I'm driving you."

"Fine."

I ignored the texts from Caleb waiting for me and called my best friend. Always a crapshoot. Ryan and I weren't attached to our phones like some people. Probably because we spent so much of our lives in service to others.

"Hey, girl. What's up?"

"Ry? Are you home?" Suddenly, a wave of emotion hit me just hearing her voice.

"No. I'm at Preston's."

"Oh." What was I thinking? Of course she was. She'd finally found a guy who could keep up with her wild and wonderful brain.

"Is everything okay?"

Banging metal on her end hit me like an ice pick to the skull. So much for that settled feeling. "No. Yes." I blew out a breath. "Yes and no. Oh, goddess. One second." I dropped the phone and raced to the bathroom again.

It was only dry heaves at this point, and yet my body didn't seem to get the freaking memo.

"Lu?"

I waved at my brother with my head in the bowl. "I'm fine."

He paced back down the hall, the click of his dress shoes fading as he neared the living room. I ran cold water over my wrists and went for another round with my toothbrush. At this rate, I was going to brush the enamel right off my teeth.

I dragged myself back into the living room and dropped onto the couch, then picked up my phone again. "Ugh. I swear, I don't have anything in my body to throw up, and yet it still keeps coming."

"Oh, hell. Are you okay? Do you have the flu?" The questions kept tumbling out of Ryan's mouth. "I can come over and bring broth or stop at Georgia's shop for supplies."

I gave a half laugh. "No, I have something a little more permanent." All the frustration I'd been tamping down seemed to bubble up now that I was actually talking to Ryan.

"I don't know what that means."

I wiped my clammy forehead with the back of my hand. "Of the demon spawn variety. Freaking teacher. Imma kill him. He's never known the hex I'm going to put on him. His ancestors for a thousand years will hate him."

Xavier whirled around, his eyes wide.

"I don't know what that means." Ryan's voice was panicked.

The moisture started again in my mouth. "Ugh. One more second." I put my head between my knees. I could hear her doing something on the other end of the line, but all I could concentrate on was keeping my stomach from spewing the whole lot of nothing left in there.

I grabbed another one of the rollerballs I had stashed all over my apartment and dragged in the clean scent of lemon oil with the tang of ginger. That combination seemed to settle me the best.

And I needed to get settled fast. The urge to get out of here was almost as overwhelming as my queasy stomach.

"Ry?"

"Here." She sounded out of breath. Then I heard Preston in the background. All of a sudden, she was clearer. "What can I do?"

"I need somewhere to crash for a bit."

"She can stay here." Preston's voice was now also more distinct. They must have their heads together.

My eyes stung. They were already such a unit.

Then the line went silent. They were probably arguing like the married couple they already were.

The ambient noise came back. "Lu? You can stay here with us." Ryan's voice was thick.

Which, in turn, put a lump in my throat. I was pretty sure it wasn't the kind that would come hurling out.

Maybe.

"Preston offered up one of his guest rooms. He's got a ton of them."

I sniffed. "With its own bathroom, maybe? I don't mean to be greedy, but the porcelain throne is my new best friend."

"Oh."

I heard the realization in her voice. I sniffed again. "Yeah. I'd handle it myself, but I just need a spot to think for a little bit."

Caleb didn't want me to handle it alone. I knew he didn't. But he was just so overwhelming right now. So sure of everything when it came to us. He kept tossing around the *love* word with such earnest happiness.

For me.

With me.

With the little family we were possibly making.

"Anything you need. Always. You don't have to handle it alone. We got you."

I swallowed down the lump and dabbed at my eyes. "I love you."

"I love you too, girl."

Simple as that, I knew Ryan had my back. No question. "I need to take a shower and clean up."

"Okay, we'll be there in a little bit. Take care of you."

"Take care of you," I said back and held my phone to my chest.

Caleb didn't deserve this. He didn't deserve me. I should be thrilled that he was so sure. So ready for this. Was he faking it? It couldn't be so easy to just accept me and an unplanned baby.

"I said I'd take you."

I blinked out of my anxiety spiral. I looked up to find my brother in front of my window, his hands on his hips. "I know, but it was just easier. They'll be here soon. I just really need to clean up."

"You're not going to pass out in the shower or something, are you?" He touched the back of his neck, rubbing at his shoulders.

"Don't worry. I don't think either of us could live that down, thanks."

Relief flooded his face. "I'm staying until they get here though."

I laughed. "I'll allow it."

He snorted. "Ass."

With a sigh, I looked at my phone and tapped on one of Caleb's half dozen texts. I couldn't even read them all right now. I just needed a second to get my head together.

My fingers shook as I typed.

I need some time to think. I'm not sure when I'll be back. Don't worry about me. I'll check in soon.

I locked the phone and flicked on the *do not disturb* option, then stood up. When Xavier rushed forward, I grabbed his hand and leaned against him. "I appreciate it."

He kissed the top of my head. "Okay, go on. You are ripe."

"Oh, I missed you so much."

He curled his arm around my neck and dragged me in until my nose was jammed against his chest. "I did miss you, Lu. I'm going to be here for you, no matter what."

I pressed my cheek against him and drew in his comforting sandalwood scent. In all these years, that hadn't changed. "Guess you're going to be an uncle. How about that?"

"That's fucking terrifying."

"Which part?" I peered up at him. "You being an uncle or me a mom?"

"Seems like they're about even."

I laughed. "I'm going to have to agree." We swayed like that for a minute before I drew back. "Okay, I'm definitely going for that shower."

"Thank God." He rubbed my arms. "Lu?"

"Hmm?"

"Is that a stripper pole?"

I swallowed a laugh. "Yep."

"Just tell me that's not how you support yourself."

I patted his cheek. "I'll be back."

"That's not an answer," he called after me.

I laughed for the first time in days as I headed down the hall.

FIFTEEN

I WAS SINGLE AGAIN.

Unofficially but really freaking officially.

She'd sent me a Dear John note. I'd heard of those on reruns of old sitcoms. Naturally, I'd never experienced such a phenomenon before in my life. I used to be the one sending those notes, full of apologies and requests to still be friends.

I was still friends with some of them. They were generally more understanding people than I was. Because if Luna dumped me, I couldn't see myself being her buddy.

Especially if she thought she was going to date and find some other dude while she was carrying my baby.

"Carrying your what?" Lucky demanded while I paced a new tread around the desk in my classroom.

It had been more than two hours since I'd received Luna's message. She'd sent it before then, when I was still fully occupied with parent-teacher meetings. The cynical part of me suspected that was why she'd sent it then. If I didn't know she was leaving, I couldn't stop her.

Not that I'd tried. I was practically a desperate, lovesick fool, but

I'd taken enough college psychology classes to know which approach would not work. If I begged her to stay, she'd run farther and faster.

So, I still hadn't responded. What the hell was I supposed to say?

Sure, fine, go ahead. Go find yourself in Joshua Tree or Salem or Hawaii or wherever. If you still need time when the birth approaches, I'm sure you can handle it without me. You know, the father.

Didn't that give me rights? I was all about a woman's body, her choice, but my kid was currently a captive to her decisions.

"Carrying what, jackass?" Lucky shouted into my ear. I'd forgotten he was even on the phone. "I must've misheard you."

I sat on the edge of my desk. "Luna's pregnant."

"Wow. Did you know she was seeing other— Oh. *Oh.*"

"Were you actually going to ask me who the father of her child is? Really?"

"Well, you didn't say it was yours," he said defensively. "And hello, I'm trying to watch the damn game. The Giants are actually up for once."

"So sorry to interrupt you." I clicked off and debated flinging my phone into the wastebasket in a proper tantrum.

But I didn't do it. I was a mature adult who'd just hung up on his best friend.

When my cell buzzed, I accepted Lucky's call. "Yeah?"

"Dude, you hung up on me."

"I know. I was there. You're my best friend, right? Aren't you honor bound to counsel me through shit?"

"Okay. If you really want me to. Hang on a second." Something banged, and then the TV went silent. "All right. So, the thing is, the rhythm method only works so well. I mean, I'm kind of an expert at it, but you're playing Russian Roulette when you time your thrusts in a town like the Cove. Of course I have exemplary staying power, so I can go much longer than you probably can. Nothing to be ashamed of. But that means—"

I laughed so loud that I worried I'd popped a blood vessel in my temple. The one that had been throbbing since I'd eagerly clicked on Luna's text.

Before I'd realized she was putting me on ice.

"She's on birth control. We used condoms every time." There was once or twice that some slippage could've happened though.

Whatever. The kid was planted. I wasn't going to Monday night quarterback the ins and outs of how it had occurred—literally.

"Huh. And you're sure it's yours."

"Lucky," I warned.

"I'm just making sure. You were right not to have sex for ages. It was like you had a premonition or something that the Cove egg dropper was hovering over your head."

"Premonition? Where did you pick up that word?"

"Macy saw a movie. Then she made Gideon watch it. Then the whole crew watched it. Some fucked up shit, man. Like this chick was married, right?"

I closed my eyes and prayed for deliverance while he blathered on about cheating husbands and funerals and Sandra Bullock. Typically, she would've triggered my interest all by herself, but I was in a bind. I was pretty sure she could've appeared naked in my classroom, and I wouldn't have so much as blinked.

Love was crap.

When he finished, he let out a breath. "So, anyway, Luna's knocked up. Congratulations?"

"Thanks."

"You don't sound overjoyed. I don't blame you. Friday beer fests are now basically cancelled forever."

"Not because of that, you dolt."

"Harsh."

"Sorry. It's just a lot. And now Luna's gone."

"Define gone."

"Not in the area."

"Did she go shopping in Syracuse?"

I explained it to him in a brief, semi-manly fashion. How she'd told me. How I'd reacted. How she'd reacted.

"So, that's why you ghosted me for dinner that night after inviting me. I had to sit with people I didn't even know. Hella awkward. And my date decided she didn't like guys before I even got to her place. I don't know what that was about."

"I can't begin to imagine."

"That Preston dude is with Ryan. She's Luna's chick, right?"

I reached up to undo the top couple buttons on my shirt. "Yeah. Her best friend."

"Ryan's guy is a lawyer. He's smart. I was shocked he didn't wear a pocket protector with his fancy suit. Complete opposite of Ryan. He was pretty funny though. Ryan kept calling him PMS. I'm sure they have a kinky sex life. They had that glow."

I'd made the mistake of sipping from my water bottle at that exact moment. The liquid went down the wrong pipe, and I started coughing. Lucky naturally took that as confirmation of his carnal theories.

"Oh, so they *do* have a kinky sex life. I knew it. Bet you it's like whips or something. She has a sexually adventurous vibe. Hot." Lucky cleared his throat. "So, ah, Luna with that pole. Bet she's the same way, huh?"

"I'm not discussing the mother of my child with you that way, pervert."

"Last month, she was the blond witchy hottie. Now she's practically sanctified."

"Pretty much. And she's gone off to find herself and I'm trying not to lose my mind."

"Why would she need to do that?"

"I don't know. I must've fucked it up somehow."

"Did you say something about not wanting the kid?"

"No. I want it so much. I want everything with Luna. And I want to tell my parents and Ivy and Rory and Aug and Kin." I released a long, uneven breath. Once I'd opened the valve, apparently there was no shutting it off. "But I can't tell them until Luna's ready for people to know, and it's killing me. They shouldn't be kept in the dark."

"Whoa."

Silence descended on the line.

I squeezed my plastic water bottle and a little dribbled out of the top onto my khakis. "You okay?"

"Yeah, I just grabbed a cold one. I thought this day would never come."

"What day?"

"The day you grew up and became a Crescent Cove daddy."

I had to laugh. "You're next, buddy."

"How dare you. Why would you curse me like that?"

"It's not a curse, man. I swear."

He made a sound that indicated he clearly did not believe me and never would.

"We haven't really planned or anything yet. But I started looking around online the other day. The clothes are so tiny. What if I accidentally drop him or her?"

"Or sit on him," Lucky mused.

"Okay, didn't think of that one, but yeah." I glanced out the window into the darkness and made myself stand from the desk. "I have to go home. Putting off facing her empty apartment isn't going to make it any easier."

"I can meet you there," he offered. "We can watch some shitty TV and get drunk until we pass out. Just like the old days."

"If by the old days you mean July," I said dryly as I put my bottle in the recycler and started stuffing papers into my briefcase.

"Before she got between us."

I set down a file full of assessment reports. "She isn't between us. We're still us. Nothing's changed."

"You know that isn't true. It can't be. You'll have all these responsibilities, and no time for your old pal Lucky." He let out a rusty laugh. "But hey, I'll be the godfather, right?"

"I can't do that to an innocent baby."

When Lucky stayed quiet, I made myself laugh. If it sounded maniacal, that couldn't be helped. "Of course you'll be his godfather. Who else would I ask than my best friend in all the world to parent a small, helpless child upon my untimely death?"

"That's better. I accept."

I had to hope when the surprise wore off, Lucky would come to his senses and admit he did not want to be my child's godfather. Problem was he always liked to be the first pick, and if he suspected I thought August was a better choice, he'd cry foul until the end of time.

Basically, baby Beck was as screwed as his daddy.

"So, are we on for crap TV and drunken antics or what?"

I started to accept, then I shook my head although he couldn't see me. I was a father now, even if the kid wasn't born yet. Drowning my sorrows when I had the tolerance of a homecoming cheerleader made no sense. On the surface, it seemed like a better plan than stationing myself outside Luna's apartment and waiting for her to emerge, but I couldn't do that either.

What I was going to do was go home alone and act like a mature freaking man.

"Nah, I'm awful company right now, but thanks. But hey, maybe you could come over tomorrow? We can throw some steaks—" nope, that was out, they made me think of Luna, "—uh, scallops on the grill on the roof."

"You know I hate seafood."

"Okay, burgers then. I found a good veggie—"

"Dude, you're sure you impregnated Luna? You're not sounding like the guy I know. Veggie burgers? Damn, son. I'll bring my own burgers if you're grilling that garbage." He clicked off and made me laugh in spite of myself.

Leave it to Lucky. As crazy as he was, I hoped he never changed. Then again, he loved his social life, especially the naked variety, and we knew what that meant for most single dudes in the Cove.

But he didn't seem worried. Perhaps he'd curtailed some of his extracurricular activities. We'd been the last two men standing—well, not really, there were far more single men in town—and look what had happened.

I glimpsed the baby book I'd shoved in my briefcase along with my school paperwork. It was already getting dog-eared. There was so much I didn't know.

I shuddered. So much I did not *want* to know.

Too bad for me. If Luna was going through this, then so was I. Every single horrifying step.

I turned out the lights and waved to Ms. Duncan who taught fourth grade across the hall. She was chatting with Mike, who was leaning over her and sniffing her hair as if she was a bucket of fried chicken.

My stomach growled. Obviously, I needed dinner. And not a veggie burger.

Sorry, Lu.

She was a carnivore like me, but she mixed it up with more "ethical options" as she called them.

My shoulders slumped where I stood outside my classroom. I really did not want to go home alone. I'd gotten too used to having Lu there. Her presence had been more sporadic over the past week, but I'd known she was across the hall. We hadn't touched each other since she'd told me about the baby. It didn't matter. I just wanted her close.

Wanted *them* close.

"Oh, hey, man, didn't see you there." Mike sounded affable on the surface as he turned his head, but I noticed the irritation in the set of his jaw.

He must think I wanted to take my turn at sniffing Ms. Duncan's hair. Since she was new this year and I couldn't even remember her first name, that was a definite no.

I nodded stiffly. I still didn't walk away. This whole "Luna taking a break" thing was going swimmingly. Now I was creeping on fellow teachers.

"You know Holly." He gestured awkwardly at the pretty brunette in her cardigan, floral dress, and sedate pumps. Nothing the least bit tight or revealing or not Catholic school approved.

I wasn't thinking of Lu again. I really wasn't.

"Sure. I'm not sure I knew her first name though. Caleb." I smiled and moved forward to extend a hand to shake.

Her grip was firm and cool. "Nice to re-meet you with actual first names." She laughed and glanced at Mike as she released my hand. "Do these parent-teacher nights get any easier?"

"Not really," I admitted just as Mike chimed in.

"Oh, yeah, they're usually a breeze."

Figured. Everything was just rainbows and glitter farts for him.

"So, Holly, our Caleb here is dating a honest-to-goodness witch."

Inwardly, I groaned. This was my own fault for lingering for non-productive chitchat. I usually knew better. Head down, out the door.

I was definitely out of sorts tonight.

"How do you know she's a witch?" I demanded.

"Everybody knows." Mike shrugged. "Someone said she has a pentagram tattoo."

"She does not."

Not that I would mind if she did. Pentagrams didn't mean what a lot of people assumed. They usually represented the elements—fire, air, water, earth, and spirit.

"A witch?" Holly's honey-brown eyes sparkled. "How fascinating. Is she meeting you here, Caleb? I'd love to meet her."

"Yeah, I wish. She's on a sabbatical. Possibly in Canada. I'm not really sure."

Holly and Mike exchanged a glance. I didn't blame them. I was nearly spiraling.

Time to leave.

"It's all good though. She's doing what's best for her. I'm sure she'll come back someday. She has to, since I knocked her up. Okay, well, nice convo. Have a good night." I pointed at Mike. "You can go back to sniffing her hair now."

I had an instant to glimpse Holly's cheeks going bright red under her freckles before I got the heck out of there.

Once I was in my vehicle in the parking lot, I called my sister on the in-dash screen. I needed to talk to someone. I wasn't supposed to be telling anyone about this baby, and here I'd just told my colleagues. Not the smartest move. They were mostly all cool people, and minds were opening up a bit even in our school, but unmarried and procreating second grade teachers weren't exactly welcomed with open arms at St. Agnes Academy.

I hadn't even thought of that until this very moment, because I didn't care. If someone had a problem with how Lu and I were living our lives, then they just would. I wasn't caving to pressure. We were on our own schedule, and no one was going to rush us.

When she came down that aisle toward me—or across that sandy dune—it was going to be because we wanted nothing else but that. Fuck society's supposed rules.

Ivy picked up, sounding harried. Rhiannon was wailing in the background. "Caleb?"

"Bad time?"

"Kinda. Rhi has decided she hates bathtime. Last week, it was her favorite thing." She sighed. "What's up?"

"Luna's having a baby." So much for easing in. And so much for keeping this news to myself.

If I couldn't have her physically with me, I had to talk about her. Talking about her meant talking about the bean burrito.

Smaller than a bean burrito right now. More like the size of a raspberry. Maybe. We didn't even know when she'd gotten pregnant. Could've been the first night. Or the next.

God, I needed answers, and they just weren't forthcoming right now.

I leaned back against the headrest and released a long, slow breath.

Patience, grasshopper. You've got probably around seven months to go in this rodeo.

If Luna was even back by then.

She had to be, right? She wouldn't just leave for good.

The woman I loved wouldn't just take off permanently. No matter how relatively new we were to being together, I knew her better than that.

Sounds of chaos came through the speaker. I'd forgotten Ivy was there. I had to stop calling people. I couldn't even focus on talking to them.

Not that my sister was speaking to me. She was whisper-shouting at someone in the background. Probably Rory. She was using the voice she typically used when dealing with her temperamental toddler —or her unhinged brother.

Ivy came back on the line after a brief howl from Rhiannon that abruptly ended, indicating she'd either been removed from the area or possibly dunked in the bathtub. "Okay, sorry," she said breathlessly. "She finally told you?"

I opened my mouth and immediately shut it again. "What do you mean finally? Did you already know?"

"Sort of."

"Ivy. Either you knew or you didn't."

"She didn't intend to tell me. She didn't even know herself. We figured it out together."

She explained the whole incident at Kinleigh's the day before our planned dinner with Ryan and Preston while I rubbed at the tension in my right shoulder. It felt as if all my muscles were seizing up.

"I knew she was getting sick a lot, but not that bad. She's not telling me stuff." I drummed my knuckles into the steering wheel. "Why isn't she telling me? Why the hell won't she let me be the father in utero of the year?"

Ivy surprised me by laughing. "Did it ever occur to you that what you think she needs isn't what she actually does?" Before I could answer, she questioned, "You didn't ask her if the baby was yours, right?"

"Why would I do that? Of course it's mine. Who else's would it be?"

"So not all men are brain dead, just your brother-in-law. Got it."

"I heard that."

I flexed my fist. "Rory asked you if Rhi was his? That bastard. I'm going to kick his ass. I'm in the mood right now. I'm on my way over."

"Cool your jets, mate," Rory answered in the background, his voice entirely too clear.

"Do you have me on speaker, Ive? What the heck. This is a private conversation."

"Sorry to inform you, but Rory is family."

"He thought you were sleeping all over the Cove. He's been ex-communicated."

"I thought nothing of the sort. We'd been apart a bit of time and not strictly together so when I came back to—you know what, mind your own relationship, Cal, how about that?"

"You know not to call me Cal."

"Oh, do I?" Rory waited a beat. "Cal."

"Boys," Ivy said mildly. "Did you tell Mom and Dad yet?"

"No. I can't." Lightly, I pounded my fist on the steering wheel. "She's not ready for everyone to know, and I already fucked up by telling teachers at work."

"At work? Oh. Um, yeah. That could be a problem."

"It's not a problem. They'll just deal with it. I'm a damn good teacher. If they're going to pitch a fit because I'm not marrying Lu yet—"

"I heard a *yet*," Rory said. "Did you hear a *yet*, Ginger Fairy?"

"Shut up. And also, ick on the nickname."

It was actually kind of cute, but not in my current gloomy mood.

"Feck off. Not relishing the oncoming birth? Afraid you'll get stuck changing nappies?"

"Hard to change a nappy when the mother isn't even here. By the way, the proper word is diaper."

"What do you mean she's not here?" Ivy asked.

As briefly as possible, I told them. I also left out most swear words in case Rhiannon was anywhere in earshot.

I was father of the year material already.

"She didn't leave you. She wouldn't do that."

Ivy's even tone annoyed me. Not a shock, since everything was annoying me right now. "What do you know about the situation?"

"She's a great woman, Caleb. You wouldn't have slept with her otherwise. You're too averse to baby fever."

"You have a point. But this isn't about me."

"Yes, it is. She's just freaked out. I saw her face when she realized. She was overwhelmed and seriously scared. Telling you terrified her, although she didn't say that. She's so strong."

"But I was fine with it. I'm fu—frigging happy. Why won't she let us be happy?"

"How long have you been together?"

"A couple months."

"Yet you expect her to trust you one hundred percent in that time. She has a baby inside her, you jerk. She's emotional and dealing with a million changes you can't even comprehend. Swollen ankles, bloating, mood swings, hemorrhoids, unexpected leakage—"

"Stop right there."

"Thanks for that, mate." Rory sounded as disturbed as I felt.

"And on top of all that, she has a fearsome need to protect her baby. Even from you. Maybe especially from you, if she isn't sure this whole child thing isn't just a temporary lark to you." She sighed. "Sorry to tell you, buddy, you don't exactly have the best track record in town for fidelity."

I didn't say anything. Her truth bomb had hit me dead on.

"But she still had no cause to leave you flat out," Rory added.

I shut my eyes. "Maybe she did. I wasn't giving her any space. If this is a big change for me, it's enormous for her. She said her back ached too much to even get up on her stripper pole."

Someone coughed, and then there were the sounds of slapping and a scuffle.

"Please do not mention stripper poles in my husband's earshot anymore, please and thank you."

I had to chuckle. "Best thing in the freaking world, man. Though my baby sister, seriously? You dog."

"Not the baby sister nonsense again," she muttered.

"Would you prefer it if I wanted to see someone *other* than your sister on the pole?"

I couldn't argue there.

"I'm going home to drown my sorrows in club soda and a little light pregnancy bedtime reading. Thanks for talking me down from the ledge."

"Anytime. She's going to be back soon, I promise. Just let her be the one who leads for a while, you know? She'll tell you what she needs. And more than anything, just love her."

"I can do that," I murmured.

"Aww. I knew it." Ivy sniffled. "My big bro's in love. Finally. I was

192

beginning to think it would never happen. Or else you'd just marry Lucky."

"He does have his uses, such as heavy duty lifting."

"And he makes a mighty cocktail. That one he made at his March Madness party got me so lit that Rory was able to talk me into going behind the gazebo and—oh, look at the time. Have to put Rhi to bed. Good luck. Talk soon, love you!" She clicked off before I could decide whether to laugh or throw up.

Family was a hell of a thing, man. But I loved mine fiercely, and I couldn't wait to expand it with Luna.

I just had to have faith that deep down, she felt the same way for me as I did for her. I'd take a reasonable facsimile until I found the key to make her fall completely for my inimitable charm.

Reversing out of my parking space, I let out a laugh. Yeah, right. If I'd been that cocky once upon a time, I definitely wasn't now.

Love had a way of humbling a guy.

I pulled up near my building and pocketed the keys as I headed inside. My back tensed as I climbed the stairs. I was already bracing to see Luna's apartment, knowing she wasn't there.

Something suspiciously like sorrow clutched my chest. I'd gone about this all wrong.

I walked up our hallway and stopped dead at the commotion around my girl's apartment. Gavin had just placed a replacement panel for the door against the wall.

"What the fuck happened here?" I dropped my briefcase and full out ran to reach them. There was a jagged crater near the knob, and the doorjamb was splintered.

Neither of the men working on the door answered me or even paid me any mind.

Pure panic drenched me in sweat as I shoved aside Gavin Forrester and came face to face with Xavier Hastings. I grabbed him by the lapels of his designer suit jacket and shook him hard enough to rattle his fillings. "Where is she? What did you do to her?"

SIXTEEN

"Easy, brother." Xavier didn't try to detangle me, just flashed me a slow smile as if we were chatting over drinks. "Gotta say I'm glad to see this display."

"I'll show you a display. And I'm not your brother."

"Good thing, or else this situation would be a bit trickier."

I glared into his smug, handsome face. He looked rather like a snootier, harder, sharper version of Luna, which was another kick in the ribs. "I'm going to say this slowly. Where. Is. She?"

"I'm just going to take a break and give you two some time." Gavin stepped back and dusted off his white dress shirt before reaching for his toolbox. I would've figured he had a handyman on call for this sort of thing, but then again, he and X had been talking quite familiarly before I arrived. "X, buzz me when we can get back to it."

I grunted. "You're doing repairs now?"

"Guess so." X hooked his thumbs in his pockets. I still had a hold of his jacket, but he didn't seem to notice. "When I cause the damage to my partner's place, especially."

"Your partner? You and Gavin are—"

"Not like that. Business partners." His smooth chuckle infuriated

195

me. "Luna is fine, by the way. I heard a bang in here, and she didn't come to the door fast enough to suit me." He shot his cuffs. "So, I made my own way in."

Finally, I let him go and took a step back. "What kind of bang?"

"The pregnancy kind."

My concern must've shown on my face, because he clapped me on the shoulder. "Come on in for a minute. The door can wait until G gets back up here."

"X. G. Are you guys too elite to use the full range of consonants and vowels?"

He ignored me as he sauntered into the kitchen. I had little choice but to follow if I wanted to ensure Luna was okay. If he even would tell me the truth.

"You know, I had every right to react like I did," I called. "This scene was like one from Asher Wainwright's True Crime podcast. Young woman says she's going away for a while, then the authorities discover her place was broken into. What was I supposed to think?"

"I'm her brother."

"Estranged brother. And family can be the most murderous of all."

He ignored me. I supposed I couldn't blame him.

Although it seemed ridiculous considering its current state, I closed the door behind me before heading into the kitchen so like my own. Luna had made it hers with soothing touches like the row of leafy plants on the windowsill and the bamboo windchimes over the island.

"I smell her here." I didn't realize I'd spoken aloud until Xavier took down a bottle from the cupboard and slid me a glance.

"Brother, you've got it bad."

"Do I need to say again you're not my brother?"

"No. I fully grasp that fact. But I have sympathy for you. Hell of a thing when a woman is carrying your baby and makes decisions without consulting you first."

I frowned. "Her body, her choice."

"That's true. But it takes two." He poured something into a short glass and slid it toward me across the island. "You look like you need this."

"Drinking isn't the answer to my problems." But my mouth was watering just the same.

"No, but it sure makes them go down easier in the short term. Bottoms up." He poured a glass for himself and knocked it back.

Ah, what the hell. I wouldn't overindulge.

I joined him and drank. And nearly coughed up a lung at the hellfire that exploded in my gut.

"What the hell is that?" I sputtered once I'd finished.

"Fireball. Awesome, right?"

"One word for it." I rubbed my throat. "It's a miracle I can still speak."

"Just wait a minute. You'll grow to appreciate its finer qualities."

It took half that. Holy shit, that was some powerful stuff.

Within five minutes, I was motioning for more.

Within ten minutes, I was loose enough to actually relax on the stool while X told me about what had happened between him and Luna years ago. How her mother had basically cut her off financially unless she toe-stepped into line.

Within twenty minutes, I was drinking my third and wondering why I hadn't proposed on the spot when Luna told me she was pregnant.

"I was in love with her from like the first day. I was moving in, and she was on her stripper pole."

X held up a finger. "No."

"Anyhoo, my best friend wanted her. I mean, who wouldn't? She's so fucking dizzying. She just makes me spin, man." Apparently, I needed to illustrate this statement by whirling around on my stool.

"I think the feeling is mutual." He leaned forward on his crossed arms. So far, he'd only had the one drink and did not seem afflicted like I was. Of course I'd tripled his intake.

I'd always been an overachiever.

"Do you think she loves me? I might throw myself off the roof if she doesn't."

X lifted a brow. "Good to leave yourself some options."

"Huh?"

He laughed and pried my half consumed drink out of my hand. "You've had enough. And yes, I'm certain she loves you. My Lulu would face the devil and not blink. She only runs when she's caught off-guard and shaken to her core."

"You're right. By God, you are." I slammed a fist on the island and jerked to my feet before promptly catching my foot on the rung of the stool and sprawling on the floor. "Ow."

Xavier sighed and came around the counter to haul me up with his hands under my armpits. "Sure you aren't pregnant too? She fell like this today too."

"Oh, fuck." My woozy head cleared immediately. "She fell? She can't fall. Let me call her. She needs to go to the doctor."

"That sobered you up impressively fast." He shook his head as he moved back. "She's fine. Trust me. Hastings aren't made of soft stuff. I guarantee that kid of hers has a head as hard as her own."

I sagged against the island. "I just really want her back. She should be spoiled right now. What if her back hurts? I give gold star massages."

"I'm pretty sure you're every pregnant chick's wet dream."

"Not hers," I said miserably.

"Give her a few days to get herself centered. That's big with her. You know, the whole one with the universe deal."

"Yeah."

"She won't be gone for long. And I'll probably be the one to give her away at your wedding, because she thinks our father is a colossal asshole. Sometimes I'm inclined to agree."

I snorted. "Wedding? She texted me to say peace out."

"Trust me. I've known her since before she was running around collecting money from our relatives for showing her bare butt."

I grimaced. "Hopefully, this was as a small child and not during her teen years."

"Yeah, she was two." He grinned. "She's strong and brave but she retreats when her foundation is shaky. When she's had time to think, she'll come roaring back." He patted my back. "You might want to get ready. Full strength Luna Hastings isn't a woman for mere mortals."

"I know. She's incredible. I don't want to change her or try to tamp her down. I just want to be with her."

"Which is exactly why she wants to be with you."

"Yeah. I probably went over the top. I just wanted her to know I would be there for the baby."

"Just don't forget to be there for her too and what she needs. And that is the literal extent of my relationship advice. I don't get involved in that shit." He walked down the hall to the bathroom, clicking the door shut.

I shook my head, smiling faintly.

So you think, pal. Wait and see.

I pulled out my phone and sent Lu a text. I tried to be casual. I'd wait for her, no matter how long she needed.

What *I* needed at the moment was a damn nap.

Yawning, I shambled to Luna's broken door and opened it to glance into the hall. At least no one had stolen my briefcase, even if the contents were spread all over.

Small favors.

"On the way out, Beck?

"Yeah."

"You okay to get home?" I looked over my shoulder and X smirked, which meant he knew quite well I lived across the hall.

"Think so, thanks."

"You're all right. If my sister had to get pregnant without a ring on her finger, I'm reasonably happy with her selection."

For some reason, that made me grin. "Same. I mean, if Luna had to have a dickhead brother."

He shrugged before I stepped into the hall. "I've been called worse."

Somehow my smile remained as I picked up my scattered belongings. I was more than a little unsteady, but that was to be expected.

Fireball. That was some crazy stuff.

But hey, maybe things weren't as dire as I'd initially assumed. I had to believe in my girl. Perhaps even in the universe. I'd been told things happened exactly as they should.

Time for me to have some faith.

I rubbed my aching head. And a couple Excedrin.

SEVENTEEN

 Luna

"You can't hide here forever."

"Yes, I can." I flipped the pillow to the cool side and dragged the covers over my head. "Did you get more of those candy things?"

"Georgia sold out of her stash because of you," Ryan said with a sigh. The rattle of paper as she shook a few out onto my bedside table soothed me.

I peeked out from my blanket fort and snatched one of the ginger candies. They were a freaking miracle. We'd found the candies at Moonstone and Obsidian the other day. Evidently, I wasn't the only one who needed a little something to help with morning sickness.

Crescent Cove's affliction was catchy all the way to Luna Falls for help in the remedy game. As an extra piece of hilarity, the candies were actually made right here in the Cove. I might have to make friends with Hannah Wainwright simply so I could maximize my supply.

Ryan sat cross-legged on the floor beside my bed. "Honestly, I'd let you stay here until the baby is born. We could do one of those cool water births or something. Imagine PMS's face?"

I flipped my blanket back so I could see her. "First of all, *ew.* Secondly, your guy would faint dead away."

"I'd pay to see that."

"You do realize the birth of my baby isn't for your entertainment in freaking out Preston?"

She propped her elbows on her knees and gave me a goofy grin. "It was just a thought."

I sighed and unearthed my phone from the depths of my bedding. Caleb had stopped texting me yesterday.

"Guess it took ten days for him to finally forget me."

Crap. I hadn't meant to say that out loud.

Ryan sat up. "Excuse me?" She snatched my phone away from me. "He's been texting you this whole time?"

I returned to my burrito status. "Yes."

He was the sweetest guy on earth, and I was petrified that I was actually in love with him. I didn't know what to do with any of this. We'd only known each other for a few months—barely. How the heck was I supposed to believe we could raise a baby together?

What if I started to lean on him and he noped out of this deal? It wasn't like I had that option.

"You are a complete ass. You didn't reply to him even one time?"

"I told him I needed time to think," I mumbled.

"Think about what? That you're an idiot?" The blankets disappeared. Ryan stood at the end of the bed with the lush bedspread in her arms. I wanted to marry those blankets, dammit. They had some sort of magical properties that stayed cool and comfy at the same time.

I sat up. "What the hell, Ry?"

She was scrolling through my phone. "'I just hope you're doing okay. I'm thinking about you. We're going to be okay, babe.'"

Tears pricked my eyes. Hearing those things out loud made my chest ache.

She locked the phone and threw it at me. "Are you kidding me? This whole time, you were just hiding here and this poor sap is pining for you?"

"He's not a sap." I grabbed the phone then pulled the pillow around in front of me to hug it.

"You let me believe he was being a jerk."

"I didn't let you believe anything." I wrapped my arms tighter around the pillow.

She dropped the duvet to the floor. "Oh, no. Don't give me that face. Out with it. You're going to tell me right now what the heck is going on."

"Can I have my blanket back first?"

"No."

"You're mean."

"No. I'm your best friend. And you're worrying me. I've been concocting ways to string this guy up by his balls."

I slumped back against the headboard. "He doesn't deserve that."

"No, he doesn't. And I'm really glad because I like him."

I lifted the pillow to my face. "Me too," I mumbled.

She climbed onto the bed to sit beside me and pulled down the pillow. "What was that?"

"Me too."

"I thought so."

I tipped my head against her shoulder. "Even worse." I huffed out a pathetic sigh. "I think I love him, Ry."

"The horror."

"Oh, shut up. I do believe you were crying in your Cheerios about PMS in the recent past." In fact, she'd interrupted a little of my stripper pole action with Caleb with her freakout a few short weeks ago. I grabbed the pillow and whacked her with it.

She laughed and grabbed one of the pillows behind her to whack me back. "Yes, but you should be learning from my mistakes."

"That is not how this works." I hit her again.

"I didn't think pillow fights were a real thing. Should I get the popcorn? You two might be wearing too many clothes for the typical fantasy, but I have a good imagination."

We both threw our pillows at Preston in the doorway.

He stepped back out of range with a laugh. "Do you two need anything?"

I sighed as a stupid tear slipped down my face. "I need Caleb. Can you do that?"

Preston crossed his arms. "Well, actually..."

I sat up and stuffed the pillow behind me. "What?"

"I'm not sure how Caleb's friend got my number. You people are phone number thieves."

I shrugged. "Best friends' phones are open season."

Preston shoved his hands into his pockets. "I don't believe that's a thing, Miss Hastings."

"Oh, you're using your lawyer voice." Ryan slid off the bed. "Stop giving her grief, PMS. Do you have a plan?"

"Well, Lucky has been checking in on Luna. Evidently, the father of your child is beside himself. I haven't given them any information about you, of course, but I did say you were safe."

I sniffed and swiped at my stupid tears.

"You're making this dude crazy. Not really like you, Lu."

"I know."

"Just go see him."

I looped my arms around my knees. I'd been in the same pajamas since yesterday. "It's not that easy."

"It really is."

"I waited too long." Guilt and fear was an ugly brew in my belly. For once, it wasn't the kind that had me sprinting for the bathroom. This one might've actually been worse.

Every night, I missed him like a limb and I hated it. Could this be any more awful than losing him for real?

My eyes burned as another tear escaped.

Ryan stroked a hand down my hair. "No, you took a time out. It's totally different. And hey, I did the same."

"It nearly killed me," Preston quipped from the doorway.

Ryan glanced at him. "But did it, really?"

He leaned on the doorjamb. "You were damn happy to see me when I arrived on that mountain, Miss Moon."

"Yeah, I was very happy to see you. But I'd also had some time to think about what we were to one another. And we'd known each other even less time. Was it any wonder I was a basket-case?"

Preston came into the room and slipped an arm around her waist. "Her situation is a little different."

"Why, because she's having a baby?" Ryan spun around to face him. "Yes."

"No. That doesn't make a bit of difference. A sperm donor is not who she is missing, you idiot."

Preston gently rubbed her arms. "I just mean she has more to think about."

She elbowed him away and turned back to me. "Is that the problem?"

"No. Well, not the only thing." I tipped my head back. "I can be both mom and dad for this baby if that was the problem. Caleb wants the baby. He's freaking thrilled. But what if he changes his mind? Then what? I get left alone again?"

"What?" Ryan launched herself at me. Her aura was glowing hot with love and the fierce protectiveness that had drawn me to her in the first place. "No. You'll never be alone again. You'll always have me. You even have PMS. He loves you too."

I wrapped my arms around her. "I know. I'm sorry. I didn't mean you. I don't know what I'm talking about. I'm so messed up."

"You meant exactly that." She pulled back and gripped my shoulders. "You have never let yourself love a guy since I've known you."

I frowned. "I've had guys in my life."

"Yeah, you've had guys. Fun. Maybe even an almost love with that rockstar guy."

I wrinkled my nose. "Dominic was just a fling."

"He was a little more than that."

I sighed. "Dom didn't have room in his life for two loves." And I'd known that within a month of going out with him. Even back then, I'd always picked guys I knew would never be more than temporary.

That was all Caleb was supposed to be too. And he'd ruined it with that clever smile and stupidly perfect green eyes. With the way he held me at night and texted me all damn day even though he faced the wrath of Sister Tobias by having his cell phone in class.

He'd brought me to the school picnic and comforted me while I freaked out and everyone was staring at us during my mini meltdown.

He didn't care.

He only saw me.

He loved me.

Loves me.

"I need to get him back," I whispered.

"I'm sure you could call him right now. He'd be here in a hot second."

"He told me he loves me."

Ryan's aquamarine eyes went shiny. "Aww, he did?"

"And I didn't say anything."

She tried to hide her wince, but I caught it before she looked away.

"I know. I'm a terrible human. I just... I've never said it to anyone. Well, but you. But you're my best bish."

"I sure am." She rubbed my arm again. "But we can fix that. We just need to do a big moment. Let him really know you love him. I mean, you do, right?"

"Yeah." I nibbled the inside of my cheek. "I do. I have for weeks—maybe even the first time I found him in my bed."

"Found him?" She frowned. "Are you not telling me all the things?"

"You've been a little busy with a certain lawyer."

"Hmm. We can't chat over wine, but maybe you can do apple juice and I'll do wine?"

I laughed. "I'll give you all the details after I get my guy back." I peeked around Ryan's voluminous dark hair. Preston was inching his way to the door. There was a lot of emotion going on in my room. He was probably ready to flee. "Did you say you had Lucky's number?"

"Yes, I do." He pulled his phone out of his pocket and texted me his contact information.

My phone buzzed under my leg. "Thanks, Preston."

"We'll do whatever we can to help." Preston's aura was a steady blue. He was the cool to Ryan's fire. A yin and yang that complemented one another.

Kinda like Caleb and I.

Goddess, I hoped the damage wasn't irreparable.

"You guys have done more than enough. Now I just need to show him how much he means to me in the biggest way possible."

Preston arched a brow. "By using the biggest human we know?"

I laughed. "I'm not exactly Lucky's favorite person. He's pretty proprietary about Caleb."

Ryan snorted as she joined Preston in the doorway. "He might out-bestie me. I wasn't sure that was possible."

"You're not wrong. But if anyone can help me pull this off, it's Lucky Roberts."

Ryan leaned back against Preston. "I'm very afraid."

"I am too."

"All right, we'll let you do your thing." She quickly moved forward to give me a hug. "Take care of you."

"Take care of you," I said back as always. Then my smile spread. That was exactly what I needed. A *Pretty Woman* moment. The bigger the better.

Ryan stepped back. "Well, there's my badass bestie. You've got a plan."

"I've got the start of a plan." I grabbed my phone. "Now I just have to see if Lucky will help me."

"He better or I'll take him out at the kneecaps."

For the first time in days, the brick that had been sitting on my chest lifted. "If anyone could take him down, it would be you, Ry."

"Damn right."

I flicked my phone awake and started a new text message using the number Preston had sent me.

This is Luna. I need your help.

Fuck off.

I huffed out a laugh. Lucky was not going to make this easy on me.

I know I screwed up, but I really need your help. Meet me at Brewed Awakening?

Eat glass.

Okay, this was going to take a little more finesse than I'd thought. I tapped my nail against my lips. I was guessing on this one, but it seemed logical.

As the future godfather of my child, I'm calling in a chip.

Low blow, Blondie. You really messed up my dude.

I know. I was stupid and scared. I want to make it right, but I need your help. I need to show him how much I care in a really big way.

How big are we talking?

Huge. Chick flick moment huge.

A'ight. Meet me in 30.

Thanks, Lucky.

Don't thank me. Just fix him. He's all broken and I don't like it. If you break him again, I'll end you.

You're a good friend, Lucky. I'm glad he has you.

Damn right. No more chick flick moments. Save it for the teacher. Cya.

I laughed and dabbed my eyes. I had enough time to take a quick shower, then I was going to get my guy back.

EIGHTEEN

Lucky

I CURLED MY HANDS AROUND THE MUG THAT WAS TOO TINY FOR MY BIG hands. Even if it seemed like one of my grandma's thimbles, I couldn't fault the brew. My boss's wife owned the main hub in Crescent Cove, Brewed Awakening. And if Macy really liked you, she would create a coffee drink just for you.

I hadn't quite made it to that level, but I was wearing her down.

"If you break one more of my chairs, I'm making you pay for it."

See how much she loves me? I hunched my shoulders at Macy's voice. "I'm a growing boy."

"HGH doesn't count, Lucky."

"Hey, I don't put any shit like that in my body." I flexed my biceps. "Just me and the Thor app, baby."

She rolled her eyes. "Sure."

I fished out my phone. "I swear. That Chris dude has a workout app. I know most chicks download it to watch Thor flex and shit, but I actually do them." I reached for the hem of my shirt. "Want to see?"

She held up a hand. "I'm good."

Jodi, the lead barista, perked up. "I'd like to see."

I stood up.

Macy pointed at me. "No."

Gingerly, I sat back down. "Next time, beautiful."

Jodi pinked up and dropped her towel. She popped back up with it in her hands and spun around once, then twice as she tried to figure out where to put herself. I hid a grin behind the lip of my cup. She was cute, but I'd learned my lesson about dating in my favorite establishments. I still couldn't show my face at The Mason Jar after hooking up with one of the bartenders.

She'd tried to de-ball me twice.

She was hot enough that I'd gone back for a second round, but she was too crazy even for me. I gave some leeway when a girl was super hot. They got a few extra rungs on the psycho scale, but damn if she didn't go nuclear last time around.

I frowned at my empty mug and was debating going up for another when Luna came through the door. She spotted me and made a beeline for my bar-top table near the windows.

Another one on the stupidly hot scale. Too bad Caleb had shut me out when we'd first met her. Then again, with the curse of the town I might've been in the same boat as he was right now. Baby mama drama with a capital B. No, thank you.

"Hey, thanks for seeing me."

"You look like crap, Blondie."

"Thanks."

I twisted my mug on the table. "You wanted to talk, so talk." As a rule, I wasn't rude to chicks, but watching my best friend spiral for the last week and change made me less than charitable to her needs.

She tried to climb up on the bar stool, but she was sprite-sized.

I stood and lifted her, plunking her onto the stool.

Her huge blue eyes went wide. "Um, thanks."

I nodded. "You better be here to tell me you got your head out of your ass."

She blinked. "Okay, so we're getting right into it."

"Look, normally I wouldn't say shit about what goes on between two people—"

"Since when?"

I shrugged and waved to Jodi for another refill. Too bad Mace didn't have a liquor license. Maybe I should've had Blondie meet me at The Haunt. "Whatever. Caleb's a fucking wreck, and it's your fault."

She looked down at her hands. "I know."

Usually, she sported a bunch of bling and looked hella cute, but she seemed to be in about the same state as my best dude. A twinge of conscience teased the middle of my shoulder blades. Enough that I gentled my voice. "We all fuck up."

I knew that more than most.

She looked up at me with watery bluebell eyes. "Yeah. I'm just used to having fun with a guy, and then we go our separate ways after a few weeks. This love stuff is a lot."

"See, I knew we were the better hookup."

She laughed. "I don't want to sound rude, but you're exactly the sort of guy I usually go for."

"All good, Blondie. We would've had a nice bounce, but we wouldn't stick. Would have been a helluva ride though."

"Thanks, I think."

I raked my fingers through my long hair. "It was a compliment. Okay, so now you got me here. What are you going to do about the sad sack upstairs?"

"I need a big gesture. A Lucky-sized one."

Jodi came over to the table with a coffee for me and a large to-go cup with a teabag tag fluttering along the side for Luna. "Here you go, guys." She blushed as our hands touched. I gave her a reassuring smile, and she brightened before letting out a high-pitched laugh. "Right. Let me know if you need anything else."

Luna took the top off her cup and blew on it. She waited until Jodi walked off then leaned forward. "You've got girls waiting in the wings everywhere."

I shook my head. "Nope. I'm not ruining my coffee."

She gave me a quizzical look.

"Another time."

"Right. Okay, so I don't really want to wait and find a skywriter to tell Caleb I love him. I was thinking something a little more *Pretty Woman*. But I don't have access to a limo with a sunroof."

"Oh, yeah. 'She saved him right back', right?"

Luna laughed. "You got the reference."

I shrugged. "I have a thing for redheads." I cleared my throat. "Anyway. I know a guy who moonlights as an Uber driver, but no one with a limo." I tapped my long finger on the edge of the mug. "Not sure a beater Honda Civic will have the same punch."

"Definitely not."

I glanced out the window and twisted in my seat as a vintage Ford truck made a turn onto Main Street. It was cherry red with flames along the hood and foot-rails. "Dare."

"What about Dare?" She frowned. "The car guy?"

I rose. "Yes. They do customs. They gotta have a badass car we can borrow. I mean, the apartments are right upstairs. We don't even need to take it off the property. It's the weekend so the street is busy, but I can take care of that."

I had orange cones in my work truck. I could totally block everything off. Fuck, this was such a moment for my TikTok channel. Romance with all the trimmings. I could see it all in my head.

My views would go through the roof.

"You can?" She slid off her stool. "I'm afraid of that look in your eyes."

"Nah. We're just going to do it up really good for my dude."

"Well."

"Well?" I scooped up my hair and pulled my elastic around it to get it out of my way.

"Never mind."

"You correcting my grammar, Blondie?"

"Caleb must be rubbing off on me."

"Obviously, since you've got a bun in the oven."

She wrinkled her nose. "Lucky."

"What? Future badass bun in the oven, girl." I grabbed her hand and dragged her through the café to the door.

"Lucky, hold up."

"No time to wait."

She laughed and her little pixie legs kept up—sort of. I stopped and picked her up and ran with her down the sidewalk to the doorway of Kramer & Burns Custom.

"Lucky, put me down."

"Sorry. I got excited." I set her on her feet. "Damn, you smell good. Lucky son of a bitch."

She lifted her hands to my bearded face. "You're a good man, Lucky. Thanks."

"Yeah, yeah. Don't get sappy. I'm only doing this because he loves you. Like big stupid love."

She sniffled. "I love him too, I promise."

"Yeah, well, you better." I held the door open.

"We're closed," a voice said in the back. It was husky and sexy enough to kick me in the chest.

"Your door is open," I replied.

"Yeah, well, my partner is a dumbass. We're closed." The voice came closer, and a fucking Amazonian queen came through the doorway. She was almost as tall as I was, and her flame-red hair was scraped back into a high tail, leaving her gorgeous face unframed.

Hell, she could be bald and still be stunning. But man, red hair. My ultimate weakness. My dick practically did a happy dance.

A slash of something black across her cheek was the only thing that marred the perfection of her face. And the scowl.

My dick got happier. I loved a grouchy fucking woman.

"Hi." I tugged my hair out of the man-bun I was sporting. I needed every edge I had. "We have an emergency."

Her dark brow lifted. "A car emergency?" She flicked her gaze over to Luna, then back to me. "Is it in a ditch or something? I can call my partner to go haul you out."

"No." I leaned my elbow on the counter. "My friend here needs help."

"Closed. We can tow your car in, and I'll deal with it Monday." She slapped her palm with the red mechanic's towel. "Best I can do."

Luna cleared her throat. "We were wondering if we could borrow one of your cars for like ten minutes. The flashier, the better."

"Excuse me?"

I straightened. "What my friend means is we need to create a moment." I gave her my most charming, dimpled smile. "For love. You know like Edward and Vi from *Pretty Woman* pow!"

"Vivian," Luna said out of the side of her mouth.

"Right, Vivian. Anyway, I saw the cherry truck go by, and I thought maybe you guys had something else here that could make a statement. She needs to grovel."

"Thanks, Lucky," Luna muttered as she shoved me aside. "I screwed up with my guy. We're having a baby, and I really need him to know how much I love him."

"Not my problem." The Amazon came around the counter and went to the door. She flipped the sign and held it open for us. "Closed."

"Oh, come on. You have to have a heart in that truly spectacular chest."

"Excuse me?" She jammed her heavy motorcycle boot against the bottom of the door to prop it open. "You know what? Never mind. I don't care. Out. Closed."

I stepped into her space. She was fucking spectacular. Curves and legs for days and fistable hair. And that scowl. She was a goddamn dream. "C'mon, my friend here wants to make a big statement, and you have the best cars around."

"Find another sucker. I want to go home and watch the game."

I frowned. "College football?"

"No, women's soccer, Thor. You know, a real sport."

I glanced down at her slash of scarlet lips. I really wouldn't mind messing up her lipstick. I didn't usually like the taste of it, but I'd make an exception. "Do you play?"

"I'd kick your ass." She straightened and crossed her arms over her stunning chest. "Regardless, I'm going home. I'm tired, and it's been a long day."

I glanced to the right where I could see into the garage. A purple Cadillac El Dorado had the hood up. "That car. Right there. Statement. It'll only take ten minutes. Half an hour max. We don't even need to go anywhere. He lives right here. We just gotta get his attention."

"Absolutely not. No one drives that but me. That's my wheels."

"Yours?" Luna hopped up so she could see from where she stood at the counter. "It's beautiful. And it's a convertible."

"No one drives Lucille but me," Amazonian girl said and lifted her chin.

"Okay. You drive."

She dropped her arms to her sides. "What? No. I told you I'm heading out."

"You know the beginning of the game is lame. You can catch up. And I'll owe you."

"I could give a crap." She tilted her head.

"I can do anything." I mirrored her folded arms.

"I'm sure you think so." She jerked her head toward the door. "Out."

"No, I mean, I can do anything. Not that I wouldn't like to try what you were thinking," I waggled my brows, "but I work for Gideon. We literally can do any job."

"Anything?"

I nodded. "I can build pretty much anything you want. I do a fair bit of plumbing, I demo like a goddamn god. Sheetrock, carpentry... you name it."

She tapped her finger on her forearm, then she grinned slowly. "You're gonna pay for this one, Thor."

I swallowed. I hoped so. "She's in love with my best friend. It's worth it."

She narrowed her gaze at me. "Hmm. Thirty minutes and not a minute longer."

"Deal." I held out my hand.

She didn't move for what felt like an ice age. Then she took it and shook. "Deal."

Goddamn what that grip would feel like on the more impressive parts of me. I grinned. "Now let's get these two crazy kids together."

Luna pushed me aside and threw her arms around the Amazon. "I don't even know your name, but I appreciate you so much."

"It's Tish." She looked like she was ready to hurl. She grimaced and patted Luna's shoulder awkwardly. "I already regret this decision."

NINETEEN

 Luna

I STOOD ON THE SIDEWALK AS THE HUGE BAY DOORS OF KRAMER & Burns Custom opened with a metallic shriek of gears, rollers, and startlingly large chains.

The most badass, feminine convertible I'd ever seen rolled out slowly. Chrome headlights arrowed back to the endless lines of the beast of a car. The top was down and the seats were a crisp glowing white leather. The afternoon rays hit the shimmery lilac finish like a spotlight. There wasn't a speck of dust or pollen on the windshield, chrome, or paint. In fact, it was probably in better shape now than when it came off the assembly line.

A murmur of voices lifted around me along with the honking of a few car horns and the distant sounds of boats on the water. It was a beautiful, crisp fall day in the Cove. People were out and about enjoying the day.

All too soon, winter would roll off the lake, and we'd all be buttoned up in our houses. But today was truly perfect.

The ideal day to do something crazy.

Heck, I'd been playing the crazy card since summer. Like this was any different. Okay, so the street was more crowded than I'd counted on.

I nibbled on my lower lip. A *lot* more crowded.

People were coming out of the diner and café to see what was going on. Foot traffic along the storefronts was getting backed up as people craned their necks to see what the commotion was.

Lucky was in the middle of the road, holding up his bear-sized paws to stop traffic while he dropped construction cones in a strategic pattern only he seemed to know. His hair whipped around his head and shoulders like sun-bleached ribbons. He waved people around his make-shift causeway with a booming laugh as he told everyone to hang out for the show.

It wasn't a show, dammit. It was my life. And was he making a video?

Goddess, what did I get myself into?

I laid my hand on my belly. "Okay, little one. We're going to go get Daddy back. I'm sorry in advance about your Uncle Lucky. He's a bit crazy. But we're stuck with him now."

At least I hoped we were.

Tish pulled up, her arm hanging out along the car window. She snapped her fingers at me. "All right, hop in so we can get this over with."

I thought about being offended for a second then decided today was only about positivity. That and her aura was crackling red. I probably shouldn't poke the dragon.

I leaped into the backseat. Not bad agility for a newly pregnant woman, if I did say so myself.

"No shoes on the leather."

I slipped off my ballet shoes and sat up on the top of the seat. We rolled out onto Main Street. Lucky was on top of his truck with a megaphone.

Seriously, this town was so unreal. I had a flashback to another day when the Chief had proposed to Gina in this same spot.

Would it be tacky to do the same? Even tackier to do the asking?

I gripped the headrests as Tish pushed the gas to get us around the throng of people. I waved with an embarrassed laugh.

"Jesus, what is this, a parade?" Tish muttered.

I stopped doing the pageant wave.

"Ladies and gentlemen, there's the star of our show," Lucky said through the megaphone.

Deputy Brady was standing on the sidewalk with his arms crossed and an indulgent smile on his face. The honking had stopped, and people were getting out of their cars.

"Lucky, I need that!"

"What?" he shouted at me through the megaphone.

I stood up on the backseat. "I need the megaphone, you dork!"

"Oh, right. Let me get things started for you." He turned toward the apartments. Caleb had a front-facing apartment, and we were right below him. "Yo, Caleb! Come to the window, dude!"

Nothing.

I twisted my fingers. Goddess, this would be insane if he wasn't even home.

Maybe we should've thought of that sooner. Too late now.

I clapped my hands, and then I held them open. Lucky tossed me the megaphone.

"Why am I doing this again?" Tish asked.

I fumbled the megaphone, but I caught it against my thighs. "Because I'm about to ask my baby daddy to marry me."

"Of course you are." She slumped down in her seat, her hand over her face.

I sat on the back of the car before inching out onto the trunk. Balance was important now. "Everyone, can you help a girl out? Honk your horns for me?"

Tish twisted in her seat and rolled her eyes. "If you dent my car, I'll be taking it out of your ass."

Rising slowly, I ignored her and lifted the megaphone. "Caleb!"

Nothing.

Tish sighed. "Squeeze the button."

"Oh, right." I clicked the button. "Caleb Beck, open your window," I yelled over the honking horns.

A window flew open, but it wasn't Caleb's. Bess Wainwright leaned out with a laugh. "You get him, girl!"

I widened my stance on the back of the car and lifted my voice again. "Caleb Beck!"

Finally, he opened his window. He looked down at the crowd then at me. "What the hell are you doing?"

"Caleb, I have something to say."

He opened the screen on his window and leaned out. "Could you possibly come up here and talk to me?" His shout sounded a wee bit shrill.

"Nope, I need to tell you now. And tell everyone."

He sat on the window ledge. "Oh, yeah? What's that?"

"I'm sorry I disappeared."

He folded his arms. "It was pretty shitty, babe."

"I know." I cleared my throat. This was more awkward than I'd thought it was going to be, but onward ho. I straightened my shoulders. "I love you!"

His face split into a smile. "About damn time."

His aura was bright blue. Happiness rolled off him and that gave me even more courage.

I laughed and glanced around at everyone. A sea of faces in pinks, oranges, and blues surrounded me, and most people were clapping.

I was pretty sure Lucky was making a video, Goddess help me.

"Can you move up a little closer, Tish? We're too far away."

"Sure. I live to serve." Tish put it in gear and slowly rolled forward.

"Luna, be careful," Caleb called. "You've got a special bit of cargo in there too."

"Thanks for announcing it to the town," I mumbled.

The clapping and cheering increased.

"About that," I said through the megaphone. "I think you should make an honest woman of me."

Caleb leaned forward and cupped his hands around his mouth. "Are you asking me to marry you?"

I clutched the megaphone. I was really doing this. Nothing had ever felt so right.

So meant to happen.

"Yes." I grinned. "I absolutely am."

When he disappeared from the window without answering, my heart plummeted. Had I gone too far?

The crowd went from cheering to chattering nervously in the span of a few minutes.

"Crap." I shielded my eyes from the late day sun.

"Always let the guy do the asking, Blondie," Lucky called.

I wiped away tears I didn't know I'd been shedding. Maybe I shouldn't have done this. I should have gone to him like an adult and talked things through.

Suddenly, cars started honking. I craned my neck to see what the excitement was about. Then I glimpsed him there on the sidewalk staring at me, his chest rising and falling. He must have run down the stairs.

I laughed and scrambled down from the trunk into the backseat.

And then he was running to me.

"You sure know how to make an entrance, Lu." He was out of breath, and exhaustion seeped through the happiness radiating from him.

I dropped the megaphone beside me on the seat. "Yeah, I figured I needed a big moment after what I did."

He walked up to the car and reached for me, lifting me out of the back. Just like a proper romantic movie hero would.

I grabbed his shoulders and curled my arms around his neck. "I'm sorry. I was stupid."

Caleb wrapped his arms around me and covered my mouth. "I don't care." He punctuated each word with kisses. "You're here. I'm never letting you go again."

I laughed and tasted tears along with the cinnamon flavor of his gum. I leaned back, my feet still dangling off the pavement. "So, is that a yes?"

"It's a yes." He kissed me again. "Always yes when it comes to you, Lu."

Relief poured through me as I pressed my cheek to his. The crowd that had gathered was still clapping, but some of the people were already dispersing. Lucky was standing on the hood of his truck with his arms up as if he was the one who was the champion.

But he wasn't.

I was.

"I love you, Luna," Caleb murmured. "Now and every day. I'll make sure to show you how much. Even if I trip and fall on my face now and then."

"We'll fall and get up together." I leaned back enough to kiss him again. "I love you too."

He gripped my butt to keep me close. "I might get overwhelming. I don't mean to be—"

I kissed him quiet. "I know." I sniffed. "I'll tell you when it's too big this time. I won't run again, I swear."

"Damn right."

"Can I go now? I'm about to drown in vomit," Tish interrupted.

I twisted my neck to smile at her. "Thank you so much, Tish."

"Oh, Thor is going to pay for this one, that's for sure. Step back. I'm not getting sued for running over toes." She leaned into the back for my shoes and tossed them at us.

Caleb laughed and kicked them back toward the sidewalk. "Thanks, Tish."

"Yeah, yeah." She put the car in reverse. "I need to get away from you two. This baby shit is catchy in this town."

"Uh oh," I said as she drove off.

"What?"

"Lucky's megaphone is still in the car."

"I have a feeling he'll get it back." Caleb waggled his brows. "One way or another."

I laughed and wrapped my legs around his waist. "How about we go inside and I'll show you just how much I missed you?"

"Now that's a plan." He gently set me down.

I slipped my shoes on and took his hand.

I had my guy and our baby. Forever was a scary word, but it didn't seem so bad when I had him by my side.

And besides, I knew how to be very, *very* flexible.

EPILOGUE

Luna

I TIPPED MY HEAD AS I LOOKED AT MYSELF IN THE MIRROR.

"Do you think it's too much?"

"I think you're going to kill him." Ryan's voice came out of my Alexa video speaker. Caleb had bought it for me so he could check on me while he was at school. Now I had one in my bedroom-slash-office and in the kitchen.

I should've been offended and worried he was being an overlord, but he was so damn cute with his check-ins. I actually looked forward to them daily.

Not that I'd tell him that.

I fussed with the white knee-high socks. "You know, is this too cliche? He's a teacher and this is…"

"A heart attack for any man with a pulse."

I turned from my mirror to find Ryan with her head propped up on her hand, her gaze focused on something else in the room. Most likely, it was centered on PMS, otherwise known as Preston to the rest of the world. He was probably doing something in the kitchen based on the heat level in her eyes.

I snapped my fingers and Ryan's turquoise eyes zeroed in on me. "Sorry."

"You can go play with your boytoy in a minute."

Ryan flushed. "I got distracted. He's wearing a pair of jeans. My guy has a superior ass."

I rolled my eyes. "I'll take your word for it."

She turned the camera. "Yo, PMS! Do a little twirl for Lu."

Preston put his hands on his hips. "Don't objectify me, Miss Moon."

"Oh, jeez." I knew that tone.

Ryan spun the video back around. "Gotta go."

I shook my head. "Are you sure?"

"Girl, Caleb is gonna be toast. Just, you know, nothing super flippy." She wiggled her long ringed fingers. "Baby and all. Keep those feet on the floor."

I laughed. "Yes, Mom."

She wrinkled her nose at me. "Have fun."

"Oh, I will." I ended the video call and blew raspberries at my reflection before I swapped out the black lace shirt for a white cropped one.

Next, I fixed my space buns. They were super big now because of the vitamins I was on for the baby. Goddess, my hair was growing like my belly.

I patted the little bump that had finally made itself known. For the longest time, I had just looked like I'd ate too much Mexican food.

It was really weird that both of us were so damn happy right now. I kept worrying about rocking the universe's boat—absolutely sure that I was way too lucky right now.

I was mending my relationship with my brother.

Slowly.

Extremely slowly.

But no matter what I said to him, he kept coming back for more. Usually, he arrived with something for the baby. Xavier figured I was having a girl. He told me I deserved a little girl just like me. I wasn't sure if that was meant to be complimentary or not, but either way, I didn't have the heart to tell him I was fairly sure the baby was male.

Caleb was convinced it was a boy. I figured that was more because he was worried Rhiannon would be jealous. She already had her cousin Vivi to compete with for time with grandma. From the get-go, wonderment had been the main element in Caleb's reaction to our pregnancy.

It had taken me some time to believe he was in it for more than loyalty's sake. Caleb was a stand-up guy with strong family values. I wasn't used to that, or to his warm, loving family who had welcomed me with open arms.

However, Caleb's overprotective instincts were driving me just a tad crazy. I needed to remind him I wasn't breakable glass.

If that took a knockoff Britney Spears outfit, then I'd take one for the team.

I fluffed the hem of the skirt and adjusted my white cotton thong. Clothing shifted in weird ways now that my curves were getting out of control.

I made a pitstop at my mostly empty dresser. Here and there, I'd been moving my stuff over to Caleb's apartment and using mine as an office of sorts. In my heart, I knew I could probably give up my apartment.

Caleb wasn't going anywhere. Especially now that I'd actually asked him to marry me. I'd been on my own for so long that the idea of moving in with anyone was overwhelming. Let alone putting a ring on it.

That and my guy kept tucking flyers for houses for sale in every available space. His hints were more like sledgehammer swings.

"Babe?"

"Coming," I called as I finished glossing on some red lipstick. I grabbed my phone and switched the music over to the playlist I'd made.

"You wouldn't believe what Maddie did today. I swear, that girl needs her own show. Unfortunately, I'm the star of her chaotic circus."

I stood in the doorway and put my hand on my waist, cocking my hip to show off the skirt to its maximum potential. Caleb had his back to me as he rolled up his shirtsleeves. A glittery handprint shimmered on his ass.

My thoughts of seduction morphed into annoyance. How dare she, whomever she was?

"Who had their hand on your ass?"

Caleb twisted his head and arched his back to see his own butt. "Dammit, how long has that been there?" He dropped his head forward—still not facing me, mind you. "I tried to get all the glitter off me."

Impatiently, I tapped my foot. "You didn't answer me."

He turned around, his cheeks red. "Holy shit."

I tipped my head. "Handprint, teach," I reminded him.

He blinked. "I...huh, what?" His confusion and slacked mouth almost made me smile.

Almost.

"Who slapped your ass, Caleb?"

"Oh, uh...me."

"Sorry I missed it." I walked into the living room.

"Holy shit. You're...um. Those. Well." He dragged his fingers through his hair and grabbed the back of his neck. "Warn a guy, would you?"

This time, I did grin. "My last client cancelled, and I had some time on my hands."

He crossed the room to me and reached down to cup my ass. "I hope more of your clients cancel. Daily."

"Not so great for the budget, buddy."

"Right." He blew out a breath and lowered his head to hover his lips over mine. "I don't really care right now."

I lifted a finger to his lips to stop him. "You need to go sit down, Mr. Beck."

Swallowing hard, he didn't move. His gaze stayed on my mouth. I knew he liked when I wore red lipstick.

I tried again. "Mr. Beck?" I twirled a loose lock of hair that framed my face. "I have a little treat for you."

He cleared his throat. "Is that right?"

I licked the little divot of my top lip. "Yes." I let the strand of hair go, and then I trailed my finger down the buttons of his gray dress shirt to his buckle. He firmed and grew under his zipper. "Oh, Mr. Beck. That looks painful."

"I'm going to hell."

I pressed my lips together against a smile. I drew a wide circle around his very stiff cock. "Can I do something to help?" I lifted my gaze to meet his and bit my lip.

"Yes, you can show me what you've got under that very, very short skirt, Miss Hastings."

I dragged the back of my knuckle over the outline of his shaft. "And that will help?"

"It can't fucking hurt any more than I am right now."

I nearly broke at his guttural tone. We'd just see about that.

Quickly, I twirled so the short skirt flipped up, creating a small breeze. And boy, did I need it, I hadn't expected to get turned on by my own show. "I'm a little embarrassed." I backed up until my ass bumped into his hard-on. I swayed back and forth, the short plaid skirt sliding higher and higher with each wiggle.

His fingers dug into my bare thighs with a groan. "Why are you embarrassed, Miss Hastings?"

I stepped forward. "They're not very sexy panties." I bent at the waist and revealed the plain white cotton thong. "See?"

"Holy hell."

I stood up and swiped the skirt back down. "See? Not sexy at all." He tried to reach for me, but I twirled away. Thank the goddess I'd practiced with the sky-high Mary Jane heels since the last time I'd tried this.

I slowly walked to the pole as the song changed from the sweeter pop song to "Stockholm Syndrome" from One Direction. The memory from when I'd first met Caleb made me put an extra twitch in my hips.

"Maybe I can make it up to you." Slowly, I walked around the pole. I'd been teaching pole dancing classes in Rylee's yoga studio, the low impact kind that anyone could do. "I've been practicing something for you." I lightly undulated against the pole before I slid toward the floor and widened my stance, only to shyly tuck the skirt between my legs. "If that's okay, Mr. Beck?"

"I would love to watch you dance." He took a quick breath and settled himself into the chair I'd set out for him. "If it's safe."

I curled my knee around the pole and did a light spin. The tip of my shoe grazed the floor as I did a flourish that sent a nice breeze under my skirt. Normally, I'd bend my waist around the pole a lot more, but our little burrito made it harder to maneuver.

Instead, I used my legs, hips, and arms for most of the twirling.

The song changed to a sexier, slower song. As Charlie Puth sung "Attention," I walked around the edges of the parquet square I'd laid around my pole. I could feel Caleb's eyes riveted on me, which made me swish my hips before I did a slow backbend and lifted one leg to show off the virgin-white panties.

Carefully, I swung in a wide arc using my knee and hand to anchor me. Then I slowly inched down the pole until my knee met the floor, and I went into a spin with one leg outstretched. I did a complicated twirl and moved into an easy backbend before straightening.

I grinned at his slack-jawed face. His white-knuckled grip on the chair made me even bolder.

Who knew being a pregnant seductress could be so fun?

I dropped to my knees and crawled toward him.

Caleb

Every fantasy I'd ever had was coming to life right before me. Between the woman I loved, that damn stripper pole that was going to put me in an early grave, and the schoolgirl uniform that would probably send me to hell, I was in Caleb-flavored heaven.

I could see down her teeny tiny T-shirt, which let me know she hadn't bothered to put on a bra. Her generous breasts swayed with each sexy little slide my way.

Everything inside me wanted to leap at her, but I also wanted to see what she had in mind. Obviously, I was a glutton for her kind of punishment.

We were heading into the second trimester, and her morning sickness had faded into morning quickies. I couldn't count the number of times I was whistling my way into school each day.

She was it for me in every way. And I was the luckiest son of a bitch on the planet.

She knelt in front of me and slowly coasted her hand up my leg to my inner thigh. I lifted my hips in reaction to her touch. The sexy song bouncing around her apartment drove up my impatience to touch her.

She straightened, her belly peeking from the short red plaid skirt. A small moon and star belly-button ring finished off the very Luna moment. The mother of my impending child, my future wife, my everything, all in one irresistible package.

Mine.

She raked her nails over my thighs and moved out to the sides of the chair.

I stiffened. *Oh, shit.*

I'd picked up her ring today. It was in my damn pocket.

I grabbed her hands and pulled them up to my stomach, and then I distracted her with a long, lingering kiss. Hell, I distracted myself. Her taste was intoxicating at the best of times.

Here and now? She tasted of sunshine and laughter, of fun and permanence. And for once, none of that scared me. I wanted more of it. Every damn day.

She undulated against my very happy pants. She dragged the moon dangle along my shaft as her clever fingers climbed into my hair.

Ring forgotten, I gathered her into my lap, my hands settling on her perfect ass. She dug her knees into the sides of the chair and straddled me.

I slid my hands under her skirt to find just her flesh.

She was wearing a thong.

Dear God, this woman was going to kill me. I coasted my fingers down the smooth shape of her to find the heat between her legs.

I flipped the front of her skirt up to feel all that heat over my cock. Her magical breasts swayed in front of me, the hard tips denting the thin cotton. I leaned in and caught one with my teeth.

She moaned as her nails dug into my shoulders. I followed the flow of the music playing, dragging her cotton-clad pussy up my erection.

I brought my hands up to her waist. My thumbs coasted over her small baby bump before I pushed up her shirt to get to her soft skin. Her nipples were already flushed in that way that told me she was closer to detonation than I'd thought.

I closed my mouth over her nipple and drew hard. She brought a hand up to the back of my head and held me there.

"Yes. Harder," she whispered brokenly.

I scraped my teeth over her skin as her belly bumped mine. I slowed at the contact, but she dug her nails into my scalp.

"No. Not gently. Take me like you mean it, Mr. Beck."

I gulped down a groan, lifted her skirt, and clapped my hand over her bare cheek.

"Yes," she groaned as she arched her back. "I've been a very bad girl, Mr. Beck."

I used my teeth again to tug at one nipple then the other, following the siren call of her body. Where we'd started. Hot for one another to a level I'd never experienced before.

I whipped the shirt over her head and inched to the edge of the chair so I could get her closer.

Her fingers fumbled with my buckle and then those strong fingers were inside, dragging me out of my boxers and the confines of my zipper. "Luna," I said against her neck. "I need to get inside you."

"Yes. Yes, I want that. Now."

She pushed at my trousers to get me totally free of the layers. I eased forward another few inches to get the pants off.

Something hit the floor.

"What was that?" she asked against my mouth.

Oh, nothing, just your freaking ring.

"Probably my wallet."

She frowned as she twisted her fingers around the base of my cock. She peered over the side of the chair.

I gripped her chin and turned her face back toward me to try to distract her with a long, slow kiss. She let out that sultry groan-slash-moan that usually meant very good things were going to happen.

Her other hand pushed at my trousers for better access, and she found my wallet. She frowned at it.

I took it and tossed it over my shoulder before reaching under her skirt to make her forget all about ring boxes.

Hopefully. I wasn't sure if my cock was more of a draw than jewelry. But I had other tricks up my sleeve.

She hissed out a moan and flung her head back as she rode my fingers. Slick heat swallowed me deeper as I curled two of them inside of her.

With a moan, she leaned back to grab the chair for purchase as she got lost in my touch. I leaned forward to take a nipple into my mouth as she breathlessly said my name in that way that indicated she was close.

I wanted to feel her coming around my cock, not my fingers. I fumbled between us and pushed her panties aside. She giggled as I tried to get our bodies to line up without dumping us both onto her wide rainbow rug.

She straightened and curled her arms around my neck. "Do you have a little treat for me?"

"Not so little," I grunted as the head of my cock bumped against the top of her slit. "Tip your hips forward, baby."

Suddenly, she frowned. "What's that?"

"My very happy cock who wants inside," I said against her neck.

"No." She nudged me back. "That." She pointed at the floor.

"You should be focused right here." I shifted to block her view.

"Oh, I will be." She wiggled back to the end of my knees, tipping me and the chair forward.

Quickly, I shifted so I took the brunt of the fall. My hip was cushioned by her rug, thankfully. She landed on me, and then she crawled right off to get to the damn ring.

I tried to catch her, but only ended up with a handful of plaid. I yanked it down her delectable hips to show off her milky white ass. "Luna," I said with a sigh.

She sat cross-legged on the rug with the ring box in her hand. "Caleb."

"You are the worst."

She looked up at me, her eyes reddened with tears. "Is this what I think it is?"

I huffed out a laugh and tucked my very lonely cock back into my boxers. "Yes."

She closed her hands over the box. "Can I see it?"

"Well, it is for you." I shook my head as I made my way over to sit next to her. "You kinda ruined my plans."

"Well, we're already engaged. I asked you already." She peered into the little cave she'd made with her hands. "But you got me a ring?"

"Of course I got you a ring. What do you take me for?"

"Well, I did the asking. I got you one, actually."

"What?" My chest tightened. "You got me a ring?"

She nodded. "I know rings are weird for dudes, but I think you'll like this one."

She handed me the blue velvet box before she stood. Then she wiggled out of the skirt and darted into her room wearing only that damn white thong.

I laughed. The woman was going to be the death of me in the very best way.

She returned without bothering to put anything on. Her perfect breasts swayed enticingly, making me forget about the box in my hand.

She dropped in front of me and dragged her feet into her typical lotus pose. She held a black box. "I have plans for our actual wedding rings, but this will fit into it."

I leaned forward until our foreheads touched. I wasn't much of a jewelry guy, but I didn't care what this thing was—I was wearing it.

For her. Always for her.

Tipping up her chin, I found more tears, but her beautiful mouth curved into a smile. "I love you more every day, Caleb."

I pressed my lips to hers. "It's only going to get better." I knew she still had some reservations. With what her family put her through, I understood and accepted that. "You're mine, and I'm yours now." I dashed away her tears with my thumb.

She nodded and laid one hand on her tiny baby bump. "We're yours."

I covered her hand with my own. "I'm going to do my best to make sure you both know how loved you are every day."

She blew out a slow breath. "I know and I will do the same." She opened the small box and turned it around. The ring was black and thin. A channel of stones was set into the jet-black piece. "I wanted to make sure you wouldn't think it was too hokey."

"No matter what it is, I would wear it, but that is...wow."

She grinned. "Yeah? It's tungsten and I picked out specific crystals for protection, love, health, and to help us understand one another."

The small stones were all in earth tones, and in between each was a black crystal. "Is that obsidian?"

"Very good." She took the ring out of the box and took my hand. "Fire agate to dispel fear and negativity, obsidian for protection, tiger's eye for balance, emerald for love and harmony." She slid it on my finger and murmured something.

I curled my fingers around her hand and pulled her wrist up to my mouth. "Thank you."

She lifted her gaze to mine. "I plan on keeping you around for a good long time."

"I was almost as thoughtful as you were with picking out this one." I grabbed the box with my other hand and flicked it open.

Her eyes widened. "Oh, Caleb." More tears started flowing as she lifted her free hand to her mouth. "It's so beautiful."

"Kin was going out for a buying trip, and I asked if I could go along. I found this, then added a little something to it." I took her left hand and slid the simple Art Deco ring over her finger. "Your name may mean the moon, but you always remind me of sunshine."

She wiggled her finger and the sunburst pattern of gold and diamonds shimmered in the late day sun. "It's so me."

I lifted her hand to kiss her fingers. "I had to make sure the ring fit just how much I love you. I asked a jewelry to add a few moonstones into the design too."

She launched herself at me, winding her arms around my neck as she kissed me fiercely.

Of course I'd had to ask her to marry me while she was nearly naked. Did anything else fit us more?

Rolling her onto her back, I grinned down at her. "Marry me?"

She pulled me down and wrapped her legs around me. "Yes. A thousand times yes." She pushed at my shirt. "Now get naked, Mr. Beck."

"Yes, ma'am."

We laughed as I shed the rest of my clothes. Achingly slowly, I slid into her on the rainbow rug with late day sunbeams streaking over her wild blond curls. I propped myself up on my forearms to watch her face as she took me in again and again.

The glide of our bodies giving and taking from one another would never be anything but sheer bliss.

She shifted and pushed me over to ride me like the goddess she was. The easy pleasure turned into wildness. I gripped her hips and we raced toward that end that we could only seem to find together. As she arched her back, I fit my hand between us to push her over with a thumb along her clit.

I sat up to surround her with my arms, holding her as she shook and cried out my name while I followed her into the sun.

When my brain returned to my body, I slumped back onto the rug, dragging her with me. She was plastered against my side, her cheek pressed into my chest.

"Wow."

"I know, right? Did you see angels?" she asked against my skin.

"Just a goddess," I said breathlessly.

She laughed. "Well, that was a good answer."

I grinned down at her. "Now that we have rings, you know my mom is going to bug us for a date."

"Do you mind if we don't do the church thing?"

"No. My family isn't overly religious."

She propped her chin on her hand over my heart. "That makes it easier. How does the winter solstice sound to you?"

"Sounds perfect."

"Yeah, it really does." She laid her cheek back down on my chest. "Caleb?"

"Yeah?"

She popped up again. Filled with endless energy, that was my goddess. "I'm freaking starving."

I laughed as she dragged me to my feet. "Can't have that."

She glanced down at her left hand and wiggled it before smiling again. We both knew this was just the beginning of our life together.

With a grin, I lifted her into my arms and headed for the bathroom. "Shower and round two first."

She dipped back her head and laughed. "Now that sounds like an even better plan."

We appreciate our readers so much!
If you loved the book please let your friends know. If you're extra awesome, we'd love a review on your favorite book site.

WANT TO KEEP UP TO DATE WITH US?

Please visit our website, tarynquinn.com, for details!

Ready to hear about Lucky and Ryan? turn the page for more details on the books for Luna's and Caleb's besties!

Now...turn the page for a special sneak peek of LUCKY BABY & HIS TEMPORARY ASSISTANT now!

LUCKY BABY

THIS MOMENT WAS PERFECTION.

The suspicious part of me wondered if it was *too* perfect.

Leaves crunched under my boots as ghostly swirls of steam rose from my oversized mug of coffee. The hazelnut blend, with whatever secret ingredient Brewed Awakening's mistress had added, was my favorite way to start the day. Even if I never quite got the milk to coffee ratio magic Macy seemed to do so effortlessly. However, it was *my* coffee blend alone.

That thrilled me more than it should, but I could own it in my own head, if nowhere else. Since my particular genius turned into one-of-a-kind car and motorcycle parts, it was only right I got a kick out of someone else's talents when it came to my coffee. Especially considering the liquid gold was my soulmate.

Coffee had kept me alive even when food had been scarce. Being a woman in the car business wasn't for the faint of heart, and I'd had to claw my way up to a living wage before I'd been able to start calling my own shots. Fast forward ten years—with quite a few crash and burns—and here I was, making an actual home in a little nowhere town as quaint as a postcard and just as family-centric.

Maybe a little too family-centric. I was tempted to get an IUD and birth control. My doctor had actually laughed when I'd tried—until she looked at my address.

Crescent Cove was legion when it came to babies.

So not in my ten year plan, thanks.

I flipped my collar up on my battered motorcycle jacket against the wind racing off the water. The sun peeked from Crescent Lake's still surface, turning the sky gold and misty blue. The air had a chilly bite that warned of the long winter coming, but the burn in my lungs made me smile over the rim of my mug. It was almost as good as the cigarettes I'd miss until my dying day.

Okay, not *as* good, but it was definitely invigorating.

I picked my way across the uneven spots of my lawn—*my* lawn. God, that felt good to say. Apartments and hand-me-downs or thrift finds had been my life for twenty-six years.

A year ago, I would have been happy with that. I never stayed in one place long enough to care about what I plunked my ass on or laid my head on at night as long as it was clean. I'd lived a transient life by choice. Job in Seattle? Yep, I was there. Car show in Miami? Sure, I could make it. Sturgis Rally? Hell yeah, I'd be there.

Now I was one-third owner in an actual company. People came to me now instead of me doing guest spots in various shops. I'd been in demand before I was legal to drink. I had an uncanny ability to fabricate just about anything. If a client dreamed up something, I could pluck it out of their mind. For years, I'd worked with any and all machines at my fingertips to make it happen. Now I had my own fabricator I'd created, down to the proprietary specs.

And I'd patented it. I'd learned the hard way that loyalty was for dreamers, not for the cold hard reality of business.

That lesson had been tattooed on my back with a blade, leaving a bonus scar that I hadn't seen coming.

But those moments had only made me stronger. Now I could charge whatever the hell I wanted for jobs. And I did. Shamelessly. I even had a company begging to license my machine. They hadn't quite come up to my number yet.

To be fair, I had a disgustingly high number in my head. I had a feeling Ramsey Inc. would get there eventually. He had a serious hard-on for Hilda, my baby.

I had a waiting list three years out to get time on my bench. They were all curated projects suited to me. I said no to people all the damn time. Did I feel bad about it? Nope. I'd worked hard to create a name for myself since I was sixteen years old.

And now I had two workshops I could outfit however I wanted.

Part of my contract with Dare and Gage Kramer had included absolute autonomy when it came to how I worked. Unique jobs were eighty percent of our income at Kramer & Burns Custom, but Dare had a special affinity for the town so we still took care of the locals.

The Kramer boys had been involved in NASCAR in a former life. Now they were happily settled with kids, but our combined reputations had resulted in a constant stream of clients and word of mouth that had only grown with each car that rolled out of our bays. Our customs had blown up so much we were looking to take over the building behind the garage to extend the space and hire on a few general mechanics. But getting Dare to move on anything was like asking a glacier to put some hustle into it.

Mostly I didn't care about that part of the company. I was more involved with the specialty projects than the everyday labor of tows and oily fingers. Unless you asked me to rebuild a British motorcycle, then I was more than willing to get my overalls on.

Like the sweet '69 Triumph Bonneville sitting in my home garage right now. I'd spent the last few months acquiring the perfect pieces, tools, and even a lift to make my home garage as effective as the one in town. To be truthful, it was the only thing I'd actually completed in my fixer-upper farmhouse.

My bedroom was as bare bones as a clichéd bachelor pad. It included my mom's old dresser my dad had shipped me, a mattress, and the badass four poster bed. Admittedly, I'd overpaid for it from August Beck, a local carpentry artist. It was a damn work of art, and I didn't mind paying for the unique, especially since sleeping was my favorite hobby.

I was still eating off a TV tray in front of my seventy-inch television in my living room three months later. My house echoed it was so damn empty, but that was a problem for future Tish.

Right now, I was going to enjoy the view and my coffee. I climbed up on my picnic table and sat on the uneven slats of the top. It was rickety as hell and probably wouldn't last the winter. Because dear God, this town was no joke when it came to winter.

The blazing summer had been full to the brim with work and somehow October had snuck in with its cool mornings made for warm coffee, and silence save for some badass birds. Just how I liked it.

I'd impulsively bought this property on the lake thanks to a little bit of right-time-right-place. Mr. and Mrs. Slide had been tired of the snow and bitter cold of Upstate New York and looking to sell the house to someone who would appreciate it. I'd lucked into the whole damn thing because I'd fabricated a hard to get part for Gary Slide's pristine all-glass hatch Pinto.

A Pinto, for fuck's sake. No one made parts for that damn car anymore, but the guy loved it—maybe even more than his wife. I was pretty sure she knew it too.

I'd volunteered to make the crazy part after he and Dare had tried to find it from one of the parts dealers we worked with. The look on the old guy's face had broken me. Actual tears because they couldn't find the rare hydraulic kit for his baby.

I'd made an exception and let him bump the line, then spent seven hours creating a new kit and actually improving the seal on the weirdly shaped glass hatch that made up the trunk. It ended up being a fun project, probably one of the best decisions I'd ever made.

Because Gary couldn't stand to be away from his baby, he sat with me as I worked on it. Once my annoyance cleared about being watched, I'd settled in and been treated to his life story.

It should have been boring, but Gary was a born storyteller and entertained me well into the night. Over a pair of hoagies from Jersey Angel's, he told me about wanting to sell his property.

After the way he'd described it, I'd ended up offering him a cash settlement for the damn thing. And now here I was, with a view that most people would kill for.

Arthur Maitland had raged at the bank as I was signing my papers. Evidently, I'd ruined his plans for another set of condos on the lake courtesy of Maitland Enterprises.

My gaze skimmed over the water to the east side where condos had been in progress for the last six months. I was pretty sure Maitland was still having a kitten about me buying up this piece of land.

I couldn't say I minded. The man was a dick.

A little meow was my only warning before a ball of fluff leaped onto the table beside me. I gave my cat a quick scratch under the chin before Dusty sprawled onto his back to play with the fringe on my jacket.

I waggled the fringe above his head and laughed at his crazy eyes and Wolverine-esque nails trying to catch them. The wind kicked up, reminding me I really did need to get a proper winter coat before the first snowfall.

"Keep Ya Head Up" blared out of my jacket pocket, startling Dusty. He flew off the table and headed for the garage for safety.

I laughed and pulled out my phone. Only one person had that ringtone. My older brother loved 2Pac.

"What do you want?"

"I can't call my baby sister?"

I spun on the picnic table and stretched out my legs, praying I wouldn't end up with a splinter in my ass. "Nope. You text, not call. Why you're usually my favorite brother."

Ezra Burns was the eldest of the Burns pack of wild dogs—my dad's name for us, not mine. But truly, he wasn't far off. Especially when we all got together, which had been harder and harder to do over the years. All of us had scattered to the four corners of the country.

"Glad I still have favorite status."

His whisky-dark voice rolled through me. A pang hit my chest like a kickback from a wrench. My brother really didn't call unless something was going on. "Depends on how this conversation goes, Ez."

"Guess I can't check in either."

I crossed my legs at the ankle. "Is that what you're doing?"

"You know me too well, Ging."

I winced. "Really?"

"You're the only redhead in the bunch."

"Because I'm the special one." The usual back and forth seemed a little forced and nerves skated up my neck, leaving bunched muscles in its wake.

"Yeah, we'll go with special."

I picked a piece of leaf off my jeans. "Not like you to try to do the small talk, bud."

He sighed. "Yeah. I suck at it."

"Indeed."

"You bought a house, right?"

I sat up and swung my feet back onto the faded wood bench. "Yeah. You gave me nothing but grief about it."

"Roots aren't for me, Ging."

"I didn't think so either." I glanced out on the lake. "They don't seem so bad these days."

Ezra was quiet for a moment. I could hear something on the other end of the line as if he'd muffled the speaker. My shoulders hunched and I braced my elbows on my knees.

I was not getting a good feeling.

"How would you feel about all of us crashing there for Christmas?"

I sat up straight. "God, why?"

He laughed. "Well, you're the first one to buy a house. You win."

"No. That's not how this works. Besides, weren't you the first one to bust my balls about my 'money pit', as you called it?"

"Well, it is."

I glanced over at the old house. The porch had seen better days, but the inside wasn't too bad. Just dated. It probably hadn't been updated since the seventies. And while I enjoyed the music, I did not love the decor.

"It's a work in progress."

"Well, can it be ready for the week of Christmas?"

"Since when do we *do* Christmas?" I pinched the bridge of my nose. Ez was being far too friendly. He had a soft spot for me, but my eldest brother was usually moving at warp speed, and niceties weren't his forte. "What happened?"

"Nothing. Well, not exactly."

"Ezra David Burns."

"Jeez."

I could see his shoulders hunching in my head. My brother was a famous photo journalist, but I was one of the few people who could crack the whip on him. Not that he'd admit it.

"Look, it's not a big deal. Don't freak out."

"Freak out?" I put my mug down, jumped off the picnic table, and stalked down to the rocky shore off the lake. "Why would I freak out?"

"I said *don't* freak. I can hear you stomping from here, you know."

"Then just tell me. Is it Dad?" The mere idea of my larger than life father being sick had me bending at the waist to drag in a breath.

"No, it's not Dad."

Relief left me with black dots in my vision.

"Breathe, Ging."

"I am," I growled before I took a deep breath. "Then what's going on?"

"It's Cohen."

Every terrible scenario blasted through my brain. My middle brother was a smoke jumper in California. He'd always been the daredevil in our family, even more so than Ezra. He'd channeled that into saving people instead of doing stunts on his dirt bike on the dangerous tracks he'd rode on during his teen years. He'd always picked out the most challenging ones to give us all nightmares.

"He's okay?"

"He's fine, Tish, I promise. Just a little messed up." He went quiet for a moment. "Okay, more than a little. He lost Jimmy on the job."

"Oh, God." I fell back on my butt on the rocks. The flash of pain up my tailbone had nothing on the vise around my heart.

.ured Jimmy's cocky swagger with his sunny
nis back. Those thick, myriad shades of blond
ıy favorite thing to tangle my fingers in.

pull when the hot fever of need had blown wild and
ı us for that secret month in July.

ımy."

He ,een my brother's best friend since they'd met during smoke jumper training. They were the youngest guys to be added to the Alpha team for his unit.

Jimmy and Cohen had been inseparable until that summer we'd had a *very* ill-advised fling that had ended in a blade I hadn't seen coming. I'd nursed the wound alone in the mountains of Colorado.

My family didn't know what he'd done. Now they never would.

And it didn't matter.

I sucked back the sob that was trapped in my chest like a frightened bird. The only thing that mattered was my brother.

Ezra's voice dragged me back from the past. "Cohen isn't doing great. We had to kick his ass to even get him into rehab."

Get it together, Burns. "Why the hell didn't you call me sooner?"

"He didn't want to worry you."

"Damn idiot." They still treated me like I was twelve. "How bad is he?"

"Just a busted leg, but it was a serious fracture so he's gotta do the whole physical therapy thing. He should be done the first week of December. I figured your place would be a good place to plant him for awhile."

"Of course."

The words came out before I could think better of it. I mean, of course I'd take in my brother and my family, but my place was definitely *not* ready for them.

At all. And neither was I.

I pushed away the memory of Jimmy's startlingly blue eyes. His laughter and the arctic chill of his deception vied for dominance. I slammed those memories back into the metal box I'd put them in years ago then hauled myself to my feet and crunched my way back over the shoreline stones to the grass strewn with leaves.

The half acre of land between the water and my house was a quick trip. It wasn't a large farmhouse by any means. In fact, it was only a three-bedroom place. Not nearly enough room for all my roughhousing brothers. Even if one was laid up and probably hurting far more than he'd let on.

"We won't need much."

"Ha." I snorted. "Right."

"Hey, you're the one who was crowing about how amazing your house was. Now I'm going to hold you to it."

Relief warred with sorrow as I tried to get my mind working again. "Yeah, yeah." I wished I could say I hadn't. But being the baby of the family and being the first to buy a house had left my ego a little unchecked. "Is Dad coming too?"

"Yep. The Burns family will be back together, baby. I'll check in later, Ging."

"Okay. Talk soon."

I shoved my phone into my pocket then tipped back my head. Tears threatened, but I wouldn't let them fall for Jimmy. Not ever again. I had one focus right now. And it was a freaking big problem because there was no way I could get this place in shape for them in less than two months on my own.

The old barn beside my garage caught my eye.

I'd had plans to call in my chip from Lucky Roberts in the spring. The dude owed me for his harebrained last minute scheme for his best friend's proposal last month.

The man was obnoxiously loud, had *player* stamped on his forehead in neon green, and was far too attractive for his own good.

He thought he could charm his way out of any problem. I knew firsthand how charm could hide a person's dark side, and could even make you think you'd imagined things that weren't there.

But I needed Lucky—well, not Lucky specifically, just his hands and his carpentry skills. I was on a budget, so I'd damn well be cashing in any favors I could to fix up the barn.

It would be the perfect place to house my brothers, otherwise known as the animals. And fixing up a guest room for my dad in my house was doable with a bit of spit and grit.

I held open the door for my cat as he zipped around my ankles. Even he seemed uncharacteristically feisty.

Did he sense that change was in the air?

No. No change. This was just a temporary speed bump. I could handle this. My brother needed me, and it just so happened I wanted to fix up my place.

If that meant I needed to deal with Lucky to get it done, then that was what I'd do. I'd make up a plan, get supplies together, and thank God I'd already started the ball rolling when it came to permits.

Now I just had to go inform Lucky it was time to pay up.

Now Available

For more information go to www.tarynquinn.com

Turn the page for Ryan & Preston's story.
*The first in our **Kensington Square** series.*

PRESTON

HIS TEMPORARY ASSISTANT

JUST WHEN I THOUGHT MY DAY—WEEK, MONTH, LIFE—COULDN'T GET any worse, my assistant said she was taking a vacation.

In a week.

Not a year.

Not a month.

A week.

"Look, sir, I'm really sorry. I never expected to get this opportunity. My grandmother was supposed to go to Fiji on her honeymoon, but they broke up, and Biff is taking the Tahoe so she's taking the vacation."

I pressed a fingertip to my aching temple. "Biff? Your grandmother? Fiji?"

"He's taking the Tahoe," my assistant April repeated slowly, leaning forward. Her blond hair fell down around her shoulders, escaping whatever pinned-up thing she'd done in the back. Unless that was the style.

Must be. April Finley was never anything but perfectly put together.

Before today, she'd also never been late. Or taken a vacation beyond a standard and reasonable long weekend. She'd called in sick precisely twice and worked from home.

"We had an agreement." My voice remained even. "I hired you on the spot approximately eighteen months ago on the condition you realized this was not a position that afforded you—"

"What, I can't take some time for myself?" Unlike my own, her voice rose in pitch to match the lifting asymmetrical hem of her dress. Not to indecent levels, mind you, because April was always proper.

Yet somehow my lack of sleep and brewing tension headache was bringing to mind ocean waters creeping higher on the Titanic.

The dress was sea blue too. Or hmm, was that more of a blue-green? I never did get why women had so many colors for things.

Look at my closet. I had black and navy suits. More navy than black because it was less severe for court. My tie collection was more colorful, but I certainly didn't know the names for the damn shades. Who had time for all that nonsense?

Not me. I didn't even have time to complete the work on my plate. I also didn't have time to further engage in this conversation.

April was still blathering on about mud masks and self-care and did I realize how long it had been since she'd even slept in?

No, I could honestly say I didn't.

"What exactly does that mean? I rise every day at precisely four."

She stopped mid-tirade and stared. "You what—why?" She tapped a glossy pale nail against her mouth. "Actually, that's better than I assumed. Rising means you sleep."

"Not necessarily," I said under my breath.

That certainly wasn't the case this month. My father was on the verge of retirement, which meant we would be looking to hire a new partner soon, and my brother and I were overloaded with work. Well, I was overloaded. Dex was strictly a nine-to-fiver—sometimes a ten-to-twoer if the water looked good. In the winter, he was all about the slopes.

I wasn't just talking about skiing. He made just as good use of the lodge as he did the hills. The guy dated more women in a year than I had in my entire life.

I was too busy working. And that was when I'd had an assistant.

Dear God, how was I going to get through a week without April? She kept my life running smoothly. Or at least it was less bumpy than it could've been without her.

"You remind me to eat," I said accusingly.

She frowned. "No, I don't. You just saw me with a donut or a sandwich a few times."

"Right, but seeing you with food reminds me I haven't eaten."

"Sir, your growling stomach should do that without my help."

As if I paid attention to such physical cues.

I would soon find out exactly how good I'd had it before.

Before vacations.

Before retirements.

Before I'd succumbed to a life of no meals and no sleep.

I grunted. "This is not enough notice. How am I supposed to hire a temp in," I consulted my Apple watch, "six days, eighteen hours, and eleven minutes?"

"I know it's short notice."

"Short? Try miniscule."

"But I have the perfect solution."

My shoulders unknotted for the first time since she'd walked into my office. "You've decided to cancel?"

April scowled. Until today, I'd never seen anything but a serene, unruffled expression on my assistant's face. That was one reason I appreciated her so much. She wasn't prone to mood swings.

Mood swings were a good part of why I was single. My mother had enough of them to change the weather from across town.

I didn't need any additional stress in my life. The calmer a woman was, the better. That went for men too, although that was a different dynamic because I didn't get naked with them.

For that matter, I didn't get naked with women much recently either.

Moving on.

"I can't cancel. My grandmother needs me. She and Biff were together for two years."

It took everything I possessed not to give a mock shudder. "I'm grievously sorry for her loss, but why does her misfortune have to become mine?"

April huffed out a breath. "Biff isn't dead. Have you been listening at all?"

"Of course I have." I adjusted my cuff links. "You're cruising to Alaska?"

"Seriously?"

"Look, I have back-to-back meetings this afternoon." Normally, at this point in a conversation I did not want to have, I would text my assistant to call me with a made-up appointment. That was hard to do when she was the one seated across from me.

One more reason I hated unplanned, unnecessary vacations.

"Not according to your Daytimer."

"There were a few last minute additions."

"Mmm-hmm. You know, I'm beginning to rethink my backup plan."

Hope bloomed inside me like a daisy in spring. "You are?"

"I always thought you were a fair, equitable boss who didn't play power games."

"I do not. Ever."

"You never so much as pinched my ass—rump," she corrected, thereby putting the image of an ass-rump in my head—luckily, not hers.

I had never so much as glimpsed her backside. I wasn't that sort of employer.

"Of course not."

"You don't take advantage of your position, and you see everyone as equals."

I couldn't help preening. Slightly. "I am careful to do exactly that."

"So, naturally, I figured Ryan would be the perfect choice to assist you while I'm away. I would never introduce you to a friend if I didn't believe you were fair-minded. Some look at having an assistant as an opportunity to lord their elevated status over them."

Why did it sound as if she was lecturing me? "I have never done such and I never will."

She rose. "Good. It's settled. Ryan will start for you next Monday at nine. Possibly nine-fifteen. No more than nine-thirty. Mornings are iffy." She crossed the office to the door. "Oh, and thanks! I'll bring you back a souvenir."

The door clicked shut on my curses.

I stalked over to the coffeemaker and discovered I was down to five pods—inhumane considering my current level of tension.

I popped one in the brewer and returned to my desk to stab the intercom button on the phone.

"Yes?"

"I'm almost out of coffee. Can you kindly place an order before your vacation?" The question held the same level of wrath as a death threat.

Preston Michael Shaw was not someone to tangle with without his caffeine.

"Already taken care of two days ago. Tracking says it should arrive by Monday afternoon. Your preferred flavor of Columbian coconut-caramel was backordered."

"Of course." I had no reason to feel ashamed I enjoyed coconut and caramel. Those were extremely manly flavors.

And Monday afternoon meant I would have to deal with April's friend who was "iffy about mornings" without the benefit of my early morning pick-me-up unless I grabbed one on the way in. My own kitchen at home was stocked with an assortment of possibilities that I rarely took time to actually make there, other than my restorative Friday night meal. For the most part, I only used my place to shower and sleep.

"I actually paid for rushed shipping."

"Why, does Ryan enjoy coffee too?" There was no keeping the edge of sarcasm out of my voice.

"Hardly. Tea is much more Ryan's speed. Coffee is a dangerous stimulant and can lead to hallucinations."

"Such as fantasizing about murdering someone when you don't have any?"

"You have five pods left," April said crisply. "Ration."

She hung up before I could reply.

In the old days before vacation, April never hung up without making sure I had everything I needed. Now she seemed dismissive. Perhaps this was her way of weaning me off the teat of capable assistantship before she took her leave.

It was hard to imagine Ryan, with his inconsistent start times and love of tea, could measure up.

Maybe I was being unfairly judgmental. Usually, water seeking its own level was a factor in friendships, but I had no idea if this was a former ex of April's or someone she merely had an acquaintance with. Many people today called everyone their friend, from the mailman to the barista who made their latte. I was far more selective.

My old school buddy, Bishop, counted as a close friend. I also had numerous acquaintances. I wasn't looking to add to the roster.

I grabbed my coffee from the brewer and disposed of the pod before sitting at my desk. I slipped on my glasses then typed a missive to April.

Memo: Ryan Moon

Ms. Finley,

Upon further reflection, while your effort to provide someone in your stead while you are vacationing is commendable, I need more information before I blindly accept someone into my employ, even temporarily. Does this individual have a CV? A work history? Applicable skills? References? I will need to see these materials before I hire anyone.

Yours,

Preston Michael Shaw, Esquire

Addressing her as Ms. Finley was a bit much, as was signing my full name and using Esquire. I was annoyed on multiple levels and needed an outlet.

I didn't believe in gyms—communal sweating had never been my kink—so I'd be going for a nice long run tonight to get out my frustrations. God knows I didn't have any other healthy outlets, other than playing Mario Kart on my ancient Super Nintendo system.

Vintage. Not ancient. I needed to learn the lingo so I didn't sound like someone caught in the past.

I drank a mouthful of hot coffee and flicked through screens until I came to my notes about one of my biggest cases, Terrance vs. Yorn, a multi-million dollar divorce with drama worthy of *Judge Judy*. I did not do drama. I also didn't relish reviewing notes that amounted to little more than a record of personal attacks rather than anything based on legal precedent.

I had pulled up my email program to dash off another email, this time to Donald Terrance, when said program dinged.

I frowned. I had turned off all notifications. How had one gotten through?

The frown grew as the most recent email in my box seemed to loom larger than all of the others. The sender? Ryan Moon.

Mental note: tell Ms. Finley not to share my email address with outsiders before asking.

Narrowing my eyes, I clicked it open.

To whom it may concern:
   I have attached my resume. References are at the bottom.
The first one is the person who got me this gig.
   Sincerely,
   Ryan G. Moon

I cocked a brow. *Gig?* That was a new one.

Rather than reply to Ryan G. Moon, I opened my email to send another memo to April.

Ms. Finley,

I just received correspondence from one Ryan G. Moon. Kindly do not share my email with strangers in the future. Also, did you make clear what sort of position this is? Your friend referred to it as a "gig."

Yours,

Preston Michael Shaw, Esquire

I'd barely hit send and sat back to drink smugly from my rapidly disappearing coffee when my email dinged.

Yet again it had bypassed my no notifications setting. How was this happening? I did not want unanticipated noises interrupting my blessed silence.

To whom it may concern:

I am well aware what kind of position this is, as April (Ms. Finley to you) has told me all about her job many, many times. I am also well-versed in the likes of you.

Sincerely,

Ryan G. Moon

I set my coffee mug down with a snap. My gaze narrowed on the jaunty saying on the side of the cup, a gift from my last secretary right before I'd fired her.

Lawyers do it in their briefs.

She'd laughed uproariously upon handing me this item at the company Christmas party. Then she'd pinched my ass. I'd been quite certain she'd dipped into the punch, but I couldn't have the other employees thinking I'd crossed a line.

As if I'd willingly have sex with a woman with nails as long as tongue depressors.

I begun to type again. Forget Ms. Finley. Evidently, Ryan G. Moon and I were meant to communicate solely with each other.

Ryan G. Moon,

What do you mean by 'the likes of me'? If you have formed a bias against me due to Ms. Finley's description of her workplace, perhaps you would like to seek employment elsewhere. Ms. Finley should also discuss any concerns she may have with me herself rather than through a questionable intermediary.

With all due respect,

Preston Michael Shaw, Esquire

I wasn't even surprised when the reply came through before I'd managed to finish even half my email to Donald. At this point, the resulting ding was also non-climactic.

Clearly, my notifications setting had gone as rogue as my obviously displeased assistant.

To whom it may concern:

April actually loves her job. I find it hard to believe, since my interactions with lawyers over the years haven't led to a feeling warmer than luke at best, but she is more generous than I. She has no concerns. I just read between the lines.

So, have you checked out my resume or what?

Sincerely,

Ryan G. Moon

What kind of feeling was *luke*? The word lukewarm was not meant to be split as if the first half counted as an adjective on its own.

I rubbed the knot in my forehead. If this was an example of Ryan's grammatical skills, I was nearly giddy with anticipation.

Also, I had forgotten to download Ryan's résumé. But I had one other salient point to attend to first.

Ryan G. Moon,

The word is resumé with the accent mark over the e. Without it, the word is simply resume. Which the dictionary defines as: to take up or go on with again after interruption; continue. Example: to resume a journey.

Sincerely,

Preston Michael Shaw, Esquire

Her response took all of three-point-five minutes.

To whom it may concern:

You forgot the accent mark on the first e. It should be résumé.

Insincerely,

Ryan G. Moon

This time, I did not answer the missive. Instead, I summoned Ms. Finley via the phone's intercom. "My office, please."

That *please* constricted my throat.

She knocked and appeared in my doorway, without seeming the slightest bit contrite. "Yes?"

"Sit."

She sat. Waited. Blinked innocently.

"Do you have some rapid-fire system that allows you to forward my emails to your friend in an instant? I've never seen anyone reply so quickly."

April's lips twitched. "She's very conscientious."

Now there was no doubting my throat was tight. "She?"

"Why, yes. Didn't you realize? Ryan is a woman." Now she did smile, widely. "She can't wait to meet you."

CRESCENT COVE

Have My Baby

Claim My Baby

Who's The Daddy

Pit Stop: Baby

Baby Daddy Wanted

Rockstar Baby

Daddy in Disguise

My Ex's Baby

Daddy Undercover

Wrong Bed Baby

Lucky Baby

Daddy on Duty

Cop Daddy Next Door

Protector Daddy

CRESCENT COVE STANDALONES & SHORTS

CEO Daddy

Fireman Daddy

Mistletoe Baby

For more information about our books visit
www.tarynquinn.com

MORE BY TARYN QUINN

OTHER SERIES

Happy Acres

Kensington Square

Afternoon Delight

Deuces Wild

Wilder Rock

Walk on the wilder side with these stories

After Dark

HOLIDAY BOOKS

Unwrapped

Holiday Sparks

Filthy Scrooge

Bad Kitty

Saving Kylie

For more information about our books visit

www.tarynquinn.com

ABOUT TARYN QUINN

USA Today bestselling author, *TARYN QUINN,* is the sexy and funny alter ego of bestselling authors Taryn Elliott & Cari Quinn. We've been writing together for years, but we have decided to pull the trigger on a combo name just for fun.

And so…Taryn Quinn was born!

Do you like ultra sexy small town romance full of shenanigans? Quirky office romances full of steam? Okay, look…we pretty much just love writing steamy stories. If you're all about that, we're your girls!

For more information about us…
tarynquinn.com
tq@tarynquinn.com

QUINN AND ELLIOTT

We also write more serious, longer, and sexier books as Cari Quinn & Taryn Elliott. Our topics include mostly rockstars, but mobsters, MMA, and a little suspense gets tossed in there too.

Rockers' Series Reading Order

Lost in Oblivion

Winchester Falls

Found in Oblivion

Hammered

Rock Revenge

Brooklyn Dawn

OTHER SERIES

Tapped Out

Love Required

Boys of Fall

If you'd like more information about us please visit

www.quinnandelliott.com

Made in the USA
Middletown, DE
26 October 2022

13572330R00156